★

"Just get me out of this bloody hole," he heard the diver say.

The diver's head appeared; he grasped the edge of the well and heaved himself out onto the floor. The worried operator sank down on his haunches beside him. "Are you all right, Mick?" he asked again. "What happened down there?"

The diver pulled off his mask and passed a hand across his face. "There's a body down there," he said shakily. "Gave me a hell of a turn." He shuddered and took a deep breath. "It's got no face," he said. "No face at all."

★

Forthcoming from Worldwide Mystery by
FRANK SMITH

FATAL FLAW

STONE DEAD

FRANK SMITH

WORLDWIDE.

TORONTO • NEW YORK • LONDON
AMSTERDAM • PARIS • SYDNEY • HAMBURG
STOCKHOLM • ATHENS • TOKYO • MILAN
MADRID • WARSAW • BUDAPEST • AUCKLAND

STONE DEAD

A Worldwide Mystery/September 1999

First published by St. Martin's Press, Incorporated.

ISBN 0-373-26320-1

Visit us at www.worldwidemystery.com

Printed in U.S.A.

STONE DEAD

ONE

PETER FOSTER swallowed hard against the taste of rising bile, and forced himself to open his eyes.

The horror was still there; naked, white as marble sprawled among the rumpled sheets. And the blood... He looked away. It was no dream; no nightmarish image that would fade and be forgotten with the coming of the dawn. This was real. What was done was done, and nothing he could do would change that.

He tried to think, but the pounding in his ears made coherent thought impossible. He felt the weight of the gun in his hands; felt it slipping from his finger but was powerless to stop it. The shotgun grazed his shins, yet he felt no pain, nor did he move as it clattered to the floor.

He closed his eyes, but the images remained: the tangled heap of clothing on the floor; the crumpled blanket tossed aside; the jagged gash across the sloping ceiling where it met the wall above the bed; the shredded pillows soaked in blood.

He squeezed his eyes tightly shut as if by doing so he could escape the pictures in his mind. A bead of moisture ran down his nose and fell without a sound. He brushed a shaking hand across his face, and was surprised to find it bathed in sweat.

He became conscious of a sound beyond the throbbing in his head. Faint, at first, but growing louder as a car began to climb the hill.

It slowed.

He almost fell, tripping on the gun as he moved swiftly to the window where he pressed his face against the glass to peer into the night. Headlights flickered through the trees between the cottage and the road. The sound grew louder. He held his breath. If it was going to turn in it would be…now!

The lights swept past and disappeared. He allowed himself to breathe again. The panes felt cool and soothing to his flesh, and for a moment he blotted out reality. But the mirrored image of the room reflected in the glass refused to go away.

He turned and snatched a blanket from the floor and flung it across the bed to hide the grisly sight, then stood there panting as if he'd run a marathon.

But the action broke the spell, and for the first time since he'd entered the room he began to think. And the one clear thought that came to him was that *nothing* had happened here. Nothing! He must hold on to that thought above all else and make it true.

He moved swiftly through the cottage; the other bedroom first, then downstairs where he went from room to room, eyes darting everywhere. He needed something… The rubber-coated apron he used in the dark-room; that would do. And the rubber gloves. And wellingtons. All of them could be scrubbed clean afterwards.

The shrill ringing of the telephone made him jump, and he felt the sweat break out once more across his brow. It rang again, but he couldn't bring himself to pick it up.

The machine clicked on and went through its programmed chatter.

'Lisa? Are you there?' a disembodied voice demanded petulantly. 'Why are you never in when I ring? Or do you just sit there and let me talk to your damned machine before you make up your mind whether to talk to me or not?'

He began to breathe again. Constance. There was no mistaking that rasping whine. Why, of all people, did it have to be her?

'Anyway, ring me back as soon as you can. I'm coming down this weekend, and I'll need someone to meet me at the station. Friday afternoon. I don't know what time, but you can always ring up and find out if you don't know.'

The machine went dead.

He had to think! What was today? Wednesday? Thursday, Fri... He had to stop her. But how? He pressed his hands to his head and tried to bring some order to his thoughts. Ring her back and tell them they had someone else coming for the weekend. No, that wouldn't do. Knowing Constance, she'd come anyway. He would have to tell her Lisa was away. Gone up to London for a few days to make the rounds. Constance would buy that. She knew how hard it was to get the top jobs these days. You had to keep after them, and it was harder for them to turn you down when you were standing there in front of them.

He'd ring Constance back straightaway and put her off. No doubt she'd whine and moan a bit, but at least he'd have her off his back, and he could get on with other calls.

IT WAS DONE. It had been easier than he'd thought. Constance had been miffed, of course, but then, when wasn't she miffed about something or other? He picked up the phone again and punched in a pre-recorded number.

'Annette? Peter here. How are you? Yes, it has been quite a while. How's Leonard? Good. Good. Tell me, is Lisa there?'

He listened to his own voice as he spoke the words. Keep it light. Don't sound worried. 'She's not.' He laughed self-consciously. 'No, nothing like that,' he said. 'It's just that she left a message for me on the machine. Yes. Wanted me to ring her back, but she forgot to say where she was. You know Lisa...' He laughed again. 'I don't suppose you have any idea where...? No. Well, never mind. No doubt she'll ring again. Say hello to Leonard. 'Bye.'

He hung up, then ran his finger down the list of numbers and picked up the phone once more.

'Ah, George. Peter here. No, just been busy—you know how it is. Tell me, George, is Lisa there?'

Thursday 14th March

MATTRESS, pillows, emulsion, brushes, wallpaper, and carpet cleaner. Sheets and pillow cases—he'd have to wash them when he got home so they wouldn't look too new— and blanket. Bought from five different shops; three in Worcester; two in Hereford. Paid cash. No name, no pack-drill, as his dad had been so fond of saying.

The rain that had fallen steadily since early morning had given way to a watery March sunshine. A good omen, perhaps? He went over everything in his mind again as he took the road for Leominster. He'd stop there and pick up more glass and frames from old Fred. Just in case anyone should ask where he'd been. Not that they would, he told himself. He'd been very careful.

He took out the list and glanced at it. Oh, yes. Gloves. He'd need another pair of work gloves. No problem. He could pick those up in Leominster.

Peter Foster crumpled the piece of paper and tossed it out of the window of the van. The wind took it, and he watched in the rear-view mirror as it skittered across the road and disappeared.

Sunday 31st March

'LISA STILL AWAY, then, is she?'

Wilf Archer walked around the billiard table, sizing up his next shot. It was a cold night, wet and miserable, and there were only a handful of people in the pub. A local farmer and his son stood chatting with Stan Trowbridge at the bar; a grey-haired couple sat quietly at a table in the corner, while their dog, a very old red setter, lay dozing beneath their seat; and two scruffy youths—a couple of right yobbos by the look of them—slouched in their seats, waiting for the game to end so they could play.

'Still away,' said Peter Foster. 'She could be away for some time. They want her to do more work for them while she's there.'

'France, wasn't it?' Archer bent low and squinted along the length of his cue.

'That's right.'

'Must be nice.' Archer moved the cue back and forth across his fingers, then played the shot. The cue ball rolled about six inches and stopped. 'Shit! Topped it,' he muttered as he stood back. 'And left you an easy pot.'

Foster chalked his cue, bent and took the shot in one easy movement. 'Thanks, Wilf,' he said, grinning as he moved around the table to take his next shot.

'What's it been? Three weeks since she left?'

A frown creased Foster's brow as he bent over the table again. Why this sudden interest in Lisa? he wondered. It wasn't as if he and Archer were close friends. He only saw the man once a week, and it was only recently that it had become a bit of a ritual to have a game of snooker on Sunday nights. Lisa had fallen into the habit of coming with him because she liked chatting with Ellen Trowbridge, Stan's daughter. Ellen still hadn't found a job since leaving university, and was working for her father behind the bar.

Steady, there, he told himself. Archer was only making idle conversation. He didn't mean anything by it. But Foster wished he'd drop the subject.

'Must be all of that,' he said, and potted the black.

'How's the new house coming along?' he asked as he stood back and surveyed the table.

Archer snorted as he fished the black out of the pocket

and set it on its mark. 'It'll be an old house by the time the bloody planners have done with it,' he said. 'Still waiting for them to decide whether they'll allow the extension on the side. Want me to lop four feet off it, they do. They say it comes too close to the orchard. If I'd known that, I'd have ripped the damned trees out before I went for approval. Bastards!'

Foster shook his head in sympathy. 'I know what you mean,' he sighed. 'I went through all that when I did the cottage up.' He lined up a red beside the centre pocket.

Archer watched as the red went down. 'Looks like your hands have healed,' he said glumly. 'You wouldn't have made that shot last week, not with all those blisters. Finished tearing down that old sheep pen, then, have you?'

Damn the man. Couldn't he think of anything else to talk about? 'All I'm going to do for the moment,' he said. 'Got too much work to do.' He glanced at his watch. 'In fact, I shall have to be going soon. I have to be up and away by six tomorrow morning. Got a job in Kidderminster, and I have to be there by eight. So we'll just finish this game out, shall we?'

One of the youths nudged the other, and sly grins spread across their faces. The older of the two winked knowingly as he picked up his glass and drank. The younger boy sniggered and quickly followed suit.

But Peter Foster saw none of this as he bent to take his shot. The black was blocked and the pink was up against the cushion. He lined up on the blue. An easy shot.

Perhaps it was the shade of blue, but whatever the reason, something made him think of Lisa. Lisa as she had looked...

He breathed in deeply; held his breath; took his shot.

'Hard luck,' Archer chuckled as he chalked his cue.

TWO

Monday 1st April

HE WAS GOING TO BE LATE.

Wilf Archer glanced at the time and put his foot down. Twelve minutes to eight, and it would take him fifteen at least to reach the station. He'd miss the train for sure. Unless it was late. It was most mornings, but just when he wanted it to be late it would probably be on time. Bloody British Rail. You couldn't depend on anything these days.

The road was narrow and winding, running between high hedges for most of the way, but he was used to it. There was never anything about at this time of day.

Christ!

He swung the wheel hard over and just scraped by the nose of the lorry stuck half-way into the road. Bloody idiot! What the hell did he think he was...?

Wait a minute. That was Foster's place. Hadn't he said he had to be in Kidderminster by eight this morning? And weren't those the two tearaways he'd seen in the pub the night before? Archer slowed as he went around the next bend. And that live-in girlfriend of Foster's was away. Gorgeous bit of stuff, she was. Lisa. Lisa Remington, that was it. Very nice. He'd seen her picture in magazines.

Those bastards were stripping Foster's house! Archer had only caught a glimpse as he flashed by, but the two of them had been struggling with a dresser or something like it, trying to get it up a makeshift ramp on to the lorry.

He made up his mind. He'd never have made the train

anyway, he told himself. There was a farm just down the road. They'd have a phone.

'THAT'S RIGHT, two of them. They're there now. No, I don't know the bloody registration, and you won't know it either if you don't get your finger out.

'All right, all right, I know you have to have information, but at least get someone on their way. What's that? I don't...' Archer turned to the farmer's wife. 'What's it called?' he asked. 'The cottage. Bracken? Right, thank you. Bracken Cottage,' he repeated into the phone. 'It's about half a mile... You know it, do you? Thank God for small mercies. Now, if you'll just get...'

He groaned. 'Oh, God, here we go again,' he said to the woman hovering at his elbow. 'Archer. As in Robin Hood. A as in apple, R as in rip-off, C as in copper...'

WILF ARCHER stood in the middle of the road and waved the police car down. 'They're still there,' he told the constable. 'I went up to the corner and had a look. Better hurry; they were pulling tarps over the load as if they were getting ready to leave.' He made as if to open the rear door and get in, but the driver stopped him.

'You remain here,' he said sternly. 'We'll take care of it.' Then, to his observer, 'Check with George and see if he's in position on the other side.'

A burst from the radio confirmed that George was in place. With a dismissive nod to Archer, the driver put the car in gear and moved off in the direction of Bracken Cottage.

The two cars came in swiftly, arriving at the same time, blocking the escape route of the lorry. The two youths were nowhere to be seen as the four policemen jumped out of their cars. One man stopped long enough to look inside the cab, saw the keys in the ignition, and took them out, then followed the others up the short driveway toward the cottage.

As the first man reached the door, the two youths came out. They had their heads down, laughing as they examined a long, slim box one held in his hands.

'Police. Stop right where you are,' commanded the constable first in line.

Astonishment barely had time to register on the faces of the youths before their survival instincts told them to run. One, the younger of the two, bolted back inside, but the older one made a break for the garden and the open fields beyond. While two men went after him, the other two split up. One went inside the cottage, while the other dashed round the back.

PC Arundel found himself in a narrow passageway with doors on either side. He stood to one side and flung open the first door on the right. The loo. No way out and nowhere to hide. Swiftly, he went through the other downstairs rooms, and met his colleague in the kitchen.

'Nothing?' he said, frowning.

The man shook his head and looked upward.

'Can't have,' Arundel said. 'We'd have heard him go up the stairs. Besides, I saw him come down the passage. He's got to be here.'

They searched the rooms again without success. Then, while his colleague remained at the bottom of the stairs, Arundel went up and searched the bedrooms. He came down scratching his head. 'He's *got* to be here,' he said again. 'You sure he didn't get out the back?'

'If he did, I didn't see him,' the man said. 'It's all open out there. Unless…'

He turned and dashed through the house to the back door and out into the open yard. Arundel followed him out. No sign of the boy there. But there was an outbuilding; a shed of some sort by the look of it. Like the house, it was built of stone, but the original roof was gone, and in its place was a covering of corrugated iron.

PC Arundel circled the shed. No back way out. He motioned for his colleague to open the door, and they both peered inside.

Nothing. Not a sign of the boy.

Arundel stepped inside. The only light came from the open door, and it took a moment for his eyes to adjust. Nothing there but garden tools and a lot of old rubbish as far as he could see. Except...

'Come here and give me a hand,' he said softly to his colleague. A circular wooden cover, about four feet across, was set in the centre of the floor. 'It's an old well, I reckon,' Arundel said. 'Let's take a look, shall we?'

Together, the two men lifted the lid. The boy, clinging to hand and footholds with fierce determination, kept his head lowered as if by not looking up he might not be seen.

'Well, well, well. What do we have here?' Arundel said heavily, chuckling at his own play on words. 'Come on, lad. Let's be having you.'

'I—I can't m-move,' the boy said through chattering teeth. 'I'll fall.'

'Serves you bloody right,' Arundel told him. 'A good dunking down there might do you a lot of good. Come on, now. Give us your hand.'

'I c-c-can't...'

'What's that you've got in your pocket, then?' said the second policeman. 'Here, let's have that up here.' He knelt down and stretched to reach the thin leather case protruding from the pocket, but just as his fingers touched it the boy moved, and the case came free. The two policemen watched helplessly as it fell. They heard the hollow splash as it hit the water far below.

Arundel looked at his colleague and slowly shook his head. 'You'd better hope you're not the one they send down after it,' he said grimly. 'You should have left the bloody thing alone.'

'It could've dropped while we were getting him out,' his colleague said defensively.

'Well, it has bloody dropped, now, hasn't it? Come on, let's get him out before he goes down as well.'

It wasn't an easy task. The boy was petrified, but between them they hauled him out, and he sat shivering on the floor.

'There must have been something very valuable in that case for you to try to hang on to it,' Arundel said as they led the boy out. 'What was it, lad?'

The boy shook his head, and Arundel sighed. 'We're going to find out sooner or later,' he said. 'You don't want to be charged with obstruction as well as thieving, do you? Somebody's going to have to go down that well, you know.' He shot a glance at his colleague, who glared back defiantly.

'Coins,' the boy said.

'What was that? Coins? What sort of coins?'

The boy shrugged. 'Dunno. Just coins, like in a set. Gold, I think. Least, they looked like gold.'

'SOMEBODY must know where this bloke, Foster, is,' said the sergeant into the phone. 'I can't just have this lorry load brought in as evidence and leave the man with hardly any furniture, now can I? Kidderminster, that's what the witness—what's his name? Archer?—said. No, he doesn't know how long he'll be away. Photographer. Freelance. We need him out here now to identify… Yes, a van. Dark blue with something about photography on the side. Fairly new. No, I don't know. Get on to Records, for God's sake!'

The sergeant paused. 'And we'll need a diver,' he said. 'No, not a *driver,* a diver. We need him to recover some of the loot that was dropped down a well. Deep? How the hell would I know how deep it is? Just get one out here along with some sort of portable winch to lower him down. It's in a confined area, so make sure it isn't too big. Got that? Good.'

THE SERGEANT and three constables clustered round as the man in the wet suit began his descent. They peered over the edge, but it was almost impossible to see anything because the diver himself blocked their view.

'Hold it. I'm at the water now,' the man operating the winch heard in his headphones. 'Steady, now. Lower away. Slowly.'

Beneath the surface of the water, the diver shone a powerful beam toward the bottom of the well. Good. It wasn't all that deep after all. He could see the case. It was open and he could see two coins glinting in the light of his lamp, but there were more than that according to the boy.

He touched bottom, but allowed himself a bit more slack before he told the man above to stop. He picked up the coins and put them in his pouch, then knelt and began to search for others. Strange. No silt. Nothing but jagged stones, and big ones at that.

Carefully, he began to move the stones aside, and found more coins. He moved more stones, but if there were more coins they must have slipped deeper into the fissures between the stones. He wished he knew exactly how many coins there were in the collection. If he had to shift this lot...

'Jesus Christ!'

The operator pressed the headphones closer to his head. 'Mick?' he enquired anxiously. 'You all right?'

'Haul me up. Haul me up, dammit. Now!' The words came out of the headphones like bullets out of a gun.

'What's wrong, Mick?' Even as he asked the question, the operator threw the winch into reverse and saw the rope begin to tighten as it took the strain. 'What is it, Mick? You in trouble?'

'Just get me out of this bloody hole,' he heard the diver say, and from then on concentrated on bringing his man safely to the top.

The diver's head appeared; he grasped the edge of the well and heaved himself out on to the floor. The worried operator sank down on his haunches beside him. 'Are you all right, Mick?' he asked again. 'What happened down there?'

The diver pulled off his mask and passed a hand across his face. 'There's a body down there,' he said shakily. 'Gave me a hell of a turn.' He shuddered and took a deep breath. 'It's got no face,' he said. 'No face at all.'

PETER FOSTER was tired and hungry. He had gone without lunch in order to finish the job and get back home before dark, but even so it was after six before he was able to get away. Fish and chips would be nice. He savoured the thought—then realized it was Monday. The chip shop was closed on Monday. Damn! He supposed he could turn off into Ludlow, but that would just take more time. It would have to be the pub in Clunbridge, then, because he didn't fancy setting to and making his own dinner when he got home. He glanced at the time. Not long now.

The police car seemed to come out of nowhere. Suddenly, it was there behind him, light flashing, and it wasn't going to pass. He felt a tremor in the pit of his stomach as he checked his speed. Oh, no! Just over. Muttering imprecations beneath his breath, he touched his brakes and slowed. Why the hell didn't they go after that black Cortina that had passed him like a rocket a few miles back?

He stopped the van and rolled the window down. He watched in the mirror as the policeman got out of the car and walked along the side of the van.

'Evening, sir. This your van, is it?'

Might as well be polite. He might get off with a warning if he was lucky. 'Good evening,' he said. 'Yes, this is my van. Why? Is there something wrong?'

'And your name is…?'

'Foster. Peter Foster. I live not far from here.'

'May I see your driving licence, sir?'

Foster dug into his wallet and handed the man his licence. The policeman studied it, then handed it back. 'On your way home, are you, sir?'

Foster nodded. 'Yes.' He might still get away with it.

'Right,' said the policeman. 'If you would be so good as to continue directly to your home, we will follow along behind you, Mr Foster.'

'Follow along behind?' Alarm bells were ringing madly somewhere in the back of Foster's head. He took a deep breath. 'Look here—' he looked for some indication of rank on the man's uniform, but could not see one '—officer. Do you mind telling me what is going on?'

'All in good time, sir,' the man said stonily. 'Now, sir, if you will…'

'But I was going to stop in at the pub in Clunbridge for a bite to eat,' Foster protested. 'I've had a long day, no lunch, and I'm starving. So, if you will kindly tell me just what it is I'm supposed to have done…'

'I'm afraid I must insist, sir,' the policeman said. 'Unless, of course, you would rather leave the van here and come with us in the car?'

Foster felt a prickle of sweat form along his upper lip, and there was a cold, hard knot in his belly. 'No,' he said curtly. 'But I intend to make a complaint about this. I see no reason to…'

'As you see fit, sir,' the man said. 'Shall we be on our way, then, sir?' Without waiting for an answer, he turned and walked back to the car.

PETER FOSTER saw the lights around the cottage as he came over the hill, and the fear that had been building inside him ever since the police had stopped him grew stronger. They *couldn't* have found out; no one else knew. No, it had to be something else. Perhaps there had been a fire. But then, why hadn't the policeman said so back there?

The driveway was completely blocked, so he had no option but to pull the van up as best he could on the grass verge behind a lorry. What was a lorry doing there, for God's sake? The lights of the police car behind him went out, and both driver and observer got out and came toward him.

'This way, sir,' said the man who had spoken to him on the road as Foster got out and locked the door behind him. The policeman placed a hand on Foster's arm.

Foster shook it off. 'I know the way into my own house without your help,' he said angrily. He made his way past several cars to the door of the cottage. Men seemed to be everywhere, and his heart sank. Conscious of the two policemen behind him, he sucked in a deep, silent breath before opening the door. The door leading to the sitting-room was open and there was someone standing in the doorway.

The policemen crowded in behind him as if they thought he might turn and run. 'Mr Foster, sir,' one of them announced.

'Sir' was a tall, well-built man of about Foster's own age. Strong face, thought Foster. The appraisal was automatic. Faces; portraits; that was a large part of Foster's business. But it was a face that gave nothing away. Foster mentally braced himself. He'd have to watch himself with this man.

'Thank you for escorting Mr Foster in, Constable,' the man said. 'I'll take it from here.' He turned his attention to Peter Foster. 'Sorry if you have been inconvenienced, sir,' he said, 'but we thought it best to have you return home as soon as possible, under the circumstances. My name is Paget. Detective Chief Inspector Paget.'

He moved aside, and Foster saw for the first time the state of the living-room.

'Good God!' He stood there in the doorway looking at the room in disbelief. Most of the furniture was gone, and it looked as if the contents of cupboards and drawers had been tipped out on the floor.

'I'm afraid you were the victim of a break-and-enter here earlier today,' Paget explained. 'Fortunately, it was foiled by a very alert gentleman who happened to be passing. He informed the police, and they arrived before the thieves had a chance to leave. Everything is quite safe, I assure you. Once it has all been itemized, and you have identified it, we will have it brought back in.'

Foster continued to stare at the room, unable to take it all in. But the one thought that kept pounding away inside his head was that he had to get this man out of here. Dimly, he became conscious that Paget was speaking to him again.

'The man who phoned us was a Wilfred Archer,' he heard him say. 'He is a friend of yours, I understand.'

'Wilf? Yes, I... Good God! My equipment. All the stuff in the dark-room. It's worth thousands!'

'Quite safe, sir, I assure you,' said Paget soothingly. Paget indicated one of the remaining straight-backed chairs that had been either overlooked or deemed to be of little value to the thieves. 'Please sit down, Mr Foster.'

Peter Foster sank into a chair, still trying to take everything in. Thank God it hadn't been any worse. But the last thing he needed right now were policemen tramping about the place. And those men outside: what were they doing out there? Best to ask the question. It would seem odd if he didn't.

'There were men outside,' he ventured. 'I saw them as I came in. What, exactly, are they doing out there?'

Paget stood looking down at him. 'Ah,' he said softly. 'Yes, I was coming to that, Mr Foster. Because that is why I am here. You see, while trying to escape, one of the suspects took refuge in your well, and he dropped this.' Paget reached behind him and picked up a clear plastic bag. 'Do you recognize it?'

Foster opened his mouth and shut it again. He felt chilled to the bone as he stared at the red leather case. What the hell was the idiot doing in the well? he thought wildly. Of all the places to hide...

He realized Paget was waiting for a reply. 'Yes,' he said in a voice barely above a whisper. He coughed, cleared his throat. 'Yes, it's my gold sovereign collection. There should be twenty-two gold sovereigns in it. It—it's quite valuable. It was my father's.'

Paget nodded. 'Then the rest must still be down there,' he said matter-of-factly. 'No doubt some slipped down between the stones, but I'm sure they will be found when all the stones have been brought up.'

Peter Foster forced himself to control his breathing. 'Brought up?' he repeated. He didn't know what else to say.

'Yes.' Paget was watching him closely. 'You see, while retrieving the coins, we found a body in your well, Mr Foster. What can you tell me about that?'

THREE

PETER FOSTER stared at Paget with unbelieving eyes. He felt as if he were about to faint. What to say? Oh, God! 'You mean someone fell down the well?' he said. 'How...? I mean, that's not possible. I don't see how...' Steady. Don't overdo it.

'It wasn't an accident,' said Paget quietly. 'The person was killed, then dumped in the well. Heavy stones were dropped in afterwards in an attempt to cover the body.

Surprise. Shock; that was it. 'Good God! But I was...' Foster stopped and looked down at his hands as if seeing them for the first time. 'But I was putting stones down the well a couple of weeks ago,' he said in a hushed voice. He looked up at Paget. 'I've been tearing down the old sheep pen at the back of the cottage, and I didn't know what to do with the stones, so I decided to fill up the old well. It hasn't been used in years. It was spring-fed, but the underground springs shifted some years ago, and the well seldom has more than a few feet of water in it now.' He lifted his face to stare at Paget. 'Do you mean to tell me that the body was down there when I was dropping stones down the well?'

He buried his face in his hands. 'That's horrible,' he whispered.

'Would you bring a glass of water for Mr Foster?' Paget said, and it was only then that Foster realized that a constable must have been standing there behind him all the time. A shiver ran through his frame as he waved a feeble hand. 'There's brandy in the kitchen,' he said weakly. 'Bottom right-hand cupboard.'

Paget hesitated, then nodded to the constable. 'A small one,' he said.

While they waited for the constable to return, Paget studied the man in the chair, mentally filing the information away. Clothing, casual but of good quality; corduroy jacket, dark green shirt open at the neck, baggy trousers, and slip-on shoes. General appearance: untidy, even unkempt. But then, it was the end of the day. The man was tired and in need of a shave. Slim, fine-boned, but his hands were broad, capable, workman-like hands. His face, beneath jet black hair and a darkening five-o'clock shadow that extended almost to his collar, was lean and pale. His eyes were dark, deep-set and watchful. His mouth, below a short, straight nose, was small, almost cherubic in the fullness of the lips. But there was a stubborn set to his chin.

An interesting face, Paget concluded, but not one he would trust. As for Foster's age, Paget judged him to be somewhere in his mid-to-late thirties.

The uniformed constable appeared with a bottle of brandy in one hand, and a mug in the other. 'I couldn't find a glass,' he said as Paget poured a careful measure into the mug and handed it to Foster.

'Thank you.' Foster took the mug in both hands and gulped the liquid down. Paget, meanwhile, capped the bottle and set it on the floor, then sat down himself.

Peter Foster had something of a reputation as a photographer, Paget recalled. He remembered seeing an article about him in the *Star*, recently. Commercial work, for the most part, but his stuff was beginning to show up in the more fashionable magazines, and his recent association with Lisa Remington, the fashion model, had done him no harm at all.

'Feeling better?' asked Paget, and received a grudging nod from Foster. 'Then perhaps you won't mind answering a few questions?'

Foster remained silent, his mind racing ahead, anticipating the questions he knew must come. Careful, he warned himself. They don't *know* anything. The trick is not to let them rattle you. Keep calm; just answer the questions. Don't, whatever you do, elaborate.

'Can you tell me how the body came to be in your well, sir?'

Foster almost laughed aloud. What a question. If only the man knew. Paget might have been asking about the weather. And so polite! He looked down at the mug in his hands and shook his head. 'I've no idea,' he said in a bewildered voice.

Paget looked sceptical. 'But you do live here, sir,' he pointed out. 'Surely you must have some idea?'

Foster shook his head in a dazed way again, then looked up. 'I don't know,' he said helplessly. 'If I knew I'd tell you, but I don't. I can't think how...' He frowned. 'How long has it been down there? I mean, it must have been there before I began to fill the well with stones.' He grimaced. 'That's a nasty thought, I must say.'

Paget ignored the question. 'Who else lives here?' he asked.

'Just Lisa—Lisa Remington. She's m-my girlfriend. But she's away at the moment. She's a model, you know. You've probably seen pictures of her.'

'Ah, yes, of course,' said Paget. 'You say she is away. When did she leave, exactly?'

Foster frowned and passed a hand across his face. 'I—I'm not sure,' he said. 'Sorry, but I can't seem to think straight. Two—three weeks ago.'

'And prior to that one or both of you were here all the time?'

'Yes. Well, most of the time. We both come and go quite a bit.'

'And when did you first start pulling down the sheep pen—and filling the well with stones?'

Foster appeared to give that some thought. 'It would be about the same time,' he said. 'Yes, that's right. I remember thinking I would try to have it all done by the time Lisa got back.' He lifted his hands. 'Unfortunately, I made a mess of my hands and I had to give it a rest. Doesn't do to have rough hands in my business, not when you're arranging things like bridal veils and delicate materials.'

'When do you expect Miss Remington back?'

'Actually, I'm not sure,' said Foster. 'She's working in France at the moment. She could be gone for some time. But you can't think that she had anything to do with this? I mean, it's ludicrous.'

'Does anyone else have access to your house while you are away?'

'No.'

'Who else would know about the well?'

'One or two friends, perhaps,' Foster said slowly, 'but I can hardly imagine that they...' He shook his head impatiently. 'No, it's too far-fetched.'

'In which case, since you say you know nothing about it, it is rather important that we talk to Miss Remington. Where can she be reached?'

'I'm not sure that she can,' said Foster slowly. 'You see, she's on location, and that could be anywhere the photographer chooses to be.'

'But there must be a base of some sort,' said Paget. There was an edge to his voice that hadn't been there before. 'She must be staying somewhere. What happens in the event of an emergency? How would you contact her?'

Foster shook his head stubbornly. 'You don't understand,' he said. 'This job came up unexpectedly. She left while I was away myself, and she didn't say where she would be. The note just said, "Off to France—good job.

I'll ring.'' Something like that.' He finished off the brandy
and set the mug on the floor beside his chair.

'You see,' he went on, 'Lisa is—well, something of a
free spirit. She becomes involved with her work. Time
means nothing to her, so she can go on for days, weeks,
even, without ringing. I don't know where she is.'

'You're saying you haven't heard from her since she
left?'

'It's not unusual for Lisa,' Foster insisted. 'She's probably rushed off her feet. It gets like that in her business,
you know.'

'Do you still have the note?'

Foster shook his head. 'Sorry,' he said apologetically.

The sound of heavy footsteps could be heard in the passageway, and a man stuck his head inside the door. He was
shorter than Paget, compact, and his face had a sort of
rumpled look about it that made him appear older than he
was. His dark hair and complexion bespoke his Cornish
ancestry, but his accent was that of a Londoner, much like
Paget's own. 'Could I have a word, sir?' he asked quietly.

'Of course,' Paget told him. 'Mr Foster, this is Detective
Sergeant Tregalles. If you will excuse us for a moment…?'

The two men acknowledged the introduction with a nod,
then Tregalles stepped back and Paget followed him out
and closed the door behind him.

'They've brought the body up,' Tregalles said quietly.
'Male, thirty to fortyish, no obvious distinguishing marks.
Dr Starkie says the body is remarkably well preserved due
to the cold water, but it's still—' he took in a deep breath
and exhaled slowly '—a God-awful mess. The face is gone,
blown away by a shotgun, according to Starkie. He says he
can see some of the pellets. And the skin—' he blew out
his cheeks '—it's sort of sliding off in places.'

Paget felt his stomach churn. This was the one part of
the job he hated. 'What about clothing?'

Tregalles shook his head. 'Naked, except for being wrapped in a sheet,' he said. 'Whoever put him down the well went to a lot of trouble to make sure he didn't come up again. He was weighted down with large stones wrapped in sheets tied to his neck and feet, then more stones were dropped on top of him.' Tregalles flicked his head toward the closed door. 'Even if Foster didn't do it himself, he has to know who did,' he concluded.

Paget was about to reply when the door opened and Foster came out into the passageway.

'Look, Chief Inspector,' he said, 'I've had a long day; I'm tired, I'm hungry, and I've had about all the questions I can take. I'm going to get something to eat.'

'Right,' said Paget. He turned to the uniformed constable. 'Please accompany Mr Foster to the kitchen and give him a hand,' he said. 'And, with your permission, Mr Foster, perhaps a cup of tea or coffee for the men in the yard?'

Foster, already moving toward the kitchen, hesitated. 'I suppose so,' he said ungraciously, and moved on. Paget watched him go for a moment, then turned back to Tregalles.

'Come on,' he said. 'Let's get it over with.'

'AT A ROUGH GUESS, I'd say he's been dead two or three weeks,' said Dr Starkie, 'but that's a *very* rough guess. I might be able to tell you more tomorrow after we've had a closer look, but I wouldn't put money on it. There's nothing more I can do here.'

'What do you say, Charlie?' Paget looked to Inspector Dobbs, the Scene-of-Crimes Officer, who hovered like a grey spectre at the edge of the pool of light surrounding the body. He was a tall, thin, gloomy-looking man, and now he came forward into the light, lips pursed, head shaking.

'We can find nothing to suggest that the killing took

place here,' he said. He eyed the cottage speculatively. 'The body was stripped, wrapped in a sheet, and weighted down with stones before it was dropped into the well,' he went on, 'and I can't see someone doing all that out here in the yard, can you?'

Almost against his will, Paget glanced at the body once again, and felt the sting of acid in his throat. 'No,' he said softly, 'I'm sure it wasn't. I think I'll have to have another word with Mr Foster.'

NONE OF THIS should be happening, Foster thought petulantly as he watched them move from room to room. He might as well not be there for all the attention they paid to him. He could have refused them permission to search, of course, but as that Chief Inspector bloody Paget had pointed out so reasonably, there were more than enough grounds for a search warrant, and he could get one, if necessary. But there might be those who would think Foster's refusal to co-operate was significant. 'And we wouldn't want that, would we, sir?'

Bastard! Seemed like a nice chap at first. Very polite. Came on smooth as silk. But questions...Christ, he never stopped! And when he did pause for breath, that other one, Tregalles, was in there right behind him.

Do you own a shotgun, Mr Foster? Ah, yes, thank you, sir. A twelve-bore; double barrel. Interesting. And loaded. A bit dangerous, don't you think, tucked in here behind the coats beside the front door? Use it often, do you? Rabbits? Do a lot of damage to the garden, do they? Of course, it's a bit early in the year for that, isn't it? Do you recall when you last used the gun, Mr Foster? Oh, yes, just one more thing: may we have the keys to your van?

On and on and on until he'd wanted to scream.

IT WAS GOING ON for eleven o'clock by the time Paget left for home. Charlie had called his people off at ten, telling them to be back there bright and early in the morning. A PC was assigned to stand watch throughout the night, and Foster had grudgingly agreed to allow him to use the kitchen. Foster himself had grown more sullen as the search progressed, and when Charlie told him he was free to go to bed, now that they were finished in the bedroom, he had gone in and slammed the door so hard that a picture had fallen off the wall.

Paget found it hard to believe that Foster did not know the whereabouts of Lisa Remington in France, and he found it more than a little strange that the man seemed to have no interest in where she was. When Paget had suggested that Lisa's agent might know how to contact her, Foster had tried to dissuade him from ringing the agent, saying that Lisa hated to be disturbed when she was in the middle of an assignment.

Was she actually in France? Paget sincerely hoped so. Because if she wasn't... He saw again in his mind's eye the decomposing body beneath the glare of the portable lamps, and quickly shut it out.

If there was anything to be found in the house, Charlie's people would find it; of that Paget had no doubt. Neither did he doubt that Foster was responsible for the body in the well. It was too much of a coincidence that the man should be dropping huge stones into the well immediately after someone else had put the body there. But whether or not they were dealing with a murder, or an accidental shooting and subsequent cover-up, remained to be seen. The search for the missing coins would continue tomorrow, and the rest of the stones would be removed from the well. He hoped that was all they would find down there.

He thought briefly of stopping at the office in Broadminster on his way through, but decided he'd had enough for one day. A light drizzle began to fall as he left the lights of the town behind, and he switched the wipers on. They thumped away hypnotically, and he found it hard to keep awake. Not for the first time, he wished he lived closer to town.

Perhaps it would be for the best if he sold the house and moved into town, he thought. Certainly it would cut his travelling time down. And yet, was it really all that much? Twenty minutes either way? That's all it was, and he *liked* the house. He *liked* living in Ashton Prior. The village was small, quiet—dead, some said—but he liked it. Besides, what would Mrs Wentworth do if he sold the house?

The house he now called home had once belonged to Mrs Wentworth and her husband. But when Bert Wentworth died she couldn't afford to keep it on, so she had moved into a maisonette and put the house up for sale. Paget's father saw it; fell in love with it and bought it, ignoring completely the fact that it was far too big for one person. A dentist, he had just recently left the London rat-race to join a clinic in Broadminster, where he would be working three days a week. It was his first step toward retirement, and toward his dream of retiring in the country after a lifetime in the city.

While negotiating for the house, he'd realized how hard it was for Mrs Wentworth to part with it, so he had asked if she would consider becoming his housekeeper. He would need someone to look after the place, and it would allow her to spend her days in the house that had meant so much to her. He even offered to make over part of the upstairs into a granny flat for her, but she had said no to that.

'It's ever so kind of you,' she told him, 'but it wouldn't be right, would it, Mr Paget? I mean, not living under the same roof like that. But I will come to work for you. It will be like I've never really left the house, won't it?'

The arrangement had worked well. Unfortunately, it

hadn't lasted long, for Paget's father had suffered a massive heart attack and died within the year.

Paget had inherited the house, and in a sense he'd inherited Mrs Wentworth along with it. Up to their ears as he and Jill were at work in London, he kept putting off going down to Ashton Prior to deal with the disposal of the house. Mrs Wentworth had agreed to stay on and look after the place until he and Jill could get time off together, but the days kept drifting on, and Mrs Wentworth, not unreasonably, wanted to know where she stood.

'It's the garden, you see, Mr Paget,' she told him on the telephone. 'I don't mind looking after the house, but I can't manage the garden as well, and I hate to see it left.'

Busy or not, he and Jill would have to make time, he decided. They couldn't go on like this. 'Next Tuesday,' he told her. 'We'll both be down. Could you book us into that pub by the church? Two nights should do, I should think.'

'Lord, bless me, there's no need for that, Mr Paget. Not when the house is empty. Don't you worry about that. I'll have everything ready.'

But next Tuesday never came. At least, not for Jill.

He felt the sting of salt behind his eyes as he relived once more those dreadful days. The explosion; the fire; Jill's torn and mangled body. The memories stopped abruptly, and no matter what he did, he could not recall a single thing for—what was it? Four weeks? Those weeks were gone, erased from his memory as if they had never been.

They said he'd carried on at work as if nothing had happened for almost three weeks before he collapsed at his desk. He remembered nothing until a week later when he found himself in hospital, and was horrified to learn he was in the psychiatric wing. Rest, they said. Get away for a while; time would heal.

He'd sought sanctuary down here in the country; fleeing

from the memories he could not bear. Mrs Wentworth had stayed on to look after him; coaxing him to eat; bullying him into taking walks when, left to his own devices, he'd have tried to lose himself in sleep.

An oncoming car came round the corner, headlights high, almost blinding him. 'Bloody idiot!' he growled as the car swept past. But the spell was broken and he was thankful, for his face was bathed in sweat.

FOUR

GRACE LOVETT stood in the middle of the back bedroom of the cottage and looked around. There was something not quite right about it, but she couldn't put her finger on it. She was still standing there when Tregalles put his head round the door.

'Everything all right?' he asked, seeing her puckered brow.

She shook her head, still frowning. 'I don't know,' she said slowly. 'Mr Foster did say this room hadn't been used since Christmas, didn't he?'

'That's right. His girlfriend's mother came down for Christmas. "She's the only one who ever uses the guest room,"' he quoted, mimicking Foster's public school voice. He came further into the room. 'Looks just like an ordinary back bedroom to me.'

'Philistine.'

'Phyllis who?'

'Point made.'

Tregalles wandered over to the window and stood looking out. To the right were trees, and beyond them the road to Clunbridge, while to the left was a large field sloping gently down the hillside to another band of trees beside the river. To the left of the trees was a farmhouse, a barn, and several outbuildings, all built, as was the cottage he was in, of local stone. As Tregalles watched, a tall, fair-haired young man came out of the barn and made his way to the house.

Beyond the river, the rolling hills lay snug beneath a patchwork quilt of fields aglow with morning sunlight. It was a beautiful view, and the kind of morning that made you want to be out there doing something. Tregalles wasn't quite sure what, for he was a city man at heart, and too much open space made him nervous.

Grace Lovett had opened the double doors of the large oak wardrobe, and had her head inside when Tregalles turned round. The wardrobe was empty, and when Grace sniffed loudly several times, it amplified the sound.

She withdrew her head. 'Stick your head in here and tell me what you smell,' she told Tregalles.

'Probably moth balls,' he said facetiously, but the expression on the young woman's face was serious. He did as she asked and sniffed several times. 'Smells like soap,' he said. 'Or perfume.'

Grace nodded. 'Perfume,' she said. 'Expensive perfume at that. Now come over here and tell me what you smell.' She led him out of the room, across the tiny landing at the top of the stairs, and into Foster's bedroom where she opened the double wardrobe there.

The wardrobe was filled with clothes. Some obviously belonged to Foster, but more than half of the space was taken up with female clothing. Tregalles leaned forward hesitantly.

'Get in there and take a good sniff,' Grace told him sharply.

'It's the same,' he said. 'At least, it smells the same to me. So what?'

'It is the same,' she told him.

'Perhaps she used the other wardrobe to hang some of her clothes in,' he offered. 'The ones she took with her. Or perhaps her mother uses the same perfume. Pinches it off her daughter, if it's that expensive.'

'Possibly,' said Grace, 'but Christmas was three months

ago. I doubt if it would be that strong. It's a very delicate fragrance. But there's something else, too. Take a look around you. What do you see? What sort of bedroom is it?'

Tregalles surveyed the room. 'It's a woman's room,' he ventured cautiously. 'Lace curtains, fancy duvet and those pillow cover things, and…'

'Shams,' said Grace. 'Those pillow cover things; they're called shams.'

'Oh.' Tregalles shrugged helplessly. 'I don't know what it is you want me to say.'

'Would you say this was done on the cheap?'

'Not my cheap, and that's for sure,' Tregalles said. 'There's more money in this room than there is in my whole house.'

'Exactly. Feel those sheets.'

Grace pulled back the duvet and Tregalles ran his fingers over the sheet beneath. 'Very nice,' he said. 'Care to slide under?'

'In your dreams, Tregalles. Now, come in here and try these.'

Tregalles meekly followed her into the back bedroom once again. She pulled back the coverlet and held up a corner of the sheet. Dutifully, he ran his fingers over it. 'Not a patch on the other one,' he declared, 'but then, this is only the guest room.'

'And yet everything else in here is just as good as in the other bedroom,' Grace pointed out. 'And, if you remember, Foster told us that it was Lisa who had all the redecorating done when she moved in. He sounded quite proud of her and the result.'

'What is it, Grace? What are you getting at?'

'Lisa Remington would never put sheets like that on this bed,' she said. 'They're cheap, they're shoddy, and they're as stiff as boards. I doubt if they've ever been used. They don't fit, Tregalles. They simply don't fit. And look at that wallpaper.'

'It looks all right to me,' Tregalles said. 'Don't you think you're getting a bit carried away, Grace? I mean, there could be any number of reasons why these sheets are different. And what's wrong with the wallpaper? It looks very like the one next door.'

'It's *like* it, yes. But look at the quality. That's not a Lisa Remington wallpaper.'

'Oh, come off it, Grace. Anyone would think you knew her personally.'

'I know her tastes,' Grace told him sharply. 'Look at her clothes, her shoes, the other bedroom, the curtains downstairs. Lisa wouldn't tolerate these things for a second. Besides, I saw the sheet the body was wrapped in, and it was top quality. I'm willing to bet a week's pay that it came off this bed.'

PETER FOSTER remained in his dark-room, pretending to work. He could hear them moving about up there in the guest room; hear the murmur of voices, but he couldn't make out what they were saying. He checked the door again to make sure it was locked, then cleared a space on his workbench. Using the stool as an aid, he climbed on to the bench, and stood with his head pressed against the low ceiling, but it was no good; the words were still muffled. Frustrated, he climbed down again and put everything back in place.

Not that he was really worried that they would find anything, he told himself. He must have been over the room a dozen times to make sure there was nothing *to* find. He wasn't out of the woods by a long shot, but without evidence they couldn't prove a thing.

So why was he sitting here sweating?

'LOOK AT THIS, sir,' Grace Lovett pulled the sheets back to reveal the mattress. 'It's brand new. The sheets are new; the pillowcases are new. They don't match the ones in the other room, and there are none like these among the linens. I've checked.'

Charlie fingered the material thoughtfully. 'You think the killing might have happened here?' he said.

'I'm sure of it,' said Grace. 'There's more. Look here.' She dropped to her knees and spread her fingers over the carpet. 'This has been cleaned recently,' she said.

'You've got better eyes than I have, then,' Charlie said as he bent closer. 'I don't see any difference.'

'Well, there is.' The young woman remembered to whom she was speaking, and modified her tone. 'I mean, I believe there is, sir. Just smell it. Someone's rubbed talcum powder or some such thing into the carpet, but you can still smell the spot cleaner underneath.' She looked up at him. 'You have to get your nose right down in it, sir.'

Muttering darkly, her boss got down on his knees beside her, groaning as he did so. 'And you can wipe that smirk off your face,' he growled. 'Just wait until you've got spikes on your knees, Lovett. You won't be smiling then.' He bent down with his nose almost touching the carpet—and sneezed. He clambered back on his feet, still sneezing.

'God, I'm getting too old for this,' he grumbled as he tried simultaneously to wipe his eyes and rub his knees. 'I couldn't smell anything but talcum powder, but I'll take your word for it. Take some fibres for analysis, then, but I doubt if we will get anything conclusive out of it.'

'Then try this, sir.' Grace ran her fingers along the skirting board. She caught the bottom of a join in the wallpaper and peeled it back several inches. 'See this wallpaper underneath?' she said. 'It's expensive like the paper next door. But this top layer isn't. It's similar, but it's not the same. It's cheap. Everything else in this cottage is expensive. According to Foster, Lisa Remington had the place redecorated when she moved in. That was less than a year ago. So why do it over with cheap wallpaper like this so soon?'

'Unless you're trying to cover something up,' Charlie finished for her. 'All right, Lovett, you've made your point. Let's hope you're right. Let's get this bed shifted and have this wallpaper off.'

FIVE

WHILE TREGALLES WENT OUT to the cottage to follow up on anything Charlie's people might find, Paget remained behind to brief Superintendent Alcott. The super had said nine o'clock, and here it was ten to ten and still no sign of him.

Not that Paget had been idle all that time. There were other matters to be attended to, and one of those matters was a phone call to Lisa Remington's agent, Sam Wiengard, in London.

'If she's in France, then she's there without my knowledge,' Wiengard told him bluntly. 'Not that I'd put it past her, but by God if her picture shows up in some Frog magazine, I'll have her. I'll have my commission *and* the penalty. It'll cost her, believe me. They all try it on sooner or later, especially when they start to lose it.'

'Are you saying she is no longer in demand?' Paget asked. 'It seems to me I've seen her picture on the cover of magazines in the shops quite recently.'

'Not on the top-line fashion magazines, you haven't,' said Wiengard. 'The ones you see her on now are second and third-raters. She's on her way down and she knows it. It's the looks, Chief Inspector; the little lines around the eyes; the neck. When they are spending more time airbrushing the lines out than they are setting up the shots, the photographers won't have it. Not when there's fresh talent coming up all the time. No, Mr Paget, Lisa Remington's on her way down, and I'd just as soon have her off my books. At least then I'd have Constance off my back.'

'Constance?'

A low chuckle rumbled down the line. 'I see you haven't met Lisa's mother,' said Wiengard. 'You've got a treat in store, Chief Inspector. A proper bitch is Constance. Sorry, got to go. Another call. If I hear where Lisa's working, I'll give you a bell.'

Alcott came breezing into Paget's office at ten past ten. 'I've got five minutes,' he told Paget briskly, 'then I'm off to another bloody meeting. Fill me in.'

Fifteen minutes later Alcott was still there. 'Nothing back from Starkie on the body, yet?' he asked. He lit another cigarette; the second since he'd been there.

'Just height, weight, age more or less—that sort of thing so far,' Paget told him, 'and Foster denies knowing anyone who fits that description. Not that I put much stock in that. If he didn't put that body in the well himself, he certainly knows who did.'

'Have you tried Missing Persons?'

'Yes. There is one possible, although there doesn't appear to be any connection. A man by the name of David Gray fits the general description. Works for a local software firm here in town. He was to be married this month, to the boss's daughter, no less, and there seems to be some thought that he might have got cold feet. Still, it's being checked out.'

Alcott glanced at the time. 'Keep me posted,' he said. 'I presume we can operate from the murder room here on this one?'

Paget hesitated. 'I'm not sure, yet,' he said slowly. 'I'm not at all satisfied with Foster's story about his girlfriend. She disappeared about the same time as the body was put in the well, and no one seems to know exactly where she is. I'm just hoping that she turns up soon. Otherwise...'

'Hmm.' Alcott ground out his cigarette. 'Let's hope it doesn't come to that,' he growled. 'Not just for the girl's sake, but for my budget. These on-site incident rooms are becoming damned expensive, and money is tighter than ever, as you well know. So, do me a favour and find the girl.'

PAGET PARKED ON THE ROAD next to the short driveway that led to Bracken Cottage, and got out of the car. The air smelt fresh and clean, and the morning sun warmed his face. March had been unusually mild, and if the forecast could be believed, the fine weather would hold throughout the first week of April at least. Fresh spring greens were everywhere; softening the dark brown latticework of hedges; filling in the winter skeletons of trees; and carpeting the meadows that swept upward to the hills. The plaintive cries of lambs broke the stillness of the air, and were answered by the deeper tones of ewes.

Paget drew in a deep breath and let it out again slowly. The air even tasted good, and he cast a longing eye at the hills that travelled westward into Wales. He really must find time for hiking this year, he told himself. Perhaps he'd take some time off when this case was over.

The warm feeling of well-being was shattered by a shout as he made his way up the driveway. 'Get in there, you great lout!' he heard someone say, and a tall, fair-haired youth burst through the wall of rhododendron bushes that lined the drive. He was followed swiftly by a uniformed PC. 'Get on there, dafty,' the PC said, shoving the lad in the back.

Despite his size, the boy looked scared to death of the smaller man.

'Just a minute, Constable. What's going on here?'

The man saw Paget for the first time. 'Oh, it's you, sir,' he said, modifying his belligerent tone. 'Caught the lad skulking in the bushes,' he explained. 'And he was carrying this.' He displayed a shotgun. It could have been the twin of the one that belonged to Foster. He gave the boy another shove between the shoulder blades. 'Get on with you, dafty,' he said roughly.

'That's enough!' said Paget sharply. He addressed the boy. 'What's your name?' he asked him. 'And what are you doing here?'

The boy looked as if he were about to cry. He opened his mouth, but only garbled sounds came out, and Paget realized he couldn't talk.

'It's Crazy Eric,' the PC said. 'He's soft in the head, if you know what I mean, sir?' He pointed a forefinger at his own head and twirled his hand back and forth. 'Lives at the farm down by the river. Tom Tyson's boy. It's Tom's land between here and the river.'

'And your name, Constable?' Paget's voice was dangerously quiet.

'Mosely, sir. PC Mosely from Clunbridge,' the man said with a self-congratulatory smirk.

'Mosely,' Paget repeated softly. 'Thank you. I'll take the gun and see to the boy.' He held out his hand for the gun, and Mosely handed it over. 'And if I ever see or even hear of you mistreating anyone like that again, especially someone who can't fight back, Mosely, I shall see to it personally that you spend the rest of your natural life patrolling Godford Ridge. Do I make myself clear?'

Mosely blanched and swallowed hard. Godford Ridge, better known among the locals as God-forsaken Ridge, was the nether end of nowhere. To be banished there was to say goodbye to any future on the force.

'But I was only...' He saw the look in Paget's eye and stopped. 'Yes, sir,' he said meekly. Paget dismissed him with an angry wave of the hand, waiting until the constable had gone before turning to the boy.

'No need to be afraid,' he said gently. 'I'd just like to talk to you for a few minutes. Eric, is it? Is that your name?'

The boy eyed him suspiciously for a moment, then nodded.

'Right, then, Eric. Do you have cartridges for your gun?' The boy delved into his pocket and held out three cartridges. 'May I have one?' Paget asked him. The boy hesitated, first looking at the cartridges, then at Paget, then back at the cartridges again. A shy smile crossed his face as he picked one out and thrust it at Paget.

'Thank you. Thank you very much, Eric,' Paget said. 'I'll let you have it back in a day or two.' The boy nodded happily.

Peter Foster appeared at the door. Eric had his back to him, and it was only when Foster spoke that he became aware of him. His reaction was immediate. He whirled, snatched the gun from Paget's hands and fled, crashing through the rhododendrons as if someone were after him. He went over the wall at the bottom of the garden and disappeared from sight.

Foster looked stunned. He stood there staring after the boy and scratched his head. 'I was just going to ask him if he wanted a cup of tea,' he told Paget. 'I saw him from the window, and he loves tea. I can't think what's got into him. That's the first time he's done that.' He shook his head in bewilderment. 'Usually, he walks right in. It's a bit embarrassing at times. He has trouble grasping the concept of privacy, and Lisa was always forgetting to lock the door.'

'What's wrong with the boy?'

'Brain damaged when he was born,' said Foster. 'He can't talk, of course, at least, not in the normal sense of the word, but we manage to communicate. He understands some things you say to him, but not others. Hard to say what his mental age would be. Three, four, something like that. It seems to change from day to day. Sometimes he seems older, but as I say, it comes and goes. We've always got along—at least, until now. Don't know what's got into him.'

'How old is he?'

'Twenty-two. Works on the farm with his dad. Hard worker, too. Loves the outdoors. Loves animals. Has a way with them. It's as if they understand he's no threat to them. Takes them under his wing if they're sick or hurt. Cares for them, and they always seem to get well. If I believed in that sort of thing, I'd say Eric is a natural healer. Except rabbits. Eric hates rabbits because they cause so much damage. Loves flowers. I don't know how he does it, but he finds flowers in the hedgerows even in the dead of winter. Tiny ones, mind you, but flowers nevertheless. He brings them for Lisa because he knows she likes them, and she makes a fuss over him when he does.'

Foster glanced over his shoulder as he heard the heavy tread of someone descending the stairs, and Tregalles appeared at his back. The sergeant looked past Foster to Paget.

'Charlie has something to show you upstairs,' he said quietly. He turned his attention to Foster. 'You might be interested in this as well, sir,' he said.

Foster saw the look on Tregalles's face, and he felt as if someone had just walked over his grave. 'Right,' he said, attempting to sound brisk. 'Shall we go and see what this is all about, Chief Inspector?'

It was a brave attempt, but his eyes betrayed him, and as he started up the stairs it was in the manner of a man condemned.

SIX

EVEN AS THEY MOUNTED the narrow stairs, Peter Foster still clung desperately to the hope that it would be something else they would want explained. It just wasn't possible, he told himself. He had been so very careful. There was no way they could tell.

But all hope vanished when he stepped into the room. The bed had been pulled aside, the newly painted skirting board pulled away from the base of the wall, and the wallpaper stripped off. No one said a word. There was no need.

The blood-spattered wall told its own story, and the last faint hope died within him. He began to cry. Tears flowed unchecked down his face as he stumbled from the room. Someone—he had no idea who it was—helped him down the stairs, and from that moment on his memory of events became a series of blurred images.

Foster was silent throughout the ride into Broadminster in the back of the police car. He dimly remembered being helped from the car, a long walk through corridors, stumbling up some stairs, and being led into a room. He sat down when someone told him to, and put his head in his hands.

So this was what it was like. He felt as if he'd been through it all before. He'd seen it on TV so many times: the bare walls; the wooden table; the hard wooden chairs. And, of course, the tape recorder. He watched dully as Paget set the tape recorder in motion and entered time and date and the names of those present. He felt quite detached. It was as if he were watching from a distance.

Paget said something to him, but it didn't register. The

chief inspector seemed to be waiting, but he didn't know what to say. No one had thought to give him a script.

So he said the first thing that came into his head. 'She didn't do it, you know. She couldn't. It must have been an accident.'

'Who didn't do it, Mr Foster?'

'Lisa. She couldn't have. Not deliberately. It was Merrick. They must have fought.'

'Let's go back to the beginning,' said Paget. 'Who is Merrick?'

'Lisa's husband. The man in the well. I put him there. It was all my doing. Lisa had nothing to do with that. She wasn't even there.'

'From the beginning, please, Mr Foster,' said Paget patiently. 'Let's start with the identity of the dead man. You say his name is Merrick, and he is Lisa Remington's husband?'

'That's right.' This was better. He didn't need a script. All Paget wanted was an explanation, and he could give him that. Suddenly, it all seemed so simple.

'See, Remington is Lisa's maiden name,' Foster said earnestly. 'And her professional name, but she was married to Merrick. Sean Merrick is a fashion designer. That's how they met. Irish. Charm the balls off a brass monkey when he's sober, but a wifebeating bastard when he's drunk. Which is most of the time these days. Lisa is divorcing him for cruelty, but Merrick wouldn't have it. Kept coming round to the cottage when I was away, pleading for her to come back to him. Said he hadn't been able to work since she left him. He even brought his latest designs to show her how bad they were. Tried to make her feel guilty so she would go back to him. When that didn't work he beat her up. He could have killed her. Didn't break any bones, but he could have done. I brought her in to the hospital. You can check. It was reported to the police; I insisted on that.' Foster's lip curled slightly. 'Not that anyone seemed very interested,' he went on. 'And Merrick lives in London, so I don't think anything was done about it.'

It was easier now that he could talk about it. Now he *wanted* everyone to know. If he could just explain.

'How long ago was this?'

Foster thought. 'Five, six weeks ago,' he said. 'That's why I made sure that Lisa kept the shotgun handy behind the door. In case Merrick decided to come back again, which of course he did.'

'When was that?'

'I don't know,' said Foster, then went on to explain as he saw the look of surprise on Paget's face. 'You see, I was away from the Monday to the Wednesday.' Foster took out a slim diary and consulted it. 'March 11th to 13th,' he said. 'I got back sometime after eight that night, and I knew something was wrong straightaway. You see, the door was open, and Merrick's design portfolio was there at the bottom of the stairs. So was the gun. It was lying on the floor just inside the door.' He was talking faster now, and colour had returned to his face.

'I was scared,' he went on. 'Afraid for Lisa. I picked up the gun and went through the house, yelling my head off, but there was no one downstairs. I felt sure that Merrick had surprised Lisa; she was always forgetting to lock the door. All sorts of things went through my mind. I was mad with worry. I was about to phone the police when I realized I hadn't been upstairs. I went up, not expecting to find anything, but then I saw the light was on in the guest room. I went in...' Foster buried his face in his hands and shuddered. 'It was horrible. I thought I was going to be sick.'

'What *did* you see, Mr Foster?'

Foster raised his head. His eyes were moist, and he stared straight ahead as if reliving the scene. 'Merrick was there on the bed,' he said. 'He was naked, and his head... Oh,

God! It was awful. I couldn't believe what I was seeing. I thought Merrick must have come back again; they must have struggled...' Foster's shoulders shook with emotion.

'And where was Lisa?' Paget asked.

Foster stared at him for a long moment. 'She wasn't there,' he said. 'She wasn't there, and I don't know where she is.'

THEY HAD BEEN THERE more than an hour. The room was warm, and both Foster and Tregalles had discarded their jackets, but Paget had kept his on. It was as if he were oblivious to everything other than Foster's testimony.

'I burned everything, scattered the ashes, then buried everything that wouldn't burn,' Foster had told them. Asked what he had done with the mattress, he said he had soaked it in petrol and burned it as well, then taken the metal skeleton to the local tip.

'Did it never occur to you to call the police?' Paget had asked.

'I couldn't, don't you see?' said Foster miserably. '*I* knew Lisa couldn't have killed Merrick deliberately, but I couldn't take a chance on you believing that. I just couldn't, that's all.'

'And you still say you have no idea where Miss Remington is?' It was Tregalles who asked the question. 'You haven't heard from her or spoken to her? She simply vanished? Doesn't that strike you as odd, Mr Foster? If what you are suggesting actually happened, don't you think she would at least ring you to say she was all right?'

Foster avoided the sergeant's eyes. 'She's frightened,' he said. 'She may think someone's listening in—I don't know.'

'Where would she go? You say you've tried all her friends and they say they haven't seen her. Where else could she go?'

'I've told you over and over again, I simply do not know!' Foster burst out. 'Perhaps one of her friends is lying. Perhaps Lisa told them not to say anything. Don't you think I've been over this in my mind a thousand times?'

'How would you describe your relationship with Miss Remington?' Tregalles asked.

'We love each other,' Foster said simply. Then, with more spirit, 'We've been living together for almost a year, for God's sake. What do you think our relationship was—is?'

'I don't know, sir. That's why I asked,' said Tregalles. 'Would you say you're a jealous man?'

Foster's eyes narrowed. 'I don't know what you mean,' he said. 'What are you getting at?'

'I just wondered how you might react if you came home to find Miss Remington in bed with her husband, that's all, sir.'

Foster half rose from his seat, his face livid. 'You bastard!' he yelled. 'Lisa would never…'

But Tregalles cut him off. 'By your own admission, sir, Merrick was in your spare bed and he was naked when he was shot. Now why would he be in bed in that condition if he were alone? Wouldn't it make more sense if someone was in there with him? Someone like Lisa Remington?'

Foster, pale now, sank slowly into his seat. 'You're suggesting that *I* killed Merrick,' he breathed. His voice rose. 'And that I killed Lisa?'

Tregalles shrugged. 'Look at it from my point of view, Mr Foster,' he said reasonably. 'Wouldn't you say it's a possibility?'

Foster clamped his mouth shut.

Paget, who had remained silent throughout the exchange, stood up. 'I think you'd better come back to the cottage with us, Mr Foster, and show us exactly where you buried everything,' he said. 'You can sign a statement later.' He paused. 'But I am curious about one thing. You say Merrick came to the cottage on more than one occasion. Came by car, did he?'

'That's right. He drives a Volvo.'

'So where is his car, Mr Foster? Obviously, Mr Merrick didn't drive it away that day, so where is it? Did you get rid of that, too?'

'No. It—I don't know. It wasn't there. He must have…I just don't know.'

PAGET SURVEYED all that remained of Merrick's clothing and possessions: a few melted buttons, tiny pieces of metal from a zip-fastener, the charred remains of leather shoes, and a few bits of cloth that had somehow escaped the fire. Neither was there much left of the man's other belongings. A melted pen, a digital watch, a pocket calculator, several coins, nail clippers, a comb, two sets of keys, and a few odd bits of leather that were once part of a wallet.

The heavy covers of the portfolio were identifiable, but there was nothing left of Merrick's designs. The metal bases of two cartridges were there as well, but they'd been hammered flat. They went over to the lab along with everything else, but it seemed highly unlikely that the lab would be able to match them to a particular gun.

'And nothing belonging to Lisa Remington,' said Paget thoughtfully as he surveyed the items spread out on a plastic sheet.

A description of both Lisa Remington and her car had gone out earlier that day, and a description of Merrick's car would be in circulation by the evening. Finding Lisa Remington had become a priority, and Paget had discussed the matter with Superintendent Alcott before returning to Bracken Cottage.

'I'm afraid we're going to need the mobile murder room,' he'd told Alcott. 'I think there's a very good chance that Lisa Remington is dead, and we are going to have to extend our enquiries.'

Alcott drew deeply on his cigarette. 'What about Foster?' he asked. 'Do you have enough to charge him?'

Paget shook his head. 'Not enough to satisfy the DPP,' he said. 'Foster has admitted concealing evidence, but we'll need more before we can pin a charge of murder on him.'

Alcott sighed. 'Very well,' he said. 'I suppose you'll want Len Ormside out there to run the mobile unit?'

'I'd appreciate it, sir. Thank you.'

'Just wrap this thing up fast,' said Alcott. 'We're already over budget for the first quarter, so for God's sake go easy, especially on the overtime.'

One of the diggers spoke to Paget. 'I don't think there is anything more to be found down there, sir,' he said. 'The ground is rock solid. Shall we fill it in?'

'Go ahead,' said Paget. He'd hoped for more; something that would at least give them a lead, but there was nothing. The well had been completely cleared of stones, and the missing coins found, but there was no sign of anything belonging to either Merrick or Lisa Remington. And the ashes of the fire in the garden had been sifted without result.

The sound of a car turning into the driveway caught Paget's attention. A door slammed, and a shrill voice could be heard demanding to know what was going on. A uniformed constable appeared, and beside him was a woman. 'Where's Lisa?' she was saying. 'And where's Peter?'

'If you'll just come with me, madam...' the constable was saying, but that was as far as he got.

'Don't you "madam" me, young man. I demand to know what's going on here. Where's my daughter?'

Constance Remington. Paget was reminded of Sam Wiengard's words, and he braced himself. Beside him Tregalles drew in his breath and said, 'Good God!'

The woman must be sixty if a day, the chief inspector thought. And thin. Excruciatingly thin. Her face was long and narrow, gaunt beneath a mass of hair whose colour defied description. Flaming brass was the closest Paget could come, and that, he felt, was being charitable. Her eyes were large and heavily made up, and her make-up looked as if it had been applied with a trowel. Her hands were skeletal, seeming to consist of little more than bones—with a ring on every bony finger.

Paget was left with the impression that he was seeing a caricature of the woman rather than the woman herself, but for all that, Constance Remington was beautifully dressed. She wore a two-piece suit of soft lilac, with a high-necked blouse to match. The jacket was slightly flared at the hips to give shape to her spartan frame, while the calf-length skirt was straight, tubular, to minimize the stick-like quality of her legs. Matching high-heeled shoes and handbag completed the ensemble.

Paget stepped forward. 'Mrs Remington?' he said. 'I'm Chief Inspector Paget. Perhaps I can help.'

The woman stopped in front of him, and the constable departed hastily. 'How do you know my name?' she demanded. 'And why are you here? Where's Lisa?'

'I was rather hoping you might be able to tell me,' Paget said. 'But first things first.' He began to walk slowly toward the house, and she fell into step beside him. An overpowering wave of perfume made him catch his breath. It was nothing like the subtle fragrance Paget had come to associate with her daughter.

'Peter Foster gave me your name,' he said, 'and we are here because we are investigating a suspicious death.'

'Who?' the woman demanded sharply.

'Sean Merrick,' Paget told her. 'Your son-in-law, or so I'm told.'

'Sean's dead? How? What happened?'

'He was shot. Here in the cottage.'

'Not by Peter, surely? He wouldn't have the guts.'

'That's what we are trying to find out, Mrs Remington.' As they rounded the corner, Paget caught a glimpse of a taxi backing into the road, and a suitcase stood on the doorstep of the cottage. 'That was your taxi, I take it?' he said.

'Yes, why?'

'Now that you're here, I would like to ask you some questions,' he said, 'but I'm afraid you won't be able to stay here.'

Constance bristled. 'Why not? I always do.'

'Because it's now a crime scene,' Paget explained patiently. 'I'm sorry, but I can have someone run you back to town.'

But Constance Remington had picked up her suitcase and marched into the house. She went straight into the living-room, set the case down, and turned to face Paget with a 'So there!' look on her face. 'Peter!' she called. The shrill voice echoed in the empty house. 'Where is Peter?' she demanded.

'He's unavailable at the moment. He's helping us with our enquiries.'

'You mean he did it? My God! I didn't think he had it in him. Good for Peter. It's time someone took care of that drunken so-called son-in-law of mine. Save Lisa a lot of time and money with the divorce proceedings, at least. Now, what's this about not knowing where Lisa is?' A wariness crept into her eyes. 'You can't think that she had anything to do with this?' Her tone threatened dire consequences if he said yes.

'Until we talk to her, we won't know whether she did or not. Tell me, when did you last hear from her?'

Mrs Remington opened her handbag, took out a cigarette, lit it, and blew out a cloud of smoke before answering. 'Peter kept telling me some cock-and-bull story about her being in France,' she said, 'but I didn't believe him. He just didn't want me coming down here.' She frowned in concentration. 'It must be all of three weeks ago when I last spoke to her. I phoned on the Sunday as I usually do—she'd never think of phoning me, of course—do you have children, Mr... What was your name again?'

'Paget,' he said. 'And, no, I don't have children, Mrs Remington.'

'You're lucky,' she told him bluntly. 'I spent the best part of my life getting Lisa to where she is today. Everything she has, she owes to me. Oh, yes, Mr Paget, it may not look like it now, but I've gone without. I know what it's like to hide behind the door when the rent man comes round, just so Lisa could have her dance lessons. And deportment, and voice. Cost a packet, that lot did, I can tell you. Not that I begrudge it, mind, but a bit of gratitude wouldn't come amiss. But then, it's the same with all of them today, isn't it? Selfish. No thought for anybody but themselves.'

Paget, who had been looking at a pocket calendar, was fast losing patience. 'Would that have been March 10th, Mrs Remington?' She looked at him blankly. 'When you last spoke to Lisa.' He offered her the calendar.

Constance Remington scrutinized it. 'Yes, that's right,' she said. She drew deeply on her cigarette, then looked round for somewhere to dispose of it. Seeing no ashtray, she dropped it on the stone hearth and crushed it with her shoe.

'Do you remember what you talked about? Did Lisa mention any plans? Anything like that?'

'Not that I remember. She did say something about coming up to town in the next week or so, but that's all. That's where she'll be now, I shouldn't wonder. She gets bored, stuck away in the country like this, miles from anywhere. I'm surprised she's put up with it for so long. Mind you—'

Mrs Remington glanced around as if afraid of being overheard '—I shouldn't be surprised if she leaves him, spe-
cially after this.'

'Leaves Peter Foster?'

Constance shrugged and waved a deprecating hand. 'You
must admit, it's a bit—primitive,' she said. 'Not Lisa's
thing at all. I knew it wouldn't last, but she thought it would
be so "romantic". All that country air; going for nice long
walks. Rubbish, I told her. Lisa wouldn't walk ten yards if
there was a car to take her. Mind you, it was the same with
the others, but at least she doesn't intend to marry Peter.
Good thing, too. No spine. No backbone at all.'

Mrs Remington paused. 'Still, he must have *some* backbone, I suppose,' she mused, 'if he killed Sean.'

'No one is suggesting that Mr Foster killed anyone,'
Paget told her. 'He is merely…'

'…helping you with your enquiries,' Constance finished
for him. 'I know, I know, but I wasn't born yesterday. It
amounts to the same thing, doesn't it?'

There was no point in arguing with the woman. 'Do you
have an address for Mr Merrick?' he asked her. 'Mr Foster
told us he moved recently to a flat in Fulham, but he didn't
know the exact address.'

Mrs Remington nodded. 'My address book is in my
case,' she told him, 'but, yes, I have it.'

'What about Mr Merrick's next of kin? Apart from Miss
Remington, of course.'

Mrs Remington grimaced. 'I don't think he had any,' she
said. 'That is, not here in England. I seem to remember his
speaking of some distant cousins in Ireland, but that's all.
He was Irish, you know. Straight out of the bog. Oh, he
was full of the blarney, and I must admit he had a talent
for design, but he had the manners of a pig. He used to
knock Lisa about, you know. That's why she left him. They
were only married six months. Charming devil when he

was sober, but a bastard when he was drunk. Lisa would have reported him, but I talked her out of it. That sort of publicity would have finished her. No one wants a battered bride as a model. He left her face alone, of course. He was clever enough to know where the bread-and-butter came from, but he used the rest of her for a punching bag.

'And he didn't take kindly to her leaving. Came down here several times trying to get her to go back to him, and I must admit I was afraid for her. I was glad when she said Peter had shown her how to use the shotgun. Give the bugger a load of shot up the arse, I told her. See how he likes it.' She stopped as she realized what she had said. 'I didn't mean…'

'I'd like Mr Merrick's address before you go,' Paget said. 'And the address of any of Lisa's friends.'

The look on Constance Remington's face hardened. 'But I'm not leaving,' she said flatly. 'I'm staying here until all this is sorted out.'

'We will need the address of where you will be staying,' said Paget, 'but I can assure you, Mrs Remington, that you are not staying here. Shall we go?'

SEVEN

Wednesday 3rd April

THE MOBILE FORWARD incident room, to give it its official name, was already in place on the strip of land immediately behind Bracken Cottage by the time Paget arrived at eight thirty. Technicians from British Telecom were busy hooking up telephone and data lines, and one computer was already up and working. And working around them were the men and women who would be interviewing the local people, preparing and writing up statements, sifting information, and co-ordinating every scrap of intelligence into a comprehensive whole.

Overseeing all this activity was Len Ormside, a sergeant with thirty years' experience, and this was what he did best. He knew the area; he knew the people; and he was very good at anticipating the needs of his superiors. Tall, thin, sharp-featured, he moved with the deliberation of a very methodical man—and being methodical was what made him ideal for the job.

'I want you to concentrate on the list Foster gave us of all the people they know and associate with round here,' Paget told him. 'I want to know if anyone saw or heard anything at all unusual during the week starting March 10th. That was when Mrs Remington last spoke with her daughter, and I'm assuming that Merrick was killed after that. Starkie cannot fix the time of death any closer than sometime in that week, so I'm afraid you'll have to cast your net wide. I want to know if anyone saw Foster during that time, and if so, exactly when and under what circumstances. I want to know when Merrick arrived and how he got here, because, according to Foster, he didn't come by car. Foster could be lying, of course, but whether he is or not, we still need to know what happened to Merrick's car.

'Even more importantly, find out anything you can about Lisa Remington. Did anyone see her leave the cottage? If so, when? Any scrap of information at all. We know she hasn't used her bank card since the end of February, neither has she used a credit card since 8th March. Tregalles is on his way to London to talk to a woman Foster tells us is Lisa's best friend, and to check out Merrick's flat. Although it seems unlikely, it's just possible that Lisa is hiding out there, but in any case we need information on the man.'

Ormside made a wry face. 'Do you really think the lass is alive?' he said, voicing the thought that had lain unspoken in Paget's mind since yesterday. 'I'd say it's much more likely that Foster came home unexpectedly, caught them at it, and blasted away with the gun.'

Paget nodded. 'You may well be right, Len,' he agreed, 'but if that's what happened, what did he do with the body? There is no evidence that anything else has been buried on Foster's land. And why, having dumped one body down the well, didn't he dump the other one down there as well? The way I see it, there are three possibilities: it could be as you said, Foster killed them both; it could also be that he killed Merrick, and Lisa ran out and got away before he could stop her; or it could be that Lisa killed Merrick herself and has gone into hiding. Or, come to think of it, there is a fourth possibility: perhaps Lisa Remington wasn't there at all when Merrick was killed.'

'What about Foster? Can't we do something about him?'

'We will,' Paget assured him. 'He'll be charged with obstruction, concealing a body, and half a dozen other things, but that's all for the moment.'

Ormside grunted. It was simpler in the old days, he

mused. Take them in for questioning and lean on them. Then chuck them in the cells and let them sweat for a day or two, then do it all over again. But you couldn't do that today. All these rules and regulations. Christ! the villains had more rights than coppers these days. He brushed the thought aside. There was work to be done, and the sooner he got on with it the better.

ORDINARILY, Tregalles would have gone directly to Merrick's flat in Fulham, but Jane Lansing, Lisa's best friend, according to Foster, lived in South Kensington, which was on his way. He had telephoned the night before to arrange a meeting, and Miss Lansing had agreed, albeit somewhat reluctantly it seemed to him, to see him at eleven.

If she had sounded reluctant on the phone, there was no sign of that reluctance when she answered the door. She invited Tregalles in and offered him a drink. 'Ordinary tea, herbal tea, or coffee?' she said brightly.

'You're having something?' he asked cautiously.

'I'm having herbal tea,' the young woman said. She saw him hesitate, and laughed. 'I have coffee made,' she told him. 'You don't look like a herbal tea man to me.'

Tregalles warmed to her. Jane Lansing was small, slim, and very attractive. She had long, flowing hair the colour of burnished copper, dark eyes that crinkled easily into a smile, a generous mouth, and a lightly freckled face. She wore a white, short-sleeved tailored shirt, open at the neck and pulled in sharply at the waist. It disappeared beneath the waistband of designer jeans that moulded to her body like a second skin. Her feet, he saw with some surprise, were bare.

'Just be a minute,' she told him as she left the room.

He barely had time to note the details of the room before she returned. Small, casually furnished, but very comfortable, with a few good prints on the walls, and a large, old-fashioned spinning wheel in one corner. A tape was playing in the background; one of those mood music things, he decided, with waves and long synthetic sighs of sound.

Jane Lansing appeared with a tray and set it on a small table between them. 'Please help yourself to milk and sugar,' she told him.

Tregalles spooned in a generous helping of sugar while Jane Lansing sipped her tea. 'I hope this isn't all a waste of your time, Sergeant,' she said. 'As I told you, I haven't seen Lisa for at least a month, so I don't know how I can help you. Is she in some sort of trouble?'

Tregalles side-stepped the question. 'Can you think of anyone she might stay with?' he asked. 'A friend, relative, anyone?'

A strange expression crossed the young woman's face. 'Has she left Peter?' she asked.

'What makes you say that?'

'Well—I don't think I'm telling tales out of school if I tell you she's been thinking about it for some time, and she was getting a bit desperate the last time she was here.'

'How, exactly, do you mean, "desperate", Miss Lansing?'

'I think it was a combination of things, really,' she said. 'I know she was bored silly down there in the country with nothing to do, and Peter was growing more and more possessive. I mean, he wanted to know where Lisa was all the time, and he didn't like her leaving the cottage even when he was away for a week at a time.'

The young woman sipped her tea. 'She did, of course. Came up to London whenever she got the chance, but she didn't always tell Peter.'

'She stayed here with you?'

Jane Lansing arched an eyebrow over her cup, and a smile tugged at the corner of her mouth. 'Sometimes,' she said guardedly.

'It *is* important, Miss Lansing. Very important.'

The young woman set her cup down. 'Look, Sergeant, if I had some idea about what Lisa's done, I might be able to help you, but I'm simply not going to talk about her behind her back.'

Tregalles set his own cup aside. 'To the best of our knowledge, Lisa Remington has been missing since sometime after March 10th,' he said. 'She disappeared at or about the same time that her husband, Sean Merrick, was killed in Bracken Cottage, and no one admits to seeing her since. So, anything you can tell me about her or where she might be would be of considerable help.'

Jane Lansing stared at him wide-eyed. 'Killed? Sean? My God! Down there at the cottage? Then he did come back. Lisa was afraid he would.' Her eyes suddenly narrowed. 'What do you mean by "killed"?' she asked.

'He was shot with a twelve-bore,' Tregalles said bluntly.

'Oh, my God! And you think Lisa did it?' She fell silent. 'Not that she wouldn't have cause,' she said softly. 'Oh, poor Lisa. But why didn't she come here? Why haven't I heard?' She looked to Tregalles for answers.

He didn't think she was acting. Jane Lansing seemed genuinely shocked by the news—and perhaps a little hurt that Lisa had not come to her for help.

'Please listen to me, Miss Lansing,' he said. 'It has not been established who killed Mr Merrick. There are several possibilities. But we are concerned about your friend, Lisa. Now, if she found herself in serious trouble, or wanted to go into hiding, would you expect her to come to you for help?'

Jane Lansing nodded, but she looked puzzled. 'I'd like to think this is the first place she would come,' she said. 'We've known each other ever since we started modelling, not that I was ever in her class, of course. But she didn't, Sergeant. I swear she didn't, and I can't understand it.'

'There is no record of her having used her bank or credit cards since she disappeared, and it seems to me that she would need money. Is there anyone she could go to for help of that nature?'

Jane Lansing shook her head. 'Lisa's line of credit is pretty thin, here in London,' she said slowly, brow furrowed as she tried to think of possibilities.

'What about her mother?'

'Constance? Lisa would die before she'd ask her mother for money,' she said emphatically. Jane's face became grave. 'Are you quite sure you've told me everything, Sergeant?' she asked hesitantly. 'Is Lisa dead?'

Tregalles hesitated only briefly. 'I'm afraid that is one possibility,' he admitted. 'But we still hope to find her alive.'

Jane Lansing shut her eyes. 'Oh, Lisa,' she breathed. Her eyes remained shut, but her voice steadied as she said, 'You said Lisa wasn't the only one who could have killed Sean. Is Peter a suspect?'

'Why do you ask that?' Tregalles countered.

'Because I'm sure that Peter must have suspected what Lisa was doing when she came up to London, and he's a very jealous man. I really don't know what he would do if he ever found out the truth.'

Tregalles picked up his coffee. It was cold. 'Don't you think it would be best if you told me everything?' he suggested. 'What *is* the truth about Lisa Remington, Miss Lansing?'

'IT'S ROUND THE BACK,' the sharp-featured woman told Tregalles as she began to shut the door. Tregalles held it open. 'When was the last time you saw Mr Merrick?' he asked her.

'I don't see him,' she said. 'I keep myself to myself, and I expect him to do the same. But you can tell him from me that if I don't have this month's rent by the end of the week, he can get out.'

'Pays by the month, does he?'

The woman scowled. 'What if he does?' she asked suspiciously.

'Then you must have seen him at the beginning of March,' Tregalles said.

'What if I did?'

'When was that, exactly? What date? Please, it's important.'

'Why? What's he done? Why don't you ask him yourself?'

Tregalles was beginning to lose patience. 'Because he's dead, that's why,' he said bluntly.

The woman stepped back. Alarm flared in her eyes. 'Here,' she said, 'what sort of game are you playing? What do you mean, he's dead?'

'Just that. He was killed about three weeks ago. Now, please, will you answer the question?'

The woman tried harder to close the door. 'I don't know what your game is,' she said, 'but if you're not out of here in ten seconds, I'm ringing the real police.'

'But I am the real police,' Tregalles said, struggling to hold the door. 'I showed you my warrant card.'

The woman thrust her face forward until it almost touched his own. 'Well, tell me this, then, Mr Policeman,' she said. 'If Mr Merrick's dead, who's been driving his car and living downstairs all this time, then? You tell me that, clever clogs!'

PETER FOSTER was in his dark-room. He'd spent most of the day in there, not so much because he had work to do, but to avoid seeing policemen every time he looked out of a window. They were a constant reminder that he was, in fact, the prime suspect in the murder of Sean Merrick.

They didn't believe him; he knew that. Oh, why, oh, why had that stupid yob chosen to hide in the well? It was as if the hand of fate had reached out, and it frightened him. The odds against something like that happening must be a million to one, but there it was, and there was nothing he could do about it.

Except stick to his story. They couldn't prove a thing if he stuck to that.

Although it was his dark-room, Foster also used it as an office, and he was sitting at his desk when the telephone rang. He scooped it up. Someone will be listening to this, he thought. In case Lisa should ring. To hell with them, he thought recklessly. Let them.

'Two-three-eight-one, Peter Foster here,' he said.

'Ah, Mr Foster. Is Miss Remington there, please?'

'No. Who is this?'

'It's me, Bill Burbridge down at the garage, Mr Foster,' the man said, and Foster recognized the voice of the owner of Burbridge Motors (Sales and Service since 1933) in Broadminster. 'Sorry it took so long,' the man said apologetically, 'but you know how it is with these foreign motors, Mr Foster, and then, of course, we had to send it out for spraying…'

Foster gripped the phone. 'What are you talking about, Bill?' he asked sharply. 'Do you mean *Lisa's* car?'

There was silence at the other end for a moment. 'Sorry,' the man said again, 'but I thought you'd know. About the accident, I mean.'

'What accident?'

'Why, the accident right outside the garage, Mr Foster. When Miss Remington tried to make that turn round the metal post on the corner. Cut it too fine; crushed the whole side in, and we had to order…'

'When was this?' Foster asked sharply.

'Like I said, about three weeks…'

'I mean what date, man? I want the exact date!'

There was a rustling of paper. 'March 12th,' said Burbridge. 'You see, it was...'

But Peter Foster had hung up, and was half-way to the door.

THE TEN-YEAR-OLD VOLVO was there in plain view beside the back gate, and the number plate matched the one being circulated. Tregalles put his hand on the bonnet. It was slightly warm.

He opened the iron gate and went down the crumbling steps. Jane Lansing had told him that Merrick had been going downhill steadily ever since Lisa left him, but he hadn't expected this. But neither had he expected to be told that someone was living in Merrick's so-called flat, and it was with a certain amount of caution that he knocked at the door.

There was no response. He knocked again, louder this time, and heard faint sounds inside. He knocked a third time and was rewarded by a bellowed 'Sod off and let me sleep!'

Tregalles knocked again, and this time he heard a rumbling behind the door, and it was suddenly flung open. A man dressed only in vest and trousers stood there, swaying. He looked as if he'd just come off a five-day binge; his eyes were bloodshot; his face unshaven, and even at that distance his breath was enough for Tregalles to turn his head aside.

He held his warrant card up and identified himself, but before he could continue, the man spewed out a torrent of abuse.

'What is it with you bastards?' he ended bitterly. 'Do you take it in turns? Christ, I've only just got back and got my head down, and here you are again. What is it, now?'

'Who are you?' Tregalles said. 'What's your name? And what are you doing here in this house?'

'Jesus, Mary!' The man looked to heaven as if for aid. 'Who the bloody hell do you think I am?' he bellowed. 'You lot have had me in often enough. Merrick, for Christ's sake. Sean Christopher Michael Merrick! All right? Or do you need it spelling for you?'

'IT'S MERRICK, all right.' Tregalles was speaking to Paget. 'I'm ringing from the local nick where he spent last night. Drunk and disorderly. He was at the cottage, though, on the Monday, March 11th. Says Lisa sent him packing with a load of buckshot, and he has the scars on his backside to prove it. And he's still limping. That's when he left his portfolio there. I have his statement, and I also have a statement from Jane Lansing.'

When Tregalles had given Paget a brief outline of what Lisa's friend had told him, the chief inspector told his sergeant not to spend any more time in London, but to get back as soon as possible. 'We have an interesting development down here,' he said. 'Tell you all about it when you get back.'

Tregalles had phoned from Worcester to tell his wife that he would be home, but it would be late, and he told her not to wait up. But when he let himself in shortly before midnight, Audrey was there waiting for him. He shrugged out of his coat and kissed her.

'You should have gone to bed,' he told her. 'I said not to wait up.'

Audrey took his coat and hung it up. 'Hungry?' she asked. 'Or did you manage to get something to eat?'

'I could go a nice cup of tea,' he said. 'I don't know what they do to the air on trains, but I'm so dry.'

Audrey went ahead of him into the kitchen and put the kettle on. Tregalles watched her with affection. A dyed-in-the-wool family man, he was glad to be home. It was all very well for those who liked a few days away on expenses, but give him home every time. For a brief moment he thought of Jane Lansing, lovely face, lively eyes, perfect body, and very nice with it, too. The sort of girl who would turn any man's head.

But he wouldn't swap his Audrey for ten Jane Lansings, he thought comfortably. He put his hands around her waist. 'Good to be home, love,' he told her.

'Good to have you home,' she responded, but there was a worried frown on her face and she seemed tense, preoccupied.

'Anything wrong?' he asked.

Suddenly, her eyes were moist and a tear trickled down her cheek. 'I'm sorry,' she said as she busied herself with cups and saucers. 'I was going to wait till morning to tell you, but...'

'What is it, then? Here, never mind those. Sit down and tell me. What's happened?'

Audrey sank into a chair. 'It's Olivia,' she began, and quickly put a hand on his arm as she saw alarm flare in his eyes. 'Oh, no, she's all right,' she assured him. 'It's just that there was this man outside the school, today. He spoke to her; walked along with her. He didn't *do* anything, but it's just the thought... Oh, John, I should have been there myself, but Joan said she'd be there all this week, and I didn't know she'd been taken ill until afterwards. I wouldn't have even known about it if Brian hadn't said something at tea-time.'

Tregalles felt as if his collar were choking him. He could feel the blood rushing to his face, and it had become unbearably hot. 'But Olivia is all right? He didn't harm her? What did he say? Did he touch her?'

Audrey put her hand out quickly and caught his sleeve. 'No, John. It's all right,' she hastened to assure him. 'Calm

down. Olivia says he didn't, and so does Brian. The trouble
is, Olivia said he was such a nice man. After all we've
said; after all the school has done...' Audrey shrugged
helplessly. 'I just don't know what else to do, John, except
to make sure that she is never on her own again.'

Tregalles sat down slowly. It was an effort, but he forced
himself to calm down. Just the thought of young, lovely,
innocent Olivia being approached by a man created a storm
inside him, but he knew there was no point in going off
half-cocked. But it was hard. He took Audrey's hands in
his.

'Did Olivia tell you what the man said?' he asked gently.

'She said he kept calling her Wendy. And he talked
about a dolls' house at home.'

Oh, God! Trying to get her interested in going with him
to see the dolls' house. 'Didn't anyone else see him? Do
anything? Ask him who he was?'

Audrey shook her head in a bewildered sort of way.
'That's the odd thing,' she said. 'Both Brian and Olivia
said there were other people about, but nobody *did* anything. It's as if the man was invisible. I don't understand
it at all.'

'Did you report it?'

Audrey nodded. 'I spoke to Jim Dean, and he sent Molly
Forsythe round to talk to Olivia, but I don't know how
much good it will do. She tried to get a description of the
man out of Olivia, but all she could tell her was that the
man was "really old like the vicar". Brian did say the man
had a dark suit on, and they both agreed he had grey hair,
but that was it. Molly was going round to see some of the
parents who meet their kids out of school, and she said
they'd do their best to have someone over there tomorrow.'

The vicar was not yet fifty, so what 'really old' meant
was open to question. Tregalles decided to try for a better
description in the morning, but he knew how hard it was

to get adults to describe someone, let alone children. Still, if Olivia had likened the man's age to that of the vicar, it was just possible that the man might resemble the vicar in other ways.

'Did you phone the school?' he asked.

'Molly did. She talked to the headmaster, and she talked to a couple of the teachers. None of them saw anything, but they are very concerned, and I'm sure they will have the patrols on alert tomorrow.' Tears welled up once more, and Audrey pressed her knuckles to her mouth. 'It's just the thought, love,' she whispered. 'It's just the thought.'

EIGHT

Thursday 4th April

'WELL, if it's not Merrick, who the hell is it?' Alcott crushed out a cigarette in the overflowing ashtray and lit another. 'What the hell am I going to tell Mr Brock?' Morgan Brock was the chief superintendent, CID, and Alcott's immediate superior. 'And what's he going to tell the chief constable?'

'I'm afraid it caught us all by surprise,' Paget said. 'I had no reason to believe that Foster wasn't telling the truth when he identified the man as Merrick. It made sense; the man's portfolio was there, so it never occurred to me to question it. Sorry, but there it is.'

Alcott puffed furiously on his cigarette. 'And what does Foster have to say about it?'

Paget spread his hands. 'He claims that he honestly believed it *was* Merrick. He says he was so shaken by the sight of him lying there naked in the bed with his face shot away, that he just assumed it was Merrick. And having seen the portfolio at the bottom of the stairs, and having had trouble with him before, he was *expecting* to see Merrick.'

'What about the man's belongings? His clothes; his wallet?'

'He says that he just wrapped everything up in a sheet without looking at any of it, then threw it all on the fire.' Alcott's expression was one of patent disbelief. 'There is some support for that,' Paget went on. 'Forensic found evidence of quite a large sum of money having been burned along with the wallet, so it looks as if he did throw everything on the fire without looking at it too closely. It's not proof by any means, but as I say, it does tend to support his story.'

'What about credit cards and that sort of thing?' Alcott asked shrewdly.

'There were several, but they were very badly mutilated in the fire. Forensic hopes to raise enough numbers to give us a lead.'

'And the body?' Smoke trickled into Alcott's eyes, and he brushed it away impatiently. 'What about dental records?'

'That is about all we have,' Paget confessed, 'and they are checking that now. We do know that the man broke his arm fairly recently—by that, I mean about six months ago. Otherwise, he was about the same height, colouring, and build as Merrick.'

'And Lisa Remington? Where do you think she is?'

Paget grimaced. 'I'm leaning more and more to the idea that she is dead, sir,' he said. 'In fact I'm obtaining a warrant to expand our search, and Sergeant Ormside is bringing in another crew to dig up the rest of Foster's garden. I think it is just possible that Lisa is buried there. Perhaps Foster didn't think the water in the well would be high enough to cover two bodies, and felt forced to bury the other one.'

Alcott sighed, and swung his chair around to face the window. He remained there for some time, staring out across the playing fields. 'You could be right,' he said at last. 'Better have a word with the Press Officer and work out what you want released.'

Paget rose to go, but Alcott swung back to face him. 'What's this I hear about Tregalles's girl being approached?' he asked. 'What's being done?'

'It's in hand, sir,' Paget told him. 'Fortunately, the man only talked to her, but he may be back.'

'How is she?'

'Apparently she's taking it all very calmly, but John and Audrey are worried sick.'

Alcott butted out his cigarette. 'I don't blame them,' he said softly. 'I'll have a word downstairs. Tell Tregalles we'll do all we can.'

'I already have, sir,' Paget told him.

GRACE LOVETT finished typing up her report. It was a long one, and it dealt as much in hypotheses as it did in fact. There was little in it that would stand up in court, but she had felt sure enough of her ground to talk to Charlie about it.

To be fair, Charlie had given her a hearing, but she could tell he thought that she was reaching, and reaching pretty far at that. 'We deal in facts, Grace,' he reminded her. 'Facts we can back up with solid evidence. I'm not saying that you're wrong; I'm merely pointing out that everything you've suggested there could be interpreted in several different ways. Stick to the facts, Grace. I know it's nice to play around with possibilities, but leave that to Paget. He's got the whole picture. We haven't. Just give him bare-bones evidence. I'm sure he'll know how to use it.'

Now, as Grace stared at the screen before her, she made up her mind. Her 'bare-bones' report had been faxed to Paget already, but now she pressed PRINT and watched as page after page of material came off the printer. When it was done, she picked it up and put it in her briefcase and snapped it shut.

'There are a couple of things I'd like to check out personally at the murder site,' she told a colleague. 'Tell Charlie I should be back by lunch-time, if he asks. I'll be on pager.'

As she drove out of the car-park, she wondered whether she was doing the right thing. How would Chief Inspector Paget react to her 'deductions'? Would he welcome her thoughts? Or would he simply see her as an interfering female who fancied herself as an amateur detective?

She almost turned back. Paget *was* a bit daunting, with that austere, almost remote look about him that set him apart from other men. But, she thought with quickening breath, there was something fascinating about the man, and she realized she was looking forward to seeing him again.

She carried on determinedly, but the closer she came to Bracken Cottage, the more she began to doubt the wisdom of her venture.

'NEITHER FOSTER nor Lisa Remington seem to have mixed much with the locals,' Ormside said. 'They were known, of course, but Foster has only owned Bracken Cottage for about eighteen months, and Miss Remington has been here less than a year, so they were still very much newcomers.'

Paget leaned back in his chair. 'They may not have mixed with the locals,' he said, 'but I'll lay odds that the locals know a lot about them. They always do in these small places.'

Ormside nodded. 'They tend to keep their distance,' he agreed, 'but they watch and they listen. It's just a matter of getting them to tell us what they've seen and heard.' He picked up a sheet of paper. 'And speaking of what they've seen, the lad from the farm up above the cottage saw a black Volvo turn into Bracken Cottage on the Monday, March 11th, which confirms what Merrick told you, Tregalles. And he says he heard what sounded like a shotgun go off just before the Volvo drove away. Said the Volvo was weaving all over the road when it left.'

'I'm not surprised,' Tregalles said. 'Merrick said he didn't believe Lisa when she threatened him with the gun. He claims, of course, that it's all lies about his beating her up; says he just wanted to talk to her and show her his new designs. But he says she began screaming at him for no reason at all, and shoved the end of the barrels in his face. Literally. He still has the marks under his nose. He said he was leaving peacefully when she followed him out and blasted him. She got him in the buttocks and the right leg, mainly. Fortunately, he had on a long anorak because it was cold that day, so the wounds were relatively superficial.'

Paget turned to Ormside. 'Didn't it strike the lad as odd when he heard the gun go off and saw the car driving erratically?' he asked.

'He says he didn't connect the two things,' Ormside said. 'It never struck him as odd at the time because he's used to young Eric firing off his gun. It was only when we started asking questions that he put them together.' He paused and scratched his chin. 'Which reminds me,' he went on, 'speaking of Eric. He was there in Foster's garden when I arrived this morning, but he took off when he saw me. Doesn't like uniforms, I suspect.'

'What was he doing there?' asked Tregalles.

'Just standing there picking blooms off the rhododendrons, as far as I could see,' Ormside said, shaking his head. 'Strange lad, but harmless enough—if you don't mind losing your rhodos.'

Paget frowned. 'I suppose he is,' he said slowly, 'but I wonder... The shot from the cartridge I took from him matches the shot taken from the dead man. But so does that taken from the cartridges in Foster's gun, for that matter, so I'm not sure whether it's relevant or not. Has Eric ever been in trouble? Real trouble, I mean.'

'Mosely had him up for discharging a firearm too close to a roadway, or some such thing,' Ormside said, 'but then, Mosely would have his mother up if he thought it would help his arrest record. Tom Tyson keeps a pretty close eye on the boy, and he's never been a scrap of trouble to anyone as far as I know.'

'Tyson lives on the farm down by the river, doesn't he?' said Paget. 'He must be able to see the cottage from his place.'

'That he can,' Ormside told him. He scratched thoughtfully at his ear once again. 'As a matter of fact, if there's anyone round here who has cause to dislike Lisa Remington, it's Tom Tyson. Not that he would do the lass any harm, mind, but according to local gossip, he was pretty upset at the time.'

Paget waited. He'd learned long ago that it didn't pay to rush Ormside.

'See, Tom had almost got Foster to sell him this bit of land we are sitting on. It only amounted to about twenty feet or so, and they had approval for it, but that was about the time that Lisa Remington came to live with Foster, and she persuaded Foster to keep the land as it was. Said it would spoil the look of the place if Tyson fenced it off.'

'But why would Tyson want it in the first place?' asked Tregalles.

'For access to the road,' Ormside said. 'Right now, the only access to the farm is by the old river road, and it would cut off half a mile if he had this bit of land. The story is that he came up to the cottage and had a flaming row with Foster over it, and said some very nasty things about Miss Remington.'

'How long ago was that?'

'Well, it was shortly after she came, so that would put it around last spring or early summer.'

'Any confrontations since that time?' Paget wanted to know.

'Hard to say. The story goes that Tyson hasn't spoken to Foster since, but I couldn't swear to that.'

'Might be worth looking into,' Tregalles said, and made a note. 'What else have you got for us, Len?'

'Not much, except the bread man—he delivers bread

twice a week along here—said he saw a blue car tucked away in Foster's driveway on several occasions when he knew Foster was away.'

'Tucked away?' said Paget. 'What did he mean by that?'

Ormside shrugged. '*He* reckons it was tucked in there out of sight because whoever owned it was having it off with Miss Remington, since her car was in the driveway, too.'

'Do you have any dates? Especially around March 11th, 12th or 13th?'

'No, no such luck. And I wouldn't put too much stock in what he said, either. I think he saw the car all right, but he admits he didn't see the driver, so it could have been anybody.' Ormside grinned. 'As for this person, whoever it was, having it off with Lisa Remington, I think that was more his imagination than anything else. Makes a better story to tell on his rounds. Still, we are asking everyone around here if they have ever seen a car like that in the neighbourhood.'

'At least this is beginning to tie in with what Merrick told me, and to some degree with what Jane Lansing told me about Lisa,' said Tregalles. 'Seems like Lisa was becoming a bit desperate about her career, and was sneaking off to London every chance she got. She'd always tell Foster she was with Jane, that is if she told him anything at all. He didn't like her leaving the cottage when he wasn't there. Very jealous; very possessive. Jane said Lisa was getting fed up with it, and she'd talked of leaving him.

'She also said she didn't like having to lie for Lisa, especially when she realized that Lisa was sleeping with anyone with influence in the trade who might help salvage her career. But it wasn't only that. Lisa let drop that she'd taken another lover; someone much closer to home, and he was coming round when Foster was away. Jane said she told

Lisa not to be so stupid; that Foster was bound to find out, but Lisa seemed to think there wasn't any danger.

'Could be the bloke with the blue car,' Tregalles went on. 'Maybe the bread man had it right after all.'

'I DON'T KNOW what you expect to find,' said Foster sullenly as he watched the men digging up his garden. 'You're wasting your time, you know. How many times do I have to tell you Lisa wasn't there when I came home that night?' He stood there just inside the door, his face pale and puffy from lack of sleep, and his hand shook as he brushed uncombed hair out of his eyes.

'I told you where I buried the clothes,' he went on. 'You found the mattress where I said it was; what more do you want? I even came straight round to tell you about Lisa's car when the garage rang yesterday.'

'It was that point as much as anything that makes us wonder whether Miss Remington ever left here at all,' Paget told him.

'But, don't you see?' said Foster desperately. 'Lisa was in town. Her car was wrecked, so she must have gone on to wherever she was going from there. She couldn't get back here without transport.'

Paget shook his head. 'Come, now, Mr Foster. Lisa's mother came out here in a taxi. Lisa could have done the same, and we're checking that possibility now. The man at the garage says she used their telephone to ring someone. He thought she was asking someone to pick her up, because when she left the garage, she went out on to the street and stood there as if waiting for someone. That someone might even have been you, sir.'

'But I wasn't here that day,' Foster protested. 'I was in Chester doing a brochure layout for British Rail.'

'Taking pictures of various parts of Chester and the surrounding countryside, I believe,' said Paget. 'Yes, you did tell us that, sir, but it is so very difficult to *prove* where you were at any given time, you see, and Chester is not exactly on the other side of the world, is it?'

Dark colour suffused Foster's face. 'Do as you bloody well please,' he muttered, and slammed the door in Paget's face.

Grace Lovett was getting out of the car as Paget was making his way back to the mobile unit. 'Do you have a minute, Chief Inspector?' she called as she locked the car door. 'I'd like to show you something.'

'Certainly,' he said. 'Come on inside.' He led the way to the mobile unit, and held the door for her. 'Down here,' he told her, edging past a WPC feeding material into a fax machine. 'We're a bit cramped for space, I'm afraid,' he went on, indicating a chair, 'but we'll be out of everyone's way here.'

Now that she was here facing Paget, Grace felt even less sure of her ground, and she began to wish she hadn't come. But the chief inspector was looking at her, waiting politely. Almost unwillingly, she took her bulky report out of the briefcase and set it on the small table between them.

'I don't know whether this will be of any help to you,' she began apologetically, 'but it seemed important when I was putting it together back at the office.' She smiled self-consciously. 'Now that I'm here, I'm not at all sure.'

Paget's face was enigmatic. 'Let's find out, shall we?' he said. He eyed the report that lay between them. 'Did you want me to read all of this?' he asked her.

Faint colour tinged her face, and she swallowed nervously. 'I—I thought you might want to skim through it when you have time,' she told him, 'but I can give you the outline now if you can spare me about ten minutes.'

Was that amusement in his eyes? Was he laughing at her? she wondered, and the colour in her cheeks became more pronounced.

He glanced at his watch. 'Go ahead,' he said.

She'd practised this in her head on her way out to the cottage, but now every carefully thought-out phrase deserted her, and she hardly knew where to begin. And he was waiting.

'I don't think Lisa Remington was sharing the same bedroom with Mr Foster at all,' she burst out. 'I think they were sleeping in separate rooms.' That was not the way she'd planned to say it, but it was out now, and the only thing she could do was go on. 'He said that back bedroom was only used as a guest room, but I think Lisa was using it, and he moved things to make it look as if they were still together.'

Paget's expression remained unchanged. 'Go on,' he said.

Grace glanced down at the report. Her reasoning seemed so flimsy in the clear cold light of day, and she could see what Charlie meant when he'd told her to stick to the evidence and the facts. But Paget was waiting, and she had little choice but to carry on.

'You see, I began to wonder at the very beginning when I looked inside the wardrobe in Foster's bedroom. If you remember, Lisa's clothes were packed in like sardines in a tin. I could hardly get my hand through between them, and Lisa Remington would never do that to her clothes. So, I began to wonder why they were packed in so tightly.'

Paget had tilted his chair back and closed his eyes. Was he concentrating on what she'd been saying? she wondered, or was he just bored?

She plunged on. 'When I checked the wardrobe, the dressing-table, and the tall-boy in the back bedroom, I found they all smelt of Lisa's perfume, and there were traces of other cosmetics. So, I took all of her clothes from the front bedroom and put them in the wardrobe in the back bedroom, and spread them out as they should be.'

Warming to her task, Grace leaned forward to emphasize
her next words. 'Now, the first thing I noticed was that,
even though the clothes had all been jammed in together,
they were not particularly wrinkled, which led me to believe that they had not been together in that state for very
long. Do you see what I'm driving at, sir?'

Paget opened his eyes and nodded. Was there a spark of
interest there? Grace couldn't be sure, but she hoped so.

'The next thing I did was examine the inside of the drawers in the back bedroom, and I found fibres that we've since
been able to match with some of Lisa's underclothes, so
they were in those drawers at some time or other.

'And there were hairs, Lisa's hairs, in the carpet, in the
wardrobe, in fact they were all over that room. It had been
vacuumed, but it's very hard to get rid of hair, so I had no
trouble finding it. I did find some of her hair in the front
bedroom, but there wasn't nearly as much of it as in the
back bedroom. And then there were the marks on the floor
beside the dressing-table. You see...'

Grace stopped short as Paget suddenly held up his hand.
'I think I get the picture,' he said quietly, 'but it would
hardly stand up in court, would it?'

Her heart dropped like a stone, and she could feel the
blood rushing to her face. She should have listened to Charlie. She was making a fool of herself.

'But I think you may be right,' he said, and smiled. It
transformed his face. Gone were the deep lines that made
his face severe, and his eyes looked less flinty as he went
on. 'It wouldn't stand up in court, but neither would most
of the conclusions we reach. What you've just told me ties
in with what a friend of Lisa's told Tregalles yesterday.
She said that Lisa was not getting along with Peter Foster,
and she was thinking of leaving him.'

He tapped the report. 'I'll have to read this later,' he

went on, 'but is there anything else you want to point out now?'

Relief swept through her. 'There are a couple of things,' she said, but even as she spoke he looked at his watch and stood up.

'Fancy a bit of lunch, do you?' he asked abruptly.

Grace Lovett didn't know quite what to say. The invitation was so completely unexpected. It didn't fit the profile she'd built up of Paget in her mind at all. He'd always seemed so aloof, so unreachable, and rumour had it that he was very much a loner. Brusque, cold, a workaholic; that was Paget. But she found herself attracted to him despite all that.

And now he'd asked her to lunch.

Grace scrambled to her feet. 'Yes, I do rather,' she said somewhat breathlessly. 'It's so…'

'Good,' said Paget. 'Bring your notes. I'll see if Tregalles is free. I'd like him to hear this as well. You are on expenses while you're out here, I presume?'

NINE

'I THINK SHE FANCIES YOU, sir,' Tregalles said, grinning. They had returned from lunch, and Grace Lovett was on her way back into town.

Paget grunted. 'I doubt that very much,' he said. 'She was just doing her job, and I must say I like the way her mind works.'

'I wasn't thinking of her mind, exactly,' Tregalles said. 'But I do like the way the rest of her works.'

Paget didn't reply, but the sergeant was right in one respect at least: Grace Lovett was an attractive woman. But as for the other nonsense…Paget dismissed it out of hand. Tregalles would have his little joke.

Audrey telephoned just after four to say that the man who had approached Olivia had not appeared that day at all. It was a relief in one way, but it only left the matter unresolved, and Tregalles would not rest easy until the man was caught.

The diggers made their discovery ten minutes before they were due to finish for the day. Two pieces of luggage buried deep beneath a clump of winter heather.

Paget was notified as soon as the discovery was made, and he, Tregalles and Ormside all trooped over to the garden to watch it being unearthed. They watched in silence as damp earth was brushed away and a large suitcase was pulled free. The second case was smaller; more like an overnighter.

'They're heavy, sir,' said one of the men. His face was pale as he looked enquiringly at Paget. 'Should I open them?'

'You reckon he chopped her up before he buried her?'

The words were spoken in a hushed whisper by one of the diggers, but Paget heard and couldn't help wondering the same. Logic told him that the cases were too small to hold a body, but there could be more buried elsewhere.

'I'll do it,' he said. He pulled on a pair of latex gloves and squatted down beside the larger case. It looked expensive. He brushed away the earth around the catches, and saw the engraved initials: L.R.

He braced himself and opened it. Clothes. A woman's clothes, and Paget had little doubt that they belonged to Lisa Remington. Something like a collective sigh escaped the watching men. He opened the overnight case, and found inside a collection of jewellery, cosmetics, and a handbag.

The handbag bulged with virtually everything he would have expected Lisa Remington to carry with her: driving licence, credit cards, compact, lipstick, keys, Kleenex, money, and a miscellaneous assortment of odds and ends including two pens, odd scraps of paper, headache tablets, a packet of mints, and so on.

No matter what, Lisa Remington would never have left the house willingly without this handbag, Paget thought.

He rose to his feet. 'Get this lot to the lab,' he instructed Ormside, 'and have someone guard the site tonight. We'll resume digging in the morning. And you,' he said to Tregalles, 'had better come with me. I think Mr Foster is going to find this lot just a little harder to explain away.'

PETER FOSTER sat with his eyes closed, waiting. He sat on the same hard chair at the same wooden table, and the same silent, uniformed constable sat in the same corner of the room. He was exhausted. Physically, mentally, every possible way. He just wanted it to be over. No more lies; no more evasions; no more having to remember what he'd just said. Just tell the truth and have done with it.

The trouble was, would they believe anything he said now? He'd tried so *hard,* but everything was coming apart. His nose began to run, and he could feel the prickle of sweat across his brow. He took out a handkerchief and wiped his face.

The man in the corner looked up. The suspect, he noted with distaste, was snuffling. He looked down at the floor again and wished they'd get on with it. He was hungry, and the canteen closed at eight.

'YOU HAVE ADMITTED burying the suitcase containing clothing belonging to Lisa Remington, together with an overnight bag containing her handbag and other personal items, Mr Foster,' Paget said. 'So will you tell me now where Lisa Remington is?'

Foster shook his head. 'I don't know,' he said miserably.

'Is Lisa Remington dead, Mr Foster?'

'No! No—I mean I don't know!' Foster burst out. 'She ran away. At least, I think she did. She must have.'

'Why would she run away?'

'Oh, for God's sake! Wouldn't you be scared if you'd just shot somebody accidentally?'

'Accidentally, Mr Foster? How do you know that? Were you there?'

Foster groaned. 'I've already told you a million times that she was gone when I came home,' he said. 'But it stands to reason. There's no other explanation.'

'I think there is,' Paget said. 'I think that when you came home you found Lisa in bed with her lover. I think you took the shotgun and killed them both in a fit of rage. I think that you tried to cover up the murder by concealing the bodies, and inventing a tissue of lies to explain the absence of Miss Remington. That's what the evidence suggests to me, Mr Foster.'

'Then where is Lisa's body?' Foster shot back. 'Tell me that!'

'That's what I'm asking you, Mr Foster.'

'I told you what happened,' Foster said dully. 'Don't you ever listen?'

'Tell me again.'

Foster shook his head helplessly. How many times did he have to go through this? he thought desperately. He cast a pleading look at Paget, but he found no comfort there in the cold and stony features.

He sighed heavily. 'As I said, it was about a week after I'd put the body down the well and cleaned up the place when I found Lisa's handbag. It was down in a corner sort of hidden behind the coats in the front passageway, and it made me think.' Foster leaned forward as he tried to make his point with Paget. 'You see, Lisa never went anywhere without that bag, and when I saw it, and saw everything that was in it, I was afraid. Even if she'd been in a blind panic, she would have taken that with her. It had her keys, her money, everything in it.'

Tears welled up in Foster's eyes. 'The only thing I could think of was that she had been taken away against her will. It was the only thing that made sense to me. But why? If it was for ransom—some people might think that because she was a top model, she had a lot of money—why hadn't I heard anything? I didn't know what to do. I'd spread the story about that Lisa was in France, but I'd always known that it wouldn't be long before someone started asking questions. Constance, Lisa's mother, was already suspicious.'

Foster drew a deep breath and let it out again. 'So, I decided to make it look as if Lisa had taken her handbag with her, and some clothes, so I picked out some things I thought she might wear, and put them in the case and buried it along with the other stuff you found. That way, it would look as if she'd left of her own accord.' He spread his hands. 'That's it, I swear.'

'What about Lisa's clothes in your wardrobe?' Paget asked.

Colour rushed into Foster's face. 'What clothes?' he asked, but he avoided Paget's eyes.

It had been a shot in the dark, based largely on Grace Lovett's instincts, but it appeared to have scored a bull's-eye, and he pressed home his advantage. 'Miss Remington was sleeping in the back bedroom,' he said flatly. 'Why was that, Mr Foster?'

Foster lifted his head and stared at Paget belligerently. 'She wasn't sleeping properly,' he said, 'so she moved in there. I offered to move, but she refused.' He shrugged. 'That's all there was to it.'

'It had nothing to do with the fact that she was about to leave you, then?'

The colour deepened in Foster's face. 'I don't know where you got that idea,' he said, 'but it's a load of rubbish. Lisa and I were very happy together.'

'That's not what she's been telling her friends.'

Foster shrugged. 'Believe what you like,' he said sullenly. 'You will anyway, but Lisa would never leave me. Never.'

'Since we now know that Sean Merrick isn't dead, who was it in that bed, Mr Foster? And how do you think he came to be there?'

Foster blinked at the abrupt switch in direction. 'I don't know,' he said. 'When I thought it was Merrick, I thought that he must have got in somehow without Lisa seeing him, got undressed and climbed into bed. It was the sort of grandstand play he would make. He thought he was God's gift to women, and he only had to crook his finger to get Lisa back. He simply couldn't get it through his thick head that she loved me.'

'But it wasn't Merrick, was it?' Paget said softly. 'So who was it? And more to the point, what was he doing in Lisa's bed?'

The colour in Foster's face grew darker. He put his hands on the table in front of him, lifted himself from the chair and thrust his face at Paget. 'If you're suggesting what I think,' he said menacingly, 'then you'd better...'

'I'd better what, Mr Foster?' said Paget mildly. 'And to make sure we understand each other, let me tell you what I am suggesting. I think that whoever the man was, he was Lisa's lover, and I think you came home and found them together. And, I think you killed them both. Now then, sir, you can save us and yourself a lot of trouble if you tell us where you've hidden Lisa's body.'

Friday 5th April

'IT'S ALL CIRCUMSTANTIAL,' Alcott said glumly. He sat back in his chair and threw the report on his desk. A cloud of ash flew up from the ashtray and a fine grey blanket settled on the polished surface. 'I don't see anything there that tells me with absolute certainty that Lisa Remington is dead. I see all sorts of evidence *suggesting* that she's dead, but nothing more.'

Paget nodded. 'Which is why I had to let Foster go again,' he said wearily. He and Tregalles had hammered away at Foster until almost midnight, but they hadn't been able to shake him. 'I'm ninety-nine per cent certain that Lisa Remington is dead. I can feel it in my bones, but I can't prove it. And yet all of the blood samples taken from the bedroom belong to the dead man. There is nothing to suggest that another person died there. So—assuming she *is* dead—I think she must have been killed elsewhere. I mean, why put one body down the well and not the other if they were both killed at the same time? God knows there was room enough.'

'You're still digging up the garden, I take it?'

'That's right. Foster swears we won't find anything, but he's changed his story so often I find it hard to believe anything he says.'

'He took the mattress out to the tip,' said Alcott slowly.

'I thought of that,' Paget told him, 'and I've had men sorting through the rubbish, but they've had no luck so far. And his van was clean.'

'Are we any closer to identifying the dead man?'

'I'm hoping we'll have some response on the dental records soon,' said Paget, 'but until then we're at a dead end there.'

'So, what's next?'

'I'm sending Tregalles to talk to this chap Tyson. Tom Tyson. He owns the farm next to Foster's place, and I gather Lisa Remington put a spoke in his wheel when he tried to buy a bit of land from Foster. If Lisa did have a lover visiting her when Foster was away, Tyson might have seen him around the place. And I'm curious about Tyson's son, Eric. The boy can't speak, and he has a mental problem, but I'm told he and his father communicate quite well. The lad—hell, I call him a lad, but he's twenty-two years old and as big as a barn door—seems to spend a lot of time roaming about the countryside, and it's possible that he knows something if only we can communicate with him.'

Alcott grunted. He had a meeting with Chief Superintendent Brock in less than an hour, and he was not looking forward to it. Brock lived by statistics: arrests, convictions, hours-per-case, overtime, and the bottom line. Graphs and charts covered the walls of his office. If it couldn't be measured, counted, or plotted on a graph, Brock wasn't interested. 'Results, Alcott, results; that's what I want. I'm not interested in explanations. That's just another name for ex-

cuses. Give me something tangible I can take to the chief
constable.'

Alcott sighed. What could you expect from someone
who'd never spent five minutes in the field? The man didn't
have a clue. A glorified accountant; that was Brock. Spent
his entire career in Administration, and thought he knew it
all. How he'd ever managed to land this job as chief superintendent was beyond...

Paget coughed discreetly. 'Was there anything else, sir?'

Alcott shook his head. 'No,' he said wearily. 'Just bring
me something Mr Brock will understand. Bring me some
results.'

THERE WAS A MESSAGE asking him to ring the pathologist
when Paget arrived back at his desk.

'We have a match,' Starkie told him when he rang back.
'We've identified your corpse. His name is David Gray,
age thirty. Went missing March 12th. At least he was last
seen on that date. Lived at 63A Runacre Road right here
in Broadminster. As a matter of fact, Missing Persons tell
me they had him on file all the time. Don't you lot ever
talk to one another?'

Paget wasn't going to let Starkie get away with that. 'As
a matter of fact, his name was mentioned earlier on,' he
said, 'but when the corpse was identified as that of Merrick,
we lost interest in Gray. Who identified him?'

'If you mean has anyone actually looked at him and said,
"Yes, that's David Gray," then I have to say no one, because there are no distinguishing marks on what's left of
the body. But I'm satisfied it is Gray. Your people had a
full-face photograph of him, and our computer mock-up fits
the facial measurements exactly; eyes, ears, nose, mouth,
etc., you know what I mean. Also, the dental records match,
and the broken arm. Gray broke his arm seven months ago

while playing squash, and his X-rays are still on file here at the hospital. They're a perfect match. Satisfied?'

'Sounds good to me, Reg. What about next of kin? Anyone spoken to them yet?'

'I shouldn't think so. I'll have a full report over to you later in the day, but I've given you the main points.'

'Right. Appreciate it, Reg. I'll talk to them downstairs. Save you a call.'

Paget caught Alcott before he left for New Street, and gave him the news. 'Thank God for that,' was Alcott's only comment, but his step was lighter as he headed for the door.

Paget had just returned to his desk when the telephone rang. It was an operator asking if he would accept a reverse charge call from Constance Remington in London.

'Put her on,' he told the girl. 'I'll accept it.'

Mrs Remington wasted no time in coming to the point. 'I want to know if it's true that Lisa's dead,' she said. 'And, if she is, why wasn't I told? I've had reporters outside my house since late last night.'

'I wish I could answer that, Mrs Remington,' Paget said. 'But all I can tell you right now is that no one has seen her since March 12th. We still hope to find her alive, but…'

'Then why are you digging up the garden at the cottage? There's a picture of it in the *Sun* this morning.'

'We have to explore every avenue…' Paget began, but Constance cut him off.

'That's a pile of shit and you know it!' she snapped. 'She's dead, isn't she? And that snivelling little sod killed her. I told Lisa he was no bloody good. Stifled her career. Smothered her. She had five good years left if she hadn't gone off with him and buried herself in the country. Undermined everything I've ever done for her. Has he confessed yet?'

Paget braced himself. 'We have no proof that your

daughter is in fact dead,' he said. 'And neither Mr Foster nor anyone else is being held at the moment.'

There was a stunned silence that was palpable at the other end of the line, but before Constance Remington found her voice again, Paget asked a question. 'Tell me, did Lisa ever mention anyone by the name of Gray to you?'

'Gray? No. Who is this Gray? And what is all this in the morning's paper about Sean being alive? You told me yourself that Sean was dead.'

'That is what we were led to believe,' Paget said patiently, 'and since we had no reason to suspect otherwise, we believed it to be true.'

'Seems to me you'll believe anything down there. My God, you let that evil little bastard lead you around by the nose. Is he still at the cottage?'

'Yes.'

'Then I'm coming down to take everything that belongs to Lisa. I want everything out of there. I don't want Peter touching them, and I'm not letting Sean get his filthy hands on any of her stuff, either. He'll try, you know. He'll reckon that because he's still her husband, he'll have a right. Some of Lisa's gowns are worth a pretty penny, and I don't intend to let that drunken bastard get his hands on them. I have a right. I'm her mother.'

'Until the case is resolved, no one has any rights to any of Lisa's belongings, Mrs Remington,' Paget told her. 'They will be released in due course, but until that time they will remain where they are. I'm sorry, but that's the way it is.'

'You'll hear more about this!' There was venom in every syllable, and it wasn't hard for Paget to imagine the distorted features of the woman at the other end. 'I'm calling my solicitor,' she went on, 'and then we'll see who has a right, Mr bloody Chief Inspector!'

The phone crashed in his ear.

'I'M GOING TO follow up on this man, Gray,' Paget told Tregalles, 'but I'd like you to have a talk with Tom Tyson. Find out whether he has seen anything that might tie in with the killing at the cottage, and see if he can get anything out of young Eric. The boy may have seen something; he seems to hang around the cottage quite a bit. It's worth a try.'

Tregalles nodded. He looked tired. 'Anything more on this business with Olivia?' Paget asked. 'How did it go this morning?'

The sergeant shook his head. 'Not a sign of him,' he said.

The man had probably been scared off by the increased activity, Paget thought, but people like that were very persistent. He'd most likely be back as soon as everyone thought the danger was over. 'Are you all right?' he asked.

Tregalles nodded. 'A bit tired, that's all. Not sleeping too well, lately.'

Paget gripped his arm. 'They'll get him, John,' he said quietly. 'I know it sounds trite, but try not to worry. What about Audrey?'

'She's worried sick,' Tregalles said. 'She tries not to show it, but she is.' He smashed a fist into the palm of his hand. 'I'd just like five minutes with the bastard!' he grated. 'Just five, that's all.'

TEN

THE MISSING PERSON report was dated March 14th, the day after Foster claimed to have discovered the body he'd sworn he thought was that of Merrick. But according to Janet Freeman, Gray's fiancée, Gray had been missing since March 12th. Gray was a software program specialist with Freeman Protronics, and shortly after two o'clock that day, he had received a telephone call at work, after which he left the office. He told his secretary that he was going out on an emergency call for assistance from a client in Bridgnorth. The client was a Mr Hambledon, owner of Travis Hambledon (Manufacturers of Fine Office Furnishings and Supplies), and Gray told the girl that he might have to stay in Bridgnorth overnight.

It wasn't until the following evening that Janet Freeman became concerned about Gray's absence. He had promised faithfully to go over the wedding invitations one last time before they were sent out, and when he failed to return to the office by five o'clock, and he hadn't phoned, she telephoned the firm in Bridgnorth, but the office had closed for the day. When David Gray hadn't appeared by nine o'clock that night, Janet Freeman telephoned Hambledon at home, only to be told that neither he, nor anyone else from the company, had called Gray. They'd had no trouble, and the last time he had spoken to David Gray was several weeks ago.

Puzzled, but not unduly worried (she said she thought the secretary must have got the message wrong), she went round to Gray's flat. When no one answered the door, she let herself in with her own key, but there was no sign of

Gray at all. Everything was as it should be. She tried to see if his car was in the lock-up garage behind the flats, but she couldn't see inside. In any case, Gray had taken a company car.

It was not unusual for any of the software people to spend long periods of time working on a tricky problem, so even then Janet Freeman was not unduly worried. More annoyed, she told the policeman who had taken her statement, because Gray hadn't phoned to tell her how long he expected to be away, and time was growing short for sending out the invitations. She also said she had tried repeatedly to call him on his pager, without result. But when questioned closely, she admitted that Gray quite often left his pager off.

When he failed to appear by Thursday morning, Janet Freeman went to the police and reported her fiancé missing.

Nothing had been done until the following day, Friday, when a detective constable was dispatched to Gray's flat. He was met there by Janet Freeman. They went through the flat together, but no clue to Gray's whereabouts was discovered. The DC questioned several people on the same floor, as well as the caretaker, and the owner of the flats, but learned nothing. The lock-up garage was opened, and Gray's car was there. The constable returned to the station where he wrote up his report, checked Gray's description against recent reports of unidentified accident victims, arrests, etc., and made a note to talk to the Freeman Protronics staff on Monday morning. A description of Gray and the company car he was driving was written up and circulated, and then he went home for a well-deserved weekend.

Paget read on. During the interviews on the following Monday, one of the clerks in the office happened to mention that the car Gray had taken on the day he disappeared was now parked in the company car-park. No one seemed to know when or how it had got there. The odometer reading showed twenty-six miles more than the last entry in the log, which was dated March 11th, so wherever the car had been, it could be no more than thirteen miles distant from Freeman Protronics.

Paget sat back and thought about that. It was roughly six or seven miles to Bracken Cottage, which left something like thirteen miles unaccounted for. But regardless of the unexplained mileage, if Gray had driven the car out there and had been killed, who had driven the car back again? And what about the keys? None were found in the car. He made a note to have the keys found at Bracken Cottage checked to see if any of them belonged to the company car.

He returned to the report. The DC had called for an examination of the car. Nothing of any apparent consequence was discovered—with one exception. There were no prints of any kind on the steering wheel or in the immediate vicinity of the driver's seat—no fingerprints; no palm prints; no hand prints—whereas the prints of several Freeman Protronics employees were found in other areas of the car. Someone had been very thorough.

The rest of the report was predictable. The lack of prints was suspicious, but it was not of itself proof that anything untoward had happened to Gray. Although it might be unusual, it was not unheard of for someone to get cold feet prior to a wedding and simply disappear. True, Gray had left everything behind, including his car, but that still didn't mean there had been foul play. The search was broadened; circulars went out across the country; friends and even distant relatives were questioned. Gray's picture appeared on TV, and the usual rash of sightings came pouring in. But when all of the supposed sightings proved false, and nothing was heard within ten days, the investigation stalled simply because no one had any idea where to look for the man.

And, thought Paget, by the time the body at Bracken Cottage turned up, no one connected the two incidents because the body had been identified as that of Sean Merrick within twenty-four hours of its discovery.

DI Abercrombie, into whose lap the Gray file had fallen, was only too happy to let Paget take it from there. It allowed Abercrombie to write off his part of the investigation, and it left Paget out there to take the flak.

Who said there was no justice in the world?

THOMAS TYSON was a dour, stocky, square-built man with the neck and shoulders of a bull. His face was weathered and what little hair he had was turning white. It was hard to tell his age: late fifties or early sixties, Tregalles guessed and left it at that.

Tregalles had telephoned ahead to make sure that both Tyson and his son would be there. Tyson had been less than enthusiastic, saying that it was his busy time, and he could spare little of it, but in the end he had agreed to be there. Now, they sat on wooden chairs in the kitchen of the farmhouse.

'I suppose you'd best come through,' Tyson had said when he answered the door. 'The wife seldom leaves the kitchen.' He led the way down a passage even narrower than that of Foster's cottage to a large, bright room. It was, in fact, two rooms knocked into one, Tregalles observed, and it was furnished as both kitchen and living-room. A squared-off bay window overlooked the field between the farmhouse and Bracken Cottage, and set in the bay was a day-bed. A woman sat half on and half off the bed, struggling to stand upright with the help of a pair of stout walking-sticks.

'This is the wife,' Tyson said brusquely as he indicated a chair and sat down himself.

Tregalles hesitated. The woman was obviously in pain,

and yet Tyson seemed oblivious to it. 'Please don't get up on my account,' he said. 'I just want to ask a few questions, Mrs Tyson.'

'There's work to be done and the Good Lord gave me two good hands to do it,' the woman said as she made her way painfully to the Aga cooker. 'You sit yourself down. Kettle's on the boil.'

Emily Tyson was a thin, wiry woman with a care-worn face and judgemental eyes. She moved about the kitchen with great difficulty, and Tregalles felt uncomfortable watching her. Tyson caught his eye and must have guessed what was going through his mind. 'Displaced hip,' he said cryptically. 'Happened when Eric was born. Nothing they can do.' He spoke softly, but his wife had sharp ears.

'Aye, it were a judgement,' she said without turning round. 'It's God's will.'

Tregalles looked around the room. Everything in it was modern and made for convenience. Handrails were placed strategically beside the bed, beside the cooker, and in various places along the walls, and Emily Tyson made good use of them as she made her painful way around the room.

'Is Eric about?' Tregalles asked.

'He'll be in shortly,' Tyson told him. 'Now, what was it you wanted, Sergeant? Something to do with the goings-on at yon cottage, I'll be bound.'

'Tea's ready,' said Emily.

Tyson rose from his chair and carried the heavy pot of tea from the cooker to the table. Cups and saucers were already set out, and he poured three cups. Meanwhile, Emily made her way back to the bed and pulled herself up until she was sitting with her back to the window. Beside her on the sill was a bible and a pair of binoculars.

'Chairs are a bit hard for Ma,' Tyson said by way of explanation. 'Help yourself.' He indicated the milk and sugar, then took a cup of clear tea to his wife.

Tregalles sipped his tea. 'Very good,' he said. 'Thank you, Mrs Tyson.' He set his cup down. 'You're right,' he went on. 'I am here about what happened at Bracken Cottage, and I'm especially interested in anything you might have seen between, say, March 11th and 15th.' He glanced at the window. 'I should think you'd have a good view of the cottage from here.'

'He's back,' said Emily.

'Sorry?'

She flicked her head in the direction of the cottage. 'He's back,' she repeated. 'Came home late last night. Why isn't he locked up? Should be after what he did.'

'You mean Mr Foster?'

'Aye. Who else?'

'What is it you think he's done, Mrs Tyson?'

'Why, murdered that girl and one of her fancy men, of course. What else would they be digging for? Caught them at it, didn't he?'

'What we need,' Tregalles said, 'are reliable witnesses.' He nodded toward the window. 'Did you, by any chance, happen to see anything that would help us, Mrs Tyson? You mentioned "fancy men". What did you mean by that?'

The woman sipped her tea in silence. Tregalles waited patiently.

'There's two at least,' she said abruptly. 'The one with the black car and the one with the blue one, although sometimes he comes in a red one.'

'Can you describe the men and the cars?'

The woman shrugged her narrow shoulders. 'The men are ordinary,' she said. 'Not much difference between them, although the one does a lot of shouting and waving his arms about. You can hear him shouting from here.'

'Would he be the one in the black car?'

Emily Tyson shot him a shrewd glance. 'Aye,' she said slowly. 'That's the one.'

'When did you last see him there?'

She thought for a moment, then glanced up at a wall calendar. 'Three, maybe four weeks ago,' she said hesitantly. She looked across at her husband. 'It was the day you said you heard someone shooting up there,' she said. 'When was that?'

Tom Tyson shrugged. 'Don't remember,' he said.

'You actually heard shots coming from the cottage?' Tregalles prompted.

'One shot,' Tyson said. 'That's all it was. Just the one. And it was outside. And then this car roared off up the road. The black one.'

'So you didn't see who actually fired the shot?'

'No.'

Tregalles looked at Emily Tyson. She shook her head. 'But the other one was there the next day,' she said. 'He had the blue car that day. They both came back together. Him and that girl. Funny, that, because she left in her own car and came back in his. I remember thinking it was funny at the time.'

'What about that night, Mrs Tyson? Were you disturbed at all? Did you happen to see or hear anything unusual?'

'Something woke me up about one o'clock in the morning,' she said. 'Don't know what it was, but I heard a car drive off shortly after. Him going home, I expect.' Her lip curled in disapproval.

'Anything else?'

The woman thought. 'Not that day, but *he* came back the next night and the lights were on half the night.'

'The same man?'

Mrs Tyson shook her head impatiently. 'No, Foster,' she said. 'I remember he had a bonfire the next day, and then he started taking down those sheep pens.' Her mouth turned down even further. 'Don't know why. Those old pens have been there more than a hundred years. Why folks have to start tearing things down for no reason, I don't know.'

'That's enough, Ma,' Tyson said. 'Time you had a rest. You'll get all tired out and then where will you be?'

Emily Tyson's eyes glittered. 'You leave me be,' she said waspishly. 'It isn't often we have visitors. More tea, Sergeant? Pour the sergeant another cup, Tom.'

'I understand you wanted to buy a piece of Mr Foster's land,' Tregalles said as Tyson filled his cup. 'For direct access to the road.'

Tyson set the pot carefully to one side. 'And what if I did?' he asked.

'I'm told that you had a deal with Foster, but Miss Remington stopped him from going ahead with it.'

Tyson eyed him over the rim of his cup. 'And what's that got to do with what's happened over there?' he asked.

'What do you think happened over there?' Tregalles countered.

Tyson shrugged his massive shoulders. 'He came home, found them in bed together, and shot the both of them,' he said. 'Word is, he stuffed them down that old well in the shed out back.'

'Didn't I say there'd be a judgement?' his wife said. 'Didn't I?'

'You did, Ma,' Tyson said.

'One man is dead,' Tregalles said, 'but we don't know what happened to Miss Remington. She is still missing.'

Tyson flicked his head toward the cottage. 'Like as not you'll find her there,' he said.

'You were not very fond of Miss Remington, were you, Mr Tyson? I believe you had words with her not so long ago.'

Tyson's eyes narrowed. 'What's that supposed to mean?'

he asked belligerently. 'Are you accusing me of something?'

'No. I'm just trying to establish what happened, that's all, sir. Did you have words with her? Over that piece of land?'

Tyson got up and went over to a shelf where he found a pipe and began to fill it with tobacco. 'Aye, I had words with her,' he said at last. 'Not that it did much good.' His expression hardened. 'Might as well have saved my breath. Bloody woman wouldn't listen.'

'Tom! Language!'

'Sorry, Ma. Got a bit carried away, that's all. But that woman would drive anyone to swearing. Not a brain in her head.' Colour was rising in his face. 'Twenty-five feet! That's all I wanted. Just twenty-five feet. The planning board approved it, and Foster was ready to let it go. It was no use to him, but then *she* came.'

Tyson suddenly spread his arms and allowed his hands to flap helplessly. 'Oh, no,' he mimicked in a high, falsetto voice, 'we simply can't have smelly tractors and cows and things going past the window all the time, can we, darling?' He dropped his arms and continued to press tobacco into his pipe.

The change in the man had been so swift and unexpected that Tregalles found it hard not to laugh. But Tyson wasn't laughing. His face was set and his jaw thrust out as he clamped the pipe between his teeth. He struck a match and sucked the flame down hard.

'Did you ever go back and try again?' Tregalles asked.

'No point,' said Tyson. 'She had him eating out of her hand.'

'She was a whore,' said Emily. 'You should have told him that, Tom. That would have changed his tune.'

Tyson sucked on his pipe. 'She was that,' he said softly.

Tregalles said nothing, but noted that both of them spoke of Lisa Remington in the past tense.

The door opened and Eric appeared. His eyes flicked in Tregalles's direction and quickly moved away. He looked toward his father as if for direction. 'Finished the wood, have you?' Tyson said. His voice had softened, and he looked upon the boy with affection.

Eric nodded vigorously. 'Good lad,' said Tyson. 'Get yourself some tea and sit down. This is Sergeant Tregalles. He's come to ask some questions. Don't be frightened, lad. He'll not harm you. Remember what I told you?'

Eric nodded and busied himself with the tea, never once looking at Tregalles. Reluctantly, it seemed to the sergeant, Eric took his seat at the table. Several spoonfuls of sugar went into his tea, and he began to slosh the tea around with his spoon.

'Don't spill it on the cloth,' his mother told him sharply. 'It's clean on.' But her warning came too late. Eric bowed his head and refused to look at anyone.

'Now look what you've done. Stupid boy. Take that spoon off him, Tom.' The words were sharp, cutting, meant to hurt.

'It'll wash, Ma,' Tyson said. 'He can't help it.'

'Of course he can!' The shrewish voice rose in anger. 'He does it to annoy me, that's all.' She sighed heavily. 'But Thy will be done,' she said resignedly. 'If this must be my burden, then so be it, Lord.'

Tyson avoided Tregalles's eyes. He looked uncomfortable. 'What was it you wanted from Eric?' he asked, obviously anxious to change the subject.

What the sergeant wanted was to find out whether Eric had seen or heard anything that might help him. But Eric seemed uneasy and, if he had been less like a child, Tregalles would have said 'evasive'. In fact, it was hardly an interview at all because Eric's answers were limited to a nod or shake of the head, and his father's interpretations of what he thought Eric meant.

'He doesn't understand days like you and me,' Tyson said when Tregalles tried to pin Eric down. 'Yesterday, last week, last month, they're all the same to him. You're wasting your time, Sergeant.'

'Perhaps,' Tregalles said, 'but tell me, why is it that we keep finding Eric in the garden up there at the cottage, Mr Tyson?'

Tyson had been relighting his pipe, but now his hands became still, and he shot a sidelong glance at his wife. Eric's head bent lower as if he sensed the stream of invective that was about to pour from his mother's mouth.

'See? I told you, Tom!' Her shrill voice rose to a screech. 'You wouldn't have it, but I told you he'd been up there, shaming us all.' She turned hate-filled eyes on her son. 'Spawn of the devil, that's what you are,' she hissed. 'Sneaking off to see that whore! You've brought God's wrath down on this house. On me! Just look at what you've done to me. Look! I tell you!'

Her face twisted in pain as she almost threw herself forward across the room. Her two sticks thudded hard against the floor with every painful step as she made her way toward her son. Her eyes glittered with pure hatred as she raised a stick above her head.

Tregalles was half out of his chair, but Tyson was quicker. He grabbed the upraised arm with one hand, and caught his wife from falling with the other. In fury, she hurled the stick at her son, but it flew harmlessly past his bowed head.

'You're evil!' she hissed. 'Evil. Do you hear?' Her eyes rolled upward and she collapsed in Tyson's arms. Tyson gathered her up as if she weighed nothing and carried her over to the bed. Spent, utterly exhausted, she lay there weeping, and when Tyson turned to face him, Tregalles saw tears in his eyes.

'I think you'd best be gone,' he said quietly. 'Ma isn't quite herself, today.'

ELEVEN

FREEMAN PROTRONICS was a small company that had found a unique niche in a highly competitive software market, and the driving force behind it was Mike Freeman. In ten short years he had come from being an unemployed programmer, having been made redundant in the latest 'reconstruction' of a major company, to the successful owner of a small but lucrative software company.

He'd known from the start that there was no point in trying to compete with the major companies, because they were very good at what they did. But there were literally thousands of small businesses out there who wanted to take advantage of the new technology, but found that the programs offered were frequently too large and cumbersome for their needs. And too expensive. They needed programs designed specifically for their particular business, and Mike Freeman was able to fill that need.

The business started slowly, but within two years he was looking for additional people, and the first person he took on full-time was his own daughter, Janet, just out of university. Guided by her father, she had spent three years specializing in industrial programming, and she turned out to have a natural aptitude for the work. Within two years, Mike was struggling to keep up with her. The industry was changing so fast that it was impossible to keep abreast of new developments. More people were taken on, young people trained in the latest technology, and Mike's business expanded rapidly.

Today, Paget was told, twenty-two people worked for Freeman Protronics. 'And that doesn't include Janet or myself,' Mike Freeman told Paget proudly. 'Couldn't have done it without Janet, though.' He beamed at his daughter, who had just joined them in his office. 'Full partner, now, is Janet. Fifty-fifty all the way. This will all be hers when I'm gone.'

'Oh, Dad, you're not going anywhere,' said Janet Freeman, obviously embarrassed.

Mike Freeman was a small, red-faced, balding, aggressive man full of nervous energy. He had been holding forth for several minutes on the evolution of the business, and he looked as if he had every intention of continuing, but Janet cut him off.

'Do you have news of David, Chief Inspector?' she asked anxiously.

Janet Freeman would be about thirty, Paget judged. She was taller than her father, and she had none of his features as far as Paget could see. Her face was long, oval and pale, framed by soft waves of chestnut hair that brushed her shoulders. Her anxious eyes were dark, and she looked tired. She wore a two-piece suit, plain, severe, and her fingers toyed nervously with the buttons of the coat.

'Won't you please sit down?' said Paget, who had risen when she came in.

She read his face. 'It's bad news, isn't it?' she said. She turned a chair so that it was facing Paget and sat down. 'Please, just tell me.'

Paget nodded. When it came right down to it, there wasn't an easy way to break the news that someone near and dear was dead. 'I'm afraid so,' he said. 'I'm afraid he's dead, Miss Freeman.'

She blinked rapidly and looked away. 'How?' she asked. 'Was it an accident?'

Paget drew in a deep breath and shook his head. 'I'm sorry, but we believe he was murdered,' he said gently.

'My God! Are you sure?' Mike burst out. He rose swiftly

to his feet and came around the desk to stand by Janet. 'I mean, who identified him? Couldn't there be some mistake? What happened?'

'There's no mistake, Mr Freeman,' Paget said. 'He was identified by his medical and dental records. Unfortunately, the body is quite beyond ordinary recognition.'

Janet Freeman drew in her breath and clutched her father's hand, but remained silent. She seemed to be holding herself tightly, afraid to speak. Mike Freeman eyed Paget narrowly. 'You don't know who did it, do you?' he said. It wasn't exactly an accusation, but it sounded like one.

'No, we don't,' said Paget candidly. 'Which is why I must ask for your co-operation. Yours and Miss Freeman's, as well as that of your staff.'

Freeman's head came up sharply. 'The staff?' he said. 'What do they have to do with it?'

'Frankly, I don't know, at the moment,' said Paget, 'but almost anything we can learn about Mr Gray's movements prior to his death could prove useful. I'm sorry, but I'm afraid it's necessary, Mr Freeman.'

Freeman opened his mouth to say something more, but Janet put a hand on his arm. 'Leave it, Dad,' she said softly. 'We will do anything we can to help you find whoever did this, Chief Inspector.'

'Thank you, Miss Freeman.'

Mike Freeman returned to his seat behind the desk. He closed his eyes for a moment, then reached for a carafe and poured himself a glass of water. He took a small box from his pocket, opened it and took out a tablet. 'Angina,' he said by way of explanation, and swallowed the tablet.

Janet Freeman was immediately concerned. 'Are you all right, Dad?' she asked anxiously. 'Do you want me to take you home?'

But Mike Freeman shook his head. 'I'm fine,' he insisted. 'It's just—well, it was a bit of a shock, hearing about

David,' he said. 'Probably sent the old blood pressure a bit over the top for a moment.'

'He's supposed to avoid stress since his heart attack,' Janet explained.

'I'm sorry,' Paget said. 'If I'd known...'

Mike Freeman waved the apology away. 'No need to concern yourself,' he said. 'It was just a twinge, and the tablets take care of that.' He turned to his daughter who was regarding him with concern. 'Don't worry, Janet,' he told her. 'Everything will be all right. I'm more concerned about you. God knows, it's worse for you than it is for me.'

Janet Freeman watched her father for a moment as if to assure herself that he was indeed all right, then turned back to Paget. 'You said you needed our help,' she said, 'and you shall have it.' Her voice shook, but there was a determined set to her mouth. 'But I must know what happened.' She took a deep breath and pushed the next words out with visible effort. 'How did David die?'

Paget quailed inwardly. He had been dreading this, and as he looked into those dark, enquiring eyes, he wished there was a way to avoid what he had to say. How did one tell a woman that the man she was about to marry had been found at the bottom of a well after having his face shot away in the bed of another woman?

You didn't. You skimmed over the details, merely saying that Gray had been shot while visiting a young woman, who had since disappeared. But Janet Freeman wouldn't let him off that easily. Her face grew paler, but her eyes never left his face as he was forced to tell her of Gray's body being concealed in the well, which was why identification had to be made by dental records. When he had finished, she just sat there, hands clasped in her lap, eyes unwavering.

'You're telling me that this woman, Lisa Remington, was David's mistress,' she said at last.

'That is the way it looks, Miss Freeman,' Paget told her. 'There is evidence to suggest that this was not their first meeting.'

'Bastard!' The word was barely audible, but Mike Freeman's face was dark with anger as he spat the word out.

'And she killed David?' said Janet. 'This Lisa Remington.'

'We don't know that,' said Paget. 'As I said, she is still missing, and we are doing everything we can to find her.'

'Seems straightforward to me,' Mike Freeman growled.

Janet Freeman's head came up, and there was pain in her eyes. 'I'm sorry,' she said to Paget, 'but I don't think I'm quite ready for questions. I—I think I would like to go home, now. Would you mind if we talked about this later, Chief Inspector?'

'Of course.' Paget got to his feet as Janet Freeman rose from her chair. Mike Freeman stood up as well, and made as if to go with her, but his daughter waved him away.

'I'd just like to be by myself for a while, if you don't mind, Dad,' she said. 'Frank will run you home if you need a ride.'

Freeman grimaced. 'Had to give up my licence after the heart attack,' he confided to Paget. 'Damned doctors should mind their own business. It's bloody inconvenient, I'll tell you. Have to be up by six to get my morning walk in.'

'I would like to talk to you and your staff first thing Monday, if that can be arranged,' Paget told him, then turned to Janet. 'Perhaps you will feel more like talking to me then,' he said.

The young woman nodded wordlessly. 'I'll go out the back way,' she told her father. 'I don't think I could walk through the front office right now.' With a brief nod to Paget, she left the room.

FRANK PORTER watched from his window as Janet Freeman walked across the parking area to her car. She walked stiffly as if holding herself in; not at all like her usual long-limbed easy stride. The word had gone round the office like wildfire that a chief inspector was in with Mike, and Frank Porter wanted very much to know what was being said.

Janet unlocked the car and got in. She sat there for some time before starting the engine. He wanted to go out to her, but he knew it would be the wrong thing to do. Wait, be patient, he told himself. God knows, he'd had enough practice. Besides, it was too late. Janet had started the car and was pulling out.

He watched until she was out of sight, then returned to his desk. His hands felt clammy, and his stomach felt decidedly uneasy. He opened a drawer and reached for the tablets he always kept there. One more shouldn't hurt. The tablet stuck in his throat and he had to swallow hard to force it down.

Porter's fingers drummed nervously on his desk. If he had known it would be like this, he told himself, he would never have gone along with Mike. But even as he formed the thought, he knew it to be a lie. He'd never had a choice, he thought gloomily. Mike always got his own way. Porter sighed heavily. He wished the chief inspector would leave so that he could find out what Mike had told him.

PC YATES was fed up with digging. He and three others had been at it for what seemed like hours; digging, sifting, refilling, then moving on to the next square. His back was killing him. This wasn't why he'd joined the force. If he'd wanted to dig gardens, he could have done that on his dad's allotment. This was just a waste of time.

He jammed his spade into the ground. 'Going for a leak,' he told the man next to him.

'Skiving off again, Yates?' the man grumbled. 'You'd

better have your waterworks seen to before you run out of piss.'

'If Yates ever runs out of piss, there'd be nothing left,' said another.

'Up yours, Thomas. And yours, too, Jack.' Yates kicked the mud from his boots and disappeared around the side of the house. He made straight for his hiding place, a niche between the chimney and a large, old-fashioned water butt. It was an ideal spot, sheltered from the wind, but more importantly, out of sight of the mobile unit.

He tucked himself in beside the wall and lit his cigarette. This was more like it. He slid down on his haunches and sat with his back propped up against the wall. The ground was a bit damp, but what the hell. His clothes were filthy after all that digging anyway.

The sun was warm on his face. Cosy little spot, this, he thought as he surveyed the tiny space. He ran his fingers over the wooden barrel, sensing the thickness of the staves, and wondered how old it was.

A piece of cloth was caught on one of the hoops of the barrel, and without thinking, he pulled it loose. He was about to drop it on the ground when something about the feel of it stopped him. It was soft, like a fine gauze but silkier to the touch, and he liked the feel of it against his fingertips. It was four to five inches long, by about two inches wide, and hemmed on one side. Obviously, torn from a piece of clothing, Yates thought, and he spent several pleasant moments thinking of the possibilities. Nice bit of material, he concluded. Sort of a peachy colour except for the dark brown stain in the corner.

He dropped the material on the ground, took another drag at his cigarette, and closed his eyes against the sun. It would be easy to go to sleep here.

Yates had almost finished his cigarette before the nagging little thought deep inside his brain managed to struggle to the surface. He picked up the piece of material and examined it carefully. Could that be blood? he wondered.

The door of the mobile unit banged, and Yates scrambled to his feet. He ground out his cigarette and scuttled out of his hiding place just in time to reach the garden as the sergeant came round the corner.

'Another rest period, is it, Yates? Just off for a smoke, were you?'

Yates looked pained. 'No, Sergeant,' he said. 'I was just going to bag this.' He held up the piece of flimsy cloth. 'Could be blood,' he said, indicating the dark stain.

The sergeant eyed Yates. The bugger had been up to something, but he wasn't sure what. 'Are you trying to tell me you dug this up?' he said scornfully.

'No, sir, of course not. It would be all muddy then, wouldn't it?' Yates glanced around. 'No, I found it there,' he said, pointing to a small shrub. 'It was caught on one of the branches underneath. I just happened to see it while I was digging.'

AUDREY TREGALLES was glad it was Friday. The bell had only just gone, but already some of the children were coming out of the door. They must fly out of their seats when that bell goes, she thought, and for a moment remembered her own school-days when Fridays meant a happy, if temporary, release.

Olivia was one of the last ones out. She had always been very deliberate in everything she did, and she could be exasperating when they were all ready to go somewhere and she was still only half dressed. It wasn't that she dawdled, exactly, it was just that she had to think about everything before she did it, and she couldn't understand why her father got so worked up about it.

'You always say you want me to look nice,' she would say to him when he was standing there fuming and looking at his watch, 'but it takes *time,* Daddy. Doesn't it, Mummy?' Audrey smiled to herself. Children! They knew exactly how to get around their parents. Sometimes you could shake them, yet five minutes later they could bring a lump to your throat and you could hug them to pieces.

Audrey left the gate and walked across the playground to meet her. Olivia paused to speak to another girl, then came on. She had almost reached her mother when her eyes opened wide in surprise, and she put up her arm and waved.

'There he is, Mummy,' she called. 'That's the man I told you about. See? He waved.'

Audrey turned, her eyes searching frantically among the children and grown-ups in the street. 'Where?' she cried. She turned back to see where Olivia was pointing.

'There. Over there across the street.'

Audrey looked to where her daughter was pointing, and saw a grey-haired man turning away. Even as she picked him out, he walked rapidly away and disappeared around a corner. Audrey dashed for the gate, but children blocked the narrow opening, and Audrey had to force her way through. 'Stay with Olivia,' she called to one of the parents she recognized. 'Please!' She thrust her way through and was out in the street. She dashed across the road in front of a man on a bicycle, and shouted, 'Sorry,' as he swerved and swore at her.

She arrived at the corner, panting. There were several people in the street, but none of them looked anything like the man she was seeking. Still gasping, she began to walk down the street, but realized there would be no point. Besides, she had left Olivia at the school gate, and what if he had somehow come back? The thought was irrational; there was no way he could do that, but still, the sooner she returned to Olivia, the better.

As Audrey made her way back across the road, heart pounding in her chest, Olivia ran to meet her. 'I've got to get more exercise, lovey,' she gasped as she hugged the child to her. 'I'll get your dad to get the exercise bike down tonight.'

Saturday 6th April

WHERE IS LISA REMINGTON? was the headline that greeted Paget when he opened his newspaper on Saturday morning. It was followed by a sub-heading: *Love Nest Stripped Bare by Police.* A picture of Lisa filled half the page. It showed her in a provocative pose, modelling black lace underwear. They must have dug it out of the archives, because it was at least ten years old. A smaller picture of Bracken Cottage appeared in the bottom corner of the page, and the accompanying story not only took up the rest of the front page, but spilled over on to page three. Four paragraphs covered the known facts of the case, but no doubt the reading public would find the other eleven paragraphs of creative speculation far more titillating.

By nine o'clock, uniformed men had to be called out to keep traffic moving past Bracken Cottage, and it became a full-time job just keeping the Press and the more daring memento-seekers off the property. Peter Foster complained bitterly to the uniformed sergeant in charge, but even he could see there was little else the sergeant or his men could do. In the end, Foster shut himself away in his dark-room, and sat hunched up in a chair, alternately cursing the world at large, and weeping piteously.

Digging had ceased—at least for the moment. Nothing, other than a scrap of material that might or might not be relevant, had been found in the garden, and careful inspection of the area in the immediate vicinity of Bracken Cottage had shown no sign of the ground having been disturbed. Now, the only course to follow was the tried and true one of knocking on doors and asking questions in the hope that someone, somewhere, had seen or heard something that would point the police in the right direction.

Tregalles had turned in his report on the interview with the Tyson family, concluding that he thought it possible that Eric Tyson might know or have seen something, but it would probably take a psychologist to winkle it out. If nothing else turned up, Paget thought gloomily, they might have to seek help in that direction.

He spent the morning catching up on paperwork, but by twelve o'clock he'd had enough. He made himself a couple of sandwiches and a pot of tea, and set them on the kitchen table. But it looked so pleasant out there in the garden that he put everything on a tray and took it outside. He settled in an old cane chair, and poured himself a cup of tea. It was warm there in the sun. Paget put his head back and closed his eyes—and promptly fell asleep.

TWELVE

Monday 8th April

PAGET TAPPED the blackboard on which he had written in bold letters, TUESDAY—MARCH 12TH, and circled it. 'To us, this case is barely one week old,' he said, 'but in fact what we're looking at is a trail that is almost a month old, and that—' he tapped the board again '—is the date we have to focus on. Because that, as far as we know, is when Lisa Remington was last seen alive.'

It was eight thirty in the morning, and members of the murder team were gathered in the operations room in Charter Lane to review the case, and to make sure that everyone knew exactly where things stood.

'If Peter Foster's description of the condition of the body is to be believed...' Paget raised his voice as a murmur of dissent arose around him. 'If Peter Foster is to be believed,' he repeated, 'David Gray was killed sometime between the afternoon of Tuesday, March 12th, and about five o'clock on Wednesday morning. Unfortunately, Dr Starkie cannot give us a more accurate time of death, so let's assume, at least for now, that Peter Foster is telling the truth.'

The murmur grew more insistent, but Paget held up his hands. 'Never mind what you *think*,' he said. 'Just bear with me for a moment. Now, let's suppose that Foster is telling us the literal truth; that he came home and found a body in the bed, and he honestly thought it was Sean Merrick. For those of you who were not there, let me remind you that the man's face was completely obliterated, and the body was naked. There was little to differentiate between Gray and Merrick under those conditions.

'So, what is Foster's reaction? He thinks that Merrick has forced his way into the cottage again, and that he has either raped Lisa or at least attempted to—remember, the man has a reputation as a bully and a wife-beater—and Lisa shot him. Where she is, he doesn't know, but on the assumption that she will get in touch with him, he sets about covering up the crime. At first he phones friends to try to find her, but when that fails, he concocts a story about her being away on an assignment, expecting her to turn up any day. But she doesn't return, and he is forced to maintain the fiction that Lisa is abroad.'

'Aren't you forgetting the stuff buried in the garden, sir?' a young DC asked.

'No, I'm not forgetting that,' said Paget, 'and I must admit it bothers me. But it is just possible that Foster is telling us the truth about that as well. Unlikely, perhaps, but possible.

'However, let's look at another possibility: the idea that Foster arrived home to find Lisa in bed with David Gray. In a fit of rage he grabs the shotgun intent on killing both of them. Now, based on the amount of shot Forensic recovered, and the grouping, two cartridges were fired from exactly the same position, suggesting that both barrels were discharged at the same time. That's why so much damage was done to Gray's face and upper body. But if Gray took the full force of the discharge, where was Lisa Remington? Was she also killed in the blast? Or did she manage to escape and slip away?'

Paget paused and looked around the room. 'If Lisa did manage to escape, then where is she? If she thought her life was in danger, wouldn't you expect her to run to the nearest place for help? Call the police? But no one admits to seeing her. No one, it seems, has seen or heard from her since that day.'

'Which suggests that Foster did kill her,' a young DC ventured.

Paget looked thoughtful. 'In that case, why didn't Foster put her body in the well along with that of Gray? There was plenty of room, so why go to the trouble of disposing of her body somewhere else? It would be more risky, so why do it?'

Ormside, who had come in for the briefing, spoke up. 'The body could still be on the property,' he said. 'From what I've seen of Foster, he's not stupid. He did a good job of doing that room over, and he went about his business as if nothing had happened. And we did find Miss Remington's handbag and suitcase buried in the garden.'

'True,' said Paget, 'but Foster claims that he didn't discover the handbag until later, and it was only then that he decided he'd better make it look as if Lisa had taken the bag and suitcase with her. It was too late to drop those down the well, so he buried them. It may not be what you or I would have done, but there is a certain logic to it.'

The noise level in the room escalated as members of the team began arguing the pros and cons among themselves. 'So what do you think happened, sir?' asked a female member of the team.

Paget shrugged. 'To be quite honest, I don't know,' he said, 'but there is another possibility, and that is that neither Foster nor Lisa Remington murdered Gray. Someone else did.'

'Who?' several voices said at once. Paget waved them to silence. 'You sound like a bunch of owls,' he growled. 'Think about it. What about Merrick himself? Once we found out that he was alive, we more or less forgot about him, but who had been coming round to try to take Lisa away? Who got a load of shot up his backside the day before? Who would have gone berserk if he'd found Lisa in bed with someone else? From what we know about him, he's capable of it, and he might well have forced Lisa to go with him. Perhaps locked her up somewhere.'

Heads began to nod, but Paget held up his hand. 'That is only one possibility,' he cautioned. 'If our information is correct, Lisa Remington was not above sleeping with men who she thought might advance her career. And bear in mind that she was entertaining one lover while living with another. Who else might have been visiting Bracken Cottage while Foster was away is anybody's guess. And I must remind you that we know nothing about David Gray, except that he was about to be married to Janet Freeman. What, for example, might happen if Janet Freeman found out about the affair? Here was her fiancé off sleeping with another woman the very day their wedding invitations were to be sent out. How do you think she might react if she found out?'

'Bloody hell!' said someone as a groan went up around the room. 'That means…'

'That means that we have a hell of a lot of work to do,' Paget cut in, 'and the sooner we get started, the better. Tregalles is on his way to London to follow up on Merrick, so that end is covered, but the rest of you will have more than enough to keep you occupied.

'Len,' he said to Ormside, 'I'd like you to extend your area of enquiry to include the villages of Brecken Cross and Chedstone, and conduct a door-to-door in both those villages. I know you've been around the farms and cottages in the area, but I'd like you to do them again. Prod their memories, and concentrate on that date of March 12th.' Paget took the chalk and circled the date heavily.

'And set up a road-block near Bracken Cottage. Ask everyone using the road whether they were on the road that Tuesday. If they were, get a statement from them. Someone has to have seen something, so let's get out there and find them.'

Paget dusted chalk from his hands. 'We've already had over forty reports of sightings of Lisa Remington since her picture was in the paper over the weekend, and Saunders, Davis and Gregson will be following those up with the local forces around the country. Meanwhile, we have work to do over at Freeman Protronics. I'll need two people this morning.' He looked around the room. 'Weller and Melrose. You will be doing interviews there with me. Be ready to go in half an hour. Anyone have any questions? No? Good. Then let's get on with it.'

IT TOOK SOME SHUFFLING on the part of Mike Freeman's staff, but by ten o'clock various people had vacated their offices to allow Paget and his two DCs to conduct interviews. Paget had looked over David Gray's office the Friday before, but it told him nothing of the man himself.

He did know, from the Missing Person report, that Gray had no close relatives. Gray was the only child of a single mother, and she had died some years ago. His grandparents were still alive, but they lived in Aberdeen, and when contacted by the police, said they had never had anything to do with David, and had no interest in him. In fact, they claimed that his mother had never contacted them again after they turned her out when she became pregnant, so they knew nothing of the boy.

As for other relatives, Gray's mother had no brothers or sisters, so it was pretty much a dead end there. Prior to joining Freeman Protronics, Gray had been employed for five years by a software company based in Manchester. His employment record with them was excellent, but as far as his personal history was concerned, they had nothing on file the police didn't already know.

So, with nothing more to go on than that, Janet Freeman

was Paget's only hope. If anyone knew anything about Gray, it should be she. After all, she had been about to marry the man, so it seemed safe to assume that she knew something about his personal life.

The trouble was, how willing would she be to talk about him under the circumstances?

JANET FREEMAN was tense. He could see it in every move, every gesture, and at least part of the reason was obvious. Two sides of her office were made of glass, and no matter how hard they tried not to, the people working in the main body of the open office kept glancing in.

'Look,' said Paget, 'I know how difficult this must be for you, Miss Freeman. Is there somewhere else we could talk? Somewhere more private?'

Janet Freeman threw him a grateful glance. 'There's a little place across the square,' she said hesitantly. 'A café. It won't be very busy, now, and they have booths.'

'Excellent,' he said. 'How's their coffee?'

'It's very good, as a matter of fact.'

Janet Freeman was right. The coffee was good, and there were only a handful of people in the place. Janet raised her cup and regarded Paget over the rim. There were dark circles beneath her eyes, and she looked as if she'd hardly slept throughout the weekend.

Paget began his questioning slowly, trying to build a picture of David Gray. But it seemed that Gray had told her very little about himself. 'It didn't seem important,' she told him. 'We were too busy planning for the future to talk much about the past. At least, I was,' she ended bitterly. 'I should have listened to Frank.'

She brushed a wisp of hair away from her face. 'He was right,' she went on, 'but I didn't want to believe him. In fact, I told him he was acting like a spiteful child.'

'This would be Frank Porter?' Paget said.

Janet nodded. 'Frank was the first one to join us when the work became too much for Dad and me, and we had to expand. Until David came along, Frank and I... Well, it was taken for granted, I suppose, that he and I would get married some day.'

'You say he was right,' Paget said. 'What, exactly, did you mean by that, Miss Freeman? What did Frank tell you about David Gray?'

Janet Freeman looked down at the table. 'He said that David was trying to worm his way into the firm; that he was more interested in Freeman Protronics than he was in me. I thought he was just saying that to get back at me, to hurt me, but it seems that he was right.'

'Did anyone else try to warn you against David Gray?'

Janet frowned and looked down at the cup in her hands. 'Not in that way, but it took Dad a while to get used to the idea of my marrying David,' she said slowly. 'We argued about it; in fact we more or less agreed to disagree, but he was coming round.'

'Why was he against your marrying Gray?'

Janet Freeman remained silent for a long moment before answering. 'I think he was frightened,' she said softly. 'Not of David, but of my leaving him. You see, he'd never admit it, but I think the heart attack made him realize that he is not immortal, and if I married David, he'd be on his own. Perhaps not right away, but we both knew that David was ambitious, and if he decided to move on and I went with him...'

Janet looked up at Paget. 'I just hope all this doesn't set him back again,' she went on. 'His blood pressure was up when he took it Friday evening, and he's been like a cat on hot bricks all weekend. I wish he'd learn to settle down. But then, that's always been his problem. He could never learn to relax.'

'Is his condition serious?'

Janet Freeman shrugged. 'If he takes care of himself, no,' she said. 'But you've seen him. He drives himself. Always has. And he won't ask for help. He could have died last time, and all because he was too stubborn to call me. He has this button beside his bed, you see. It's connected to a buzzer in my room, and he only has to push it for me to be there in seconds. But will he do it? Not him! "Don't like to disturb you, Janet," he tells me. "You needed your sleep."'

Janet shook her head despairingly. 'So he ends up in hospital with a broken rib as well as blood pressure off the end of the scale.'

'What happened?'

'He had a bad attack during the night,' she said. 'He took his tablet, but it didn't work, so instead of ringing for me, he got up, even tried to dress himself, then started down the stairs to ring the doctor. I've tried to get him to have a telephone extension in his bedroom, but it's like talking to the wall. Anyway, he tripped over his trousers at the top of the stairs and fell. That's how he broke his rib. If it wasn't so serious, it would be laughable. I asked him why he got dressed, and do you know what he said?'

Paget waited.

'He said he thought the doctor might send him to hospital, so he wanted to be ready.' Janet closed her eyes and clenched her fists in a gesture of frustration. 'He also said he would have left me a note so I wouldn't worry. What do you do with a man like that, Chief Inspector?'

Paget chose to regard the question as rhetorical. He caught the eye of the waitress, and motioned to their cups. She was a young girl, not long out of school, and she seemed more interested in a group of young people gathered around the till than in serving paying customers. She came grudgingly, and poured the coffee, slopping it over into his saucer. The girl turned to Janet, but she put her hand over her cup and shook her head.

Paget slipped a paper napkin beneath his cup to soak up the excess coffee. 'Take me back to March 12th,' he said. 'The day David left the office. I've been over the report several times, but there may be something, some little detail that I've missed or that you'll remember. As I recall, he received a telephone call just after two o'clock that day, and he left the office shortly afterwards.'

'That's right. I was out at the time, so I didn't know David had gone until I came back about four thirty.'

'And it was only when he failed to appear by the following evening that you became concerned?'

'Yes. David had promised faithfully to go over the invitation list with me, and when he didn't come, and didn't answer his phone, I thought he must still be at Bridgnorth. I tried his pager, but when he didn't answer that, I wasn't too surprised. He was always leaving his pager in the car.'

The pager, Paget remembered, had been found in the company car.

'So you went to David's flat later that evening,' he said. 'What time was that? It wasn't clear in the report.'

Janet thought about that. 'It must have been after ten,' she said. 'I didn't like to leave before that because of Dad. I wanted to make sure he had settled down. I have a key to David's flat, so I went in and checked to see if he'd left a message on his phone, but there was nothing. But even then I wasn't really worried. It was only the next morning that I realized that something must be wrong.'

'You say you wanted to make sure your father was all right,' Paget said. 'Had he had another of his attacks?'

Janet seemed surprised by the question. 'That was the one I told you about,' she said. 'He had the attack that morning.'

'This would be the morning of the 13th?' said Paget.

'That's right. That's when he fell. It was about two o'clock in the morning. He was in such a state I didn't dare wait for the ambulance, so I rushed him over to the hospital myself. They checked him over and rang me to come and pick him up about four o'clock that afternoon. I had hoped they'd keep him in at least overnight, but I suppose they need the beds. So I took him home and made him go to bed. Then I...' She stopped. 'I'm sorry, Chief Inspector,' she said apologetically. 'I know this has nothing to do with what you want to know, but I worry about Dad. He could have killed himself on those stairs.'

Paget steered Janet Freeman back to the matter at hand, but learned nothing that wasn't in the original report.

'I wish I could help you more,' she said as they left the café, 'but I don't know what else to tell you.'

'You mentioned that you were out of the office when David Gray received the phone call the day he disappeared,' Paget said. 'Do you mind telling me where you were?'

'I was doing some shopping. Why do you ask?'

'And I believe you said you were gone from lunch-time until about four thirty. Is that right?'

Janet Freeman looked puzzled. 'Yes, but I don't see what that has to do with anything.'

They reached the office and Paget held the door for her to enter. 'Do you know Burbridge Motors?'

She stepped inside and turned to face him, her frown deepening. 'Yes, of course.'

'Were you anywhere near there that afternoon?'

Janet Freeman seemed baffled by his questions. 'I was in the shopping precinct,' she said. 'That's just around the corner. Why?'

'I just wondered whether you might have seen David Gray while you were out,' Paget said. 'We have reason to believe that he went there to meet Lisa Remington.'

Janet Freeman's face became a mask. 'No,' she said shortly, and looked pointedly at her watch. 'And if that is all, Chief Inspector, I have a great deal of work to do.' She smiled mechanically. 'Thank you for the coffee.'

'Just one more thing, Miss Freeman,' he said as she turned to go. 'I'd appreciate it if you could give me a list of the shops you went to that afternoon. And the approximate times you were there. It helps if we know where everyone was that day.'

'Suspects, you mean,' she said icily. 'Why don't you come right out and say it? You think I might have killed David, don't you?'

Paget met her gaze head on. 'To be honest, Miss Freeman, I don't know,' he told her. 'But I will have a better idea once I can eliminate those who could *not* have done it—which is why I would like that list.'

THIRTEEN

'OH, CHRIST! You again. That's all I need. What the hell do you want?'

Sean Merrick glowered at Tregalles through red-rimmed eyes. His shoulder was wedged hard against the door, barring the way.

'I'd like to come inside and talk to you,' the sergeant said. 'About Lisa.'

Merrick's eyes narrowed. 'What about Lisa?' he demanded. 'Have you found her?'

'No. That's what I want to talk to you about.'

'It's no good talking to me,' Merrick snarled. 'It's that prick, Foster, you want. He's the one. He turned her against me. He's hiding her. I'd like to kill the little bastard!'

Merrick's hand on the door began to shake. He turned away and limped inside. The sergeant took it as an invitation and followed Merrick inside.

The entrance was in fact the back door, and Tregalles found himself in a large, old-fashioned kitchen. The place was a tip. Merrick was living like a pig. Take-away food wrappers were everywhere, as were crushed beer cans, newspapers, and an assortment of discarded clothing. Pots and pans piled high in the sink looked as if they hadn't been washed for a month, and the table was littered with dirty plates and cups and saucers.

Through an archway, Tregalles could see what was obviously a workroom. A large drafting table stood beneath an unlit bank of fluorescent lights. Shelves lined the walls, and a cutting table took up one whole side. Fashion books lay everywhere, and fabrics of every colour and texture spilled out of boxes stacked one on top of another beneath the tables. All this Tregalles saw at a glance, but his attention was riveted on the sketches—or what was left of them.

They had been torn to shreds, literally ripped from the walls and scattered about the room like huge pieces of confetti.

Merrick stood there in the middle of the room, swaying slightly as he watched Tregalles. 'I might as well burn the bloody lot for all the good they are,' he said peevishly. 'Christ! It isn't as if she loves the stupid little bastard. What is he, anyway? A third-rate photographer buried away down there in the country. He'll never amount to anything. He's got no talent; no imagination. She's living a bloody fantasy. Country cottage. Roses in the garden. That's all it is, a bloody fantasy.'

Merrick raised a finger and shook it at Tregalles. 'She'll come back,' he shouted. 'You mark my words, she'll come back.' He lowered his voice and his lip curled contemptuously. 'And when she does come crawling back,' he went on ominously, 'the bitch'll pay. By God! she'll pay for what she's done to me. She'll pay for every job I've lost; every insult I've taken on account of her. It's her fault I can't work. Look at it!' Merrick swept an arm toward the workroom. 'Nothing! Nothing since she left. I can't work; I can't sleep; I can't even think! And it's all her fault.'

He swung round to face Tregalles, head thrust forward, chest heaving with anger. His eyes glittered. 'Oh, yes, my friend,' he whispered. 'When she comes crawling back to me, you'll see. She'll pay, believe me.'

'That's enough of that,' said Tregalles sharply. 'I want to ask you some questions.'

'Sod you and your questions.' Merrick turned to the fridge and took out a can of beer. He pulled the tab and raised the can in mock salute.

'To retribution,' he said softly. 'You'll see.'

Tregalles moved swiftly to his side. He took the can from Merrick's hand and slammed it on the table. Merrick, already unsteady on his feet, fell back against the fridge, eyes wide in sheer surprise. 'You cheeky sod!' he breathed. His mouth twisted into something like a grin. 'You cheeky sod,' he said again—and slammed his fist into the sergeant's unprotected stomach.

PEGGY OWEN was supposed to be Mike Freeman's secretary. At least, that's how it started out, she told Paget. In fact, she worked for Janet Freeman and Frank Porter as well. 'And, of course, I worked for Mr Gray before he—aahh—left,' she ended.

Mrs Owen was a widow. Lost her husband five years ago, she told him. Industrial accident. Freak thing; couldn't be helped. She was short, plump, fair-haired, and fortyish. She had an open face, and a mind like the computer that took up a good part of her desk. She fielded all the incoming calls for the senior members of Freeman Protronics, she told Paget, took dictation, typed their letters, and allotted work to the other members of the clerical staff. She had been with the company since its inception, she said proudly, and there was virtually nothing she did not know about Freeman Protronics and its employees.

Paget mentally rubbed his hands together. People like Peggy Owen were invaluable to a firm—and to investigating policemen. It was his experience that secretaries often knew more about what was really going on than their so-called superiors.

He began by taking her back to the afternoon of March 12th. 'According to the Missing Person report, you took the call Mr Gray received just before he left,' he said.

The woman nodded. 'That's right. It was a woman who rang, and she asked to speak to David. That's what she said, "David". Then she sort of coughed and corrected herself, you know, the way people do when they've made a mistake, and she said, "I mean Mr Gray."'

'Young voice?'

Peggy Owen hesitated. 'Not really young,' she said. 'Not old either. It's a bit hard to tell, but I'd put her down as in her late twenties or early thirties.'

'Did she say anything else?'

'No.'

'Mr Gray didn't have his own line, then?'

They were in Gray's office, and Mrs Owen indicated the six buttons on the phone, two of which were lit up. 'This was Mr Gray's number,' she said. 'Four-two-four-nine. The prefix is the same for all of them, of course. But each of the others—that is Mr Freeman, Miss Freeman and Mr Porter—also have the same numbers on their phones so that they can get on the line together if they need to.'

'And the woman who called in that day used Mr Gray's line?'

'Yes.'

'Had you ever heard her voice before?'

Mrs Owen's brows drew together. 'I think I have,' she said hesitantly. 'I couldn't swear to it, mind, but I think she rang Mr Gray once before. It was about a week... No, it would be more than a week before.' Her brow cleared as she mentally counted backward. 'It was the Monday. March 4th.'

Paget stared at her. 'How can you be so sure?' he asked. 'You must take a lot of calls each day.'

Peggy Owen smiled. 'I remember because Mr Gray was just leaving the office and I had to call him back because the woman insisted on talking to him. He was going to McGregor and Speers. We're designing a new system for them, and they have a meeting every Monday afternoon; their staff and ours.'

'Did the woman identify herself in any way?'

'No. But I knew she wasn't one of our regular clients. That's why I was a bit surprised when Mr Gray said the call was from Travis Hambledon, and he had to go out there.'

'But you didn't question it?'

'Good heavens, no. She might have been a new girl at T.H. for all I knew. It was just… Oh, I don't know. There was something about the way she asked for Mr Gray that made me think that perhaps she knew him.'

'Knew him, Mrs Owen?'

Peggy Owen looked down at her hands and shook her head as if to deny her words. 'It was just a feeling,' she said. 'As if she knew Mr Gray, well, personally, if you know what I mean.'

Paget thought he knew very well what Mrs Owen meant.

'How long after the call was it that Mr Gray left here?' he asked.

'Ten minutes. No more, I'm sure. He told me he was going out to Bridgnorth and might not be back until the following day. He asked me to get him the spare set of keys Mr Freeman keeps in his desk, because he couldn't find his own, and then he left.'

'Miss Freeman was out of the office at the time, I believe?'

'That's right. When she came back about four thirty, she asked if I knew where Mr Gray was, and I told her.' A troubled expression appeared in her eyes, and she looked away.

'What is it, Mrs Owen?'

Peggy Owen remained silent for some time. Some internal struggle had to be resolved. Office loyalties? Personal friendships? Paget waited.

'Janet was so excited,' she said at last. 'You see, she'd just bought all her…night things. For her wedding, if you know what I mean, and she wanted to show them to me. I wanted to feel happy for her, but, well, it's just that I didn't want her to be hurt.' Her eyes grew moist as she looked at Paget. 'Janet and her father are like my own family, and David Gray was…'

Peggy Owen pulled herself up short. 'I'm sorry, Chief Inspector,' she said primly. 'I shouldn't have spoken like that.'

Paget smiled understandingly. 'I wish more people would be as frank with us,' he said gently. 'There is nothing wrong with caring for a friend. But tell me, what was it you didn't like about David Gray?'

The woman shook her head and frowned. 'That's just it,' she said. 'I don't really know. There was just something about him. I know it probably sounds silly, but he was *too* good in many ways. He was brilliant at his job, and our clients seemed to like him, but the way he went after Janet was, oh, I don't know—so deliberate, if that makes any sense.'

'I think it does,' Paget told her. A picture of the man was beginning to take shape in his mind. But he wanted to steer her away from that subject. 'Who else was in the office when Mr Gray left?' he asked.

Mrs Owen thought. 'Everyone, except Jan—' office protocol reasserted itself '—Miss Freeman, of course. Mr Freeman and Mr Porter left just after, but…'

'What do you mean by "just after"? Mrs Owen?'

The question seemed to bother her, and she looked uncomfortable. 'A few minutes,' she said at last, but she avoided looking directly at him.

'Are you telling me that they *followed* Mr Gray?'

'Oh, no. It wasn't…I mean, no, it was just that something came up and…' She stopped. 'It was the car,' she said suddenly. 'That's what it was. Something came up and Mr Freeman wanted Frank to take him somewhere in the car, and Mr Gray had just taken it, so they had to go in Mr Porter's car.'

'I see. Did they say where they were going?'

'No. Mr Freeman went into Mr Porter's office, then they both dashed out, so there wasn't time to tell me where they were going.'

'You say they "dashed" out. Was that because they were trying to catch Mr Gray before he took the car?'

Mrs Owen shrugged. 'It must have been, mustn't it?' she said. Her eyes met his own. 'You see, we only have the two company cars, and Mr Gray was about to go off in the one, and the other one was in Cheltenham where Mr Parkinson had it for the week.'

'I see. But Mr Gray had gone by then, had he?'

'He must have done. As I said, they took Mr Porter's car.'

'How do you know they took Mr Porter's car, Mrs Owen?'

The woman bridled. 'Because I watched them leave from Mr Porter's window,' she said stiffly. Paget remained silent, but his very silence was a question. 'I was worried,' Mrs Owen said defensively. 'Mr Freeman hadn't been back all that long after his heart attack, and I didn't like to see him dashing about like that.'

'Ah, I see. How long were they gone?'

'Not long. Perhaps an hour at the outside.' The woman looked puzzled. 'But what has that got to do with Mr Gray?'

'Probably nothing,' Paget confessed. He gathered up his notes and stood up. 'But one never knows, does one?' he said with a smile. 'Thank you, Mrs Owen. You have been a great help to me.'

Peggy Owen returned his smile, but she looked anything but happy as she left the room.

EMILY TYSON lowered the binoculars. 'They've stopped digging up there,' she said. 'They're shifting all those loose stones around the sheep pen now.'

Tom Tyson grunted. 'It'll do them no good,' he said as he stirred his tea.

Emily's features became even more pinched than usual. 'He was up there again this morning,' she said. 'I told you he'd go. Like to like, that's what I say. That's why he goes.'

'For God's sake, woman,' Tyson burst out, 'how many times do I have to tell you? He didn't go up there to...'

Her shrill voice cut across whatever he was going to say. 'Don't you blaspheme in this house, Tom Tyson. Haven't I enough to bear? He must go! I'll not have him under this roof any longer. As long as he is here, this house is cursed, and well you know it.'

Tyson groaned inwardly. It was getting worse. Much worse. Something had to be done. And soon. Thank God she didn't know the truth.

'THE MAN'S a bloody nutter,' Tregalles said into the phone. He was speaking to Len Ormside. 'I had to take him in. They're holding him for assaulting a police officer for starters. But there's nothing in his place to suggest that Lisa was ever there. Merrick swears he doesn't know where she is, but he could have gone back to the cottage the day after she sent him packing and killed both her and Gray. He says he can't remember where he was after Lisa shot him. Says he got drunk and stayed over at a pub somewhere down the road, but he can't tell me where or how far down which road. I tried tracing his movements through his credit cards, but there's no record of him using them that day, and he says he probably paid cash.'

Ormside sighed. 'Then we'll just have to do it the hard way,' he said heavily, 'and check out all the likely pubs. Are you sure you're all right?'

'I could use a refresher on self-defence,' Tregalles said ruefully. 'The bastard's as strong as a bloody ox, and he took me by surprise, but I'll live.'

'Good. Did Merrick give you any idea how far he might have gone before he stopped?'

'No, but I doubt if it was far. The man can't go ten minutes without a drink, and with a load of buckshot up his arse, I doubt if it would be very comfortable driving.'

'You're probably right. I'll get someone on it right away. Anything you want me to tell Paget when he checks in?'

'Just tell him I'm on my way back. The locals can take care of things at this end. Oh, and Len, perhaps you could let Audrey know I'll be back this evening.' Tregalles paused. 'I don't suppose you've heard anything? About Olivia, I mean.'

Ormside smiled into the phone. 'I spoke to Jim Dean,' he said. 'He sent Molly Forsythe over there this afternoon. Nothing to report so far. He says he'll let me know if there is.'

Tregalles's sigh of relief could be heard over the phone. 'Thanks,' he said simply. 'Tell Jim I owe him one. On second thoughts, I'll tell him myself when I get home.'

FOURTEEN

FRANK PORTER was nervous. He tried to appear relaxed, tilting back in his office chair behind the desk, but his big hands moved constantly as he talked. His broad, square fingers ran lightly over the ends of the armrests of the chair; traced the edges of his desk; moved a memo pad a millimetre this way, then a millimetre back.

'Tell me what you know about David Gray,' Paget said.

Porter's mouth turned down at the mention of Gray. He was a big man, heavy-set, and would probably run to fat by the time he was fifty. In fact, he was only thirty-five, but he had the settled look of middle age, and his hair was already turning grey.

'Can't say I know much about him at all,' he said heavily. 'He was good at his work; I'll give him that, but...' He shrugged as if to say that was as far as he was prepared to go.

'But what?' Paget prompted him. 'If my information is correct, the two of you have worked together for something like two years now, so you must have learned something about the man; formed some opinion.'

Porter's fingers slid along the edge of the desk and back again. 'I don't really know what it is you're after,' he said. 'Yes, I worked with him; so did a lot of others, but I know virtually nothing of his personal life, and I assume that's what you're interested in.'

Paget tried another tack. 'Did you like him, then?'

Porter grimaced and fiddled with the memo pad. 'He was all right,' he said grudgingly.

'So you didn't like him.'

'I didn't say that. I said he was…'

'I know what you *said*, Mr Porter,' said Paget testily. 'You said absolutely nothing. Did you dislike him because he was about to marry Miss Freeman?'

Porter looked startled. His big hands stopped moving, and his face began to turn colour. 'I don't think that is any of your business,' he said huffily. 'And I'll thank you to keep Miss Freeman's name out of this.'

Paget leaned back in his chair and steepled his fingers. 'Let me put it this way, Mr Porter: David Gray was murdered; killed by someone who disliked him intensely. Now, I'm told that you and Miss Freeman enjoyed a close relationship for several years before David Gray came along and took her away from you. If I were in your shoes, I wouldn't be too happy about that. Especially if the girl I'd hoped to marry was half owner of the business where I worked.'

Porter's face grew red. 'That is insulting!' he said hoarsely. 'If anyone was trying to get his foot in the door, it was Gray.' His voice shook. 'I tried to tell Janet. I tried to warn her about him, but she wouldn't listen. Gray wasn't in love with her. He was using her. She was a means to an end, that's all.'

'How do you know that?'

Porter opened his mouth, then clamped it shut again. His fingers played with the memo pad, then slid back and forth along the edge of the desk. 'The circumstances of his death,' he said at last. 'That shows what he was like.'

'What do you know about the circumstances of his death?' asked Paget sharply.

Porter looked startled. 'Just what Mike…I mean, he said that Gray was involved with some girl.'

'But you said you warned Miss Freeman about him before that,' Paget said. 'Did you offer her any proof?'

'He was ambitious,' Porter muttered.

'A lot of people are ambitious, Mr Porter. Aren't you?'

Porter scowled. 'Yes, of course, but Gray was different. Always out for the main chance. Cut-throat. That was his style.'

Paget shrugged. 'I'm given to understand that this is a highly competitive business,' he said. 'And I've also been told that David Gray was good at his job. According to Mr Freeman, he brought in more new business than anyone else. Isn't that right?'

'But at what cost?' Porter burst out. 'Tell me that. He'd cut corners, lie, cheat, do anything to get a contract. You ask any of our competitors.'

'Isn't that the way of business today?' Paget asked, deliberately goading the man.

'Not for Freeman Protronics, it isn't,' said Porter stoutly. 'Mike Freeman built this business on honesty, and Gray was dragging the name of Freeman Protronics into the mud. Yes, he brought in new business; yes, he was probably the most innovative program designer we've ever had, but he had the morals of a bloody tom-cat. He...'

'Morals?' said Paget softly. 'Are we still talking about business, Mr Porter? Or are we talking about something else?'

'Both,' snapped Porter harshly. He glanced at the closed door as if to satisfy himself that no one outside the office could hear him. 'I know for a fact that he got the Robinson contract by—' Porter raised his hands and curled his index fingers to indicate quotes '—"chatting up" their systems manager, Freda Lyndhurst.'

Paget pretended not to understand. 'Isn't "chatting people up" normal in business?' he asked.

Porter shook his head angrily. 'You know what I mean. Screwing the systems manager to get a contract isn't what I regard as normal. And before you ask, I was *there*, Chief Inspector.' He stabbed a stubby finger into the surface of the desk. 'We'd been trying to get that contract for close to six months, but Cycom had the edge. Mike sent Gray and me into Birmingham to try one last time. We spent the whole day trying to convince them that we could do a better job for them in the long term, even if our price was a bit higher, but we were getting nowhere.

'I was ready to come home, but Gray persuaded Freda to have dinner with him. He told her I had to get back, but he was free for the evening, and he wanted to show her there were no hard feelings. I didn't have to get back, but what could I say? Anyway, the long and the short of it was that he took her out and didn't come back until the next morning. But he had the contract.' Despite his obvious disapproval, Porter's face registered something akin to grudging admiration.

'This was before he became engaged to Miss Freeman?' Paget said.

Porter nodded. 'Three weeks before,' he said. 'I had no idea at the time that they were even thinking of becoming engaged. But don't you see? He must have been on the point of proposing when this happened, but it didn't stop him.'

'Is that when you warned Miss Freeman about him? Did you tell her about that particular incident?'

Porter's hands began their rapid play along the edge of the desk once more, and his face grew sullen. 'No,' he said. 'I mean, how could I? Mike was so pleased that we'd got the contract, he gave both of us a bonus. Gray never mentioned how he'd got it, so Mike assumed we were both responsible.' Porter shrugged in a helpless fashion. 'I see now that it was Gray's way of keeping me quiet. His letting Mike think it was a joint effort.'

The picture of the man who had died in Lisa Remington's bed was becoming clearer. Gray had been an opportunist and a manipulator, and a man like that could have many enemies. There could be little doubt that Porter resented him, possibly even hated him, but whether that hatred could be translated into murder was open to question.

'When David Gray left the office on the afternoon of March 12th, you were here in your office, I believe,' said Paget.

'That's right.'

'And you followed him out?'

Porter looked startled. 'No,' he protested. 'No, that's not right. It was a few minutes after; several minutes after. It was Mike who…who came in and suggested going for a ride. We didn't leave until some time after Gray.'

Paget sighed. 'Which was it, Mr Porter? A few minutes? Several minutes? Some time after? Could you be more specific? I have been led to believe that Mr Freeman was anxious to stop Gray before he left because he wanted to use the company car—or have you drive him, at least.'

Porter seemed at a loss for an answer. The memo pad was moved a fraction of a millimetre once more as Porter's brows drew together in a worried frown. 'I—I'm not sure,' he said. 'It's possible. I don't remember exactly.'

'Was it usual for Mr Freeman to suggest going for a ride in the middle of the afternoon?'

Porter flushed. 'Well, no, not ordinarily,' he admitted. 'But he wanted to discuss something with me, and he didn't want to do it in the office. He can't drive since he had the heart attack, so he asked if we could take my car.'

'If that was the case, then why the big rush to stop Gray from using the company car? Especially if he had to go out on a service call.'

Porter's frown deepened. 'As I said, I don't remember, exactly. You'd have to ask Mike about that.'

'Where did you go?'

'Eh?' Porter looked up at the ceiling for inspiration. 'Oh, yes. I see.' He lowered his voice and leaned forward across the desk. 'We didn't actually go anywhere,' he said, then corrected himself. 'What I mean is, we just drove around.'

'Following Gray?'

Colour flooded into Porter's face. 'Of course not. We were talking, that's all.'

'Talking?'

'Yes.'

Paget looked sceptical.

Porter leaned closer. 'I must insist that you keep this to yourself,' he said conspiratorially. 'You see, Mike has been toying with the idea of opening up a new office in Bristol, and he wanted to talk it over with me away from the office. It would mean that we might have to move some of the people from here to Bristol, and Mike doesn't want anything to leak out until the plans are finalized.'

'I see. You say you just drove aimlessly around,' Paget said. 'Around town? Out in the country?'

'No! I—I mean, no, of course not.' Porter sat back and put his hands together as if to keep them still. 'We drove around town for a while, then parked by the river for a few minutes. That's all. We were only gone for about an hour.'

'And you didn't see Gray while you were driving around?'

'No. Absolutely not.'

'So you have no idea where he went?'

Porter passed a hand through his hair. He looked a bit desperate. 'I've told you everything I know,' he insisted. 'I can't tell you anything else.'

Paget didn't believe him. Porter was a poor liar, but with so little to go on, there was nothing to be gained by pressing him. His dislike for Gray was evident, but had he hated the man enough to kill him? It was certainly not out of the question. Gray had come along and taken everything away from him: his girl, his preferred status in the company, and his future prospects. Together, they might prove a powerful motive for getting rid of Gray, and if the opportunity presented itself…

But if that were the case, where did Mike Freeman fit in?

'YOU CAN WAIT by the gate for your dad,' Audrey said, 'but don't go outside. Remember what I told you, Olivia? I don't want you out on the street alone.'

'Yes, Mum.' Olivia Tregalles made her way down the path to the iron gate and lifted the latch. She couldn't see all the way down the road unless she stepped outside, and it was only a few steps. With one eye on the front window to see if her mother was watching, she stepped outside on to the pavement and closed the gate behind her. With one hand still on the latch ready to jump back inside if she heard her mother coming, she waited.

The wind had changed, and with it came the smell of far-off rain. Clouds thickened in the evening sky, and street lights flickered, undecided whether to stay on or not. A slanting ray of sunshine broke through the shifting clouds, illuminating the chalked outlines of hop-scotch squares a few yards away.

Olivia looked up and down the road. There wasn't a sign of anyone. With a backward glance at the window, she ran to the chalk-line and hopped through the squares. She needed a stone. There was one in the gutter; a small one, but it would do. Olivia went through the squares again; toppled half-way through and began again.

The grey-haired man in the car a few houses down the street watched her. The familiar feeling gripped him and he stirred restlessly. Back and forth the girl skipped and hopped; back and forth, concentrating on getting it right.

He opened the door of the car and got out. The sun had gone, and it was almost dark. He felt the prickle of sweat across his brow as he walked slowly in the shadows before crossing the road. Don't move too quickly, he warned himself. Don't frighten her.

He stepped off the kerb.

The lights of a car came round the corner, sweeping the other side of the road. The girl looked up—and scurried back to the gate as she recognized her father's car.

The grey-haired man stepped back on the pavement and walked back to his car. He got in, started the engine, and pulled away from the kerb as Tregalles got out of the car.

PETER FOSTER put the phone down. Another cancellation. That was the fifth one. He sank back into the padded leather chair. He had done almost nothing all day, and yet he felt exhausted. His hand shook as he scratched the name from his appointment book. Christ, if this kept up he'd have no business left.

The police had packed it in for the night, but they'd be back tomorrow. Sergeant Ormside had made a point of telling him that. They'd have the road-block up again; stopping people; asking their endless questions.

Foster rubbed his face with his hands. Ormside was as bad as that bloody chief inspector, in his own way. Always respectful, never hurried, but questions... There was no end to them. Seemingly innocuous questions, many of them—until you realized that you'd just contradicted something you'd said the day before, and it was too late to do anything about it.

He knew Ormside was convinced he'd killed both Gray and Lisa. He could see it in the sergeant's eyes every time he spoke to him; lurking there behind that bland expression; waiting for him to make that one, fatal mistake.

Would it never end?

He should go away. But where? And would the police let him?

There'd been another call from Constance this morning.

Threatening; abusive. He hated that woman. How she could be Lisa's mother was beyond him.

He'd hung up on her. Slammed the phone down, panicking as the thought occurred to him that the police might be listening and believe the things she was saying. Could they do that? Didn't they have to have a warrant? But then, they might have grounds. If they thought that Lisa was still alive and might contact him, they could probably get one.

He screamed in terror as glass exploded into the room. He cowered in the chair, arms and hands covering his head, as if expecting blows to rain down on him. It took him several seconds to realize what had happened, but he seemed frozen in that position. Dimly, he heard voices; young voices. Kids!

He couldn't hear what they were saying. He didn't *want* to know. He just wanted them to go away; to leave him alone. It was too much.

He leapt from the chair and ran to the door. It crashed against the wall as he flung it open and screamed obscenities into the night.

But the only response was the roar of an engine and the squeal of tyres as a car roared off into the darkness.

IT WAS COLD. Eric Tyson shivered. And the floor was hard. He turned over and pulled the blankets around himself, but it made no difference. He frowned into the darkness, trying to remember what his father had said, and at last it came to him.

'Put plenty of straw under you, Eric,' he'd told him. 'It's not so much what's on top; it's what's underneath that counts. You'll be all right. It's only for a while, Eric. I promise. And tomorrow I'll bring the old paraffin heater up, then you'll be warm enough. And I don't want you going over there to the cottage again. Understand? You stay away from there.'

The young man got up and pulled straw from the bale and spread it liberally on the hard-packed earth. He liked it up here in the old barn. This was *his* barn; his father had told him that when they built the new one closer to the house. He spent most of his time here when he wasn't helping his father. But he'd never slept here before, and he didn't understand why he had to sleep here now.

He'd spilled his tea again. Ma had screamed at him again, but he couldn't help it. He didn't spill things when he was with his dad. Only in the kitchen where his mother was. But she always screamed at him. He couldn't remember when she had not screamed at him.

Perhaps it was because of the lady. His father had said it wasn't, but Eric knew that people didn't always say what they meant.

He settled uneasily into the straw and pulled the blankets over himself. He must have done something very bad because he was being punished. Punished by his dad. A tear rolled down his cheek. He stuck his thumb in his mouth and began to rock gently back and forth.

FIFTEEN

Tuesday 9th April

MOLLY FORSYTHE slumped back in her chair and stared at
the screen. Nothing. Absolutely nothing. She'd tried every
possible combination she could think of, but the answer
was still the same. Nowhere in the system did they have
anyone matching the description Olivia and Audrey Tregalles had given of the man who had spoken to Olivia. Nor
had the name 'Wendy' produced any results.

'Sorry, Jim,' she said to the sergeant standing behind her.
'I think he must be new. If he's here, I haven't been able
to find him, and I've tried everything I can think of.'

Sergeant Dean swore beneath his breath. That meant
there was nothing for it but to send the watchers out again.
The trouble was, he didn't have enough people to do the
job properly. Neither was there a good observation post
overlooking the school. No empty premises; no rooms
above shops with convenient front windows; nothing.

They'd already done a door-to-door in the area, warning
people and asking them to report anyone loitering near the
school. But the description was so vague. Since Olivia had
said the man looked a bit like the local vicar, he and Molly
had called on the vicar to get some idea of age, height,
build and colouring in order to write a description at all.

Scared the poor devil half to death, Dean recalled. He
thought they were accusing *him* of being a child molester,
and he'd gone so white they thought he was going to faint.

Molly switched off the screen. 'I don't understand why
Olivia wasn't more frightened of the man,' she said. 'She
seems to understand the danger, and yet it's almost as if

she makes an exception in this man's case. It worries me, and I know it worries Audrey.'

'It scares the hell out of me,' Dean said flatly. 'I've got kids of my own. I think you'd better have another talk with Olivia. I *want* her to be scared. I want her screaming her head off the moment that man comes near her.'

Molly drew in her breath. 'Touchy,' she said. 'Very touchy. We don't want to give the kid nightmares.'

'I know, I know,' Dean said grimly, 'but give it your best shot. I don't care how you do it, but make sure she gets the message.'

MIKE FREEMAN came round his desk to greet Paget and usher him to a seat.

'Sorry I had to go out yesterday afternoon,' he said. 'I'm told you were looking for me.' He returned to his seat behind the desk. 'I'll have Peggy bring coffee.' He pressed a button on the phone. 'How do you take yours, Chief Inspector?'

'Black. Thank you.' He really didn't want coffee, but on the other hand he didn't want to start off the day by rejecting Freeman's hospitality.

Freeman relayed the information to Peggy Owen, then sat back in his seat, wincing slightly as he put his hands behind his head. He looked at Paget expectantly. His face was slightly flushed and it crossed Paget's mind that the man was secretly excited about the prospect of being interviewed. His eyes followed Paget's every move, anticipating the first question.

'Ribs still a bit painful, are they, Mr Freeman?' Paget asked.

The anticipatory light in Freeman's eyes flickered. Whatever the question the man had expected, this was not even close.

'On the mend,' he said cryptically, dismissing the question as hardly worthy of an answer.

A brief tap on the door announced the arrival of Peggy Owen. Obviously, the coffee had been ready and waiting for Mike Freeman's call. She set the tray on the desk between them, smiled mechanically at Paget, and retreated without a word. Mike Freeman pulled open a drawer and reached inside. 'Like a little drop of something to liven it up?' he asked, displaying a bottle of cognac.

'It's fine the way it is, thank you,' said Paget.

Freeman nodded and pursed his lips judiciously. 'Perhaps you're right,' he conceded as he slid the bottle back into the drawer. 'Now, then, what can I do for you, Chief Inspector?'

'Tell me what you thought of David Gray,' said Paget.

Freeman frowned. 'In what context?' he asked cautiously.

'In any context,' Paget said. 'As an employee; as a prospective son-in-law; or as a friend, perhaps.'

Mike Freeman sipped his coffee. 'He came highly recommended,' he said carefully, 'and he certainly knew his job. He was one of those rare people who not only understand all of the technical aspects of the job, but the role of marketing and sales as well. In that respect, we will miss him. He was an asset to the company.'

His voice became hard. 'As for his treatment of Janet, the bastard deserved everything he got, and I for one won't shed any tears for him. Not that I'm suggesting he should have been killed for what he did,' he added hastily, 'but how would you feel if it were your daughter? How would you feel? Here they were sending out wedding invitations, and the bastard's off screwing this tart! Christ!'

'You had no idea that this was going on?'

'No, of course I didn't know,' Freeman said dismissively. 'Do you think I'd have kept quiet if I did?'

'What about Gray as a son-in-law? How did you feel about that?'

Freeman's face became set. 'To be honest, I wasn't in favour of it,' he said, 'and Janet and I had a few words about him. But Janet is a grown woman; I realized it had to be her decision.'

'But you didn't like the decision she made,' Paget persisted.

A flicker of annoyance crossed Freeman's face. 'I don't see what this has to do with anything,' he said. 'How does this help find out who killed Gray?'

'I won't know until I hear your answer, will I?' Paget said quietly. 'What was your objection to Gray as a son-in-law?'

Freeman was becoming angry. 'Not that I think it's any of your business,' he said testily, 'but Janet and I are...well, close; always have been since her mother died when she was fourteen. There's just been the two of us. We're a team. We work well together; we worked together to build up this business, and I could see that relationship changing. Call me selfish if you like, but it's hard to lose a daughter, especially one like Janet.'

'But there was more to it than that, wasn't there, Mr Freeman? You didn't like the man she was marrying, did you?'

Freeman scowled. 'All right, no,' he growled. 'I thought she could do better than Gray. Much better. But that doesn't mean I set out to kill him.'

'According to my information, you and Frank Porter followed Gray out of the office the day he disappeared,' Paget continued. 'Why was that, Mr Freeman?'

Freeman eyed Paget stonily. He appeared to be having difficulty holding his temper in check. 'We didn't "follow him out", as you put it,' he said thinly. 'It just happened that I wanted to talk to Frank in private, that's all, and we left a few minutes after Gray. I didn't even know he'd gone, to tell you the truth.'

'Oh?' Paget looked surprised. 'Didn't Mrs Owen come into your office to ask for the spare set of keys to the company car just before you left?'

Freeman shook his head impatiently. 'She may have done,' he said, 'but I was probably busy or on the phone. I don't really remember.'

'Why did you leave the office so suddenly, sir?'

Mike Freeman bristled. 'I don't know where you get the idea that it was a sudden decision,' he growled. 'I wanted to talk to Frank privately about opening another office in Bristol, and I didn't want it known around the office. At least, not until all the details were ironed out. So, I suggested going out in the car where we wouldn't be overheard or interrupted.'

'In the company car?'

Freeman shook his head impatiently. 'Of course not,' he said. 'Gray had taken that. In Frank's car.' He looked at Paget as if he felt the chief inspector were being particularly obtuse.

'I see. And have all the details been ironed out?'

'No. I've decided not to go ahead. Though what the hell that has to do with all this, I'm damned if I know. And I'll thank you not to mention that to anyone else in the office.'

Unperturbed by Freeman's truculent attitude, Paget continued. 'Did you see David Gray in the parking area—or anywhere else, for that matter—when you left in Mr Porter's car?'

Freeman shook his head emphatically. 'No. He must have been well away by the time we got there. The car was gone. I remember that.'

'And it reappeared sometime during the weekend,' Paget said.

'That's right. God only knows how it got there.'

'How do *you* think it got there, Mr Freeman?'

Freeman looked mystified. 'Whoever murdered David must have brought it back, I suppose,' he ventured.

Paget remained silent for a moment. 'That is certainly a possibility,' he agreed. 'Why do you think he—or she—would do that?'

Freeman shrugged. 'You tell me,' he said. There was a wariness about him now that hadn't been there when Paget first sat down.

'It makes me wonder what happened to his or her—let's stick to "his" for the moment—own transportation,' Paget said musingly. 'You see, if the murderer drove the car back here after killing Gray, how did he get out to Bracken Cottage in the first place? And if the killing was done by someone who was already at the cottage, how did he get back there after dropping off the car? Unless, of course, he had an accomplice.'

Freeman remained silent, gently rocking back and forth in his swivel chair.

'This business of the car has me puzzled,' Paget went on, musing aloud. 'The killer might well have wanted to get Gray's car away from Bracken Cottage, but how did he know exactly where to take it? The Freeman Protronics logo was on the car, so he could have found the address by looking in the telephone book, but why return it at all? Why not just abandon it somewhere? David Gray died sometime between the late afternoon of Tuesday, March 12th, and the morning of Wednesday, March 13th. So where was the car between then and when it appeared in its regular slot during the weekend? And why the delay?'

'Perhaps he thought he would be seen if he put it back before the weekend,' Freeman offered. 'Several of our offices overlook the car-park.'

Paget nodded. 'That may well have had a lot to do with

it,' he agreed. 'And perhaps he was afraid of being recognized.'

Freeman sat up straight. 'Recognized?' he repeated. 'Are you suggesting what I think you are?'

'That it might have been someone from here?' Paget said. 'Oh, yes, Mr Freeman. I think it's quite possible.'

BEFORE RETURNING to his office, Paget went into the operations room where he stood looking at the large-scale map of the town. Gray had left the office in the company car on Tuesday, March 12th. Foster claimed it was not at Bracken Cottage when he came home on Wednesday, March 13th, and yet it had not appeared in the car-park behind Freeman Protronics until sometime after the close of business on Friday March 15th.

So where the hell had it been? There wasn't much mileage on it, so it hadn't been far.

It was while he was still trying to solve that puzzle that he noticed something else. Mike Freeman's house was just around the corner from that of Frank Porter. Not cheek-by-jowl, exactly, but there couldn't be more than six or seven houses separating them. And both were no more than a five-minute walk away from the office. It probably meant nothing, but now that his attention had been drawn to it, Paget checked Peggy Owen's address.

She lived across the river in one of the older parts of the town, and he remembered hearing her mention to one of the girls in the office that she'd had to run to catch the bus that morning.

'Melrose,' he called, still looking at the map. 'I've got a job for you,' The man had been pouring coffee from a flask, and now he came over to stand beside Paget, mug in hand.

'Sir?'

'I want you to talk to everyone in the premises overlooking the back of Freeman Protronics, and I want you to talk to all the neighbours in the immediate vicinity of these three houses.' Paget indicated the locations on the map. 'I want to know if they noticed anything unusual happening in the area between Tuesday March 12th and Monday March 18th. And don't tell them the real reason you're asking. I don't want this getting back to the people involved, at least not for now.'

Melrose studied the map. 'What am I supposed to be looking for?' he asked, not unreasonably.

'I don't know,' said Paget slowly. 'I wish to hell I did. Unusual activity; cars parked where they shouldn't be; noises in the night; anything at all. And make sure you read all of the interviews we did at Freeman Protronics before you go. The background might prove useful.'

'When...?' Melrose began, but Paget was ahead of him.

'Now,' he said as he made for the door. 'You can start reading while you finish your coffee.'

It was almost one thirty by the time Paget reached his office, and he was looking forward to lunch. Just a couple of phone calls to make, then perhaps he would nip across the road for a pint and something to eat.

But Grace Lovett was waiting for him outside his office. He suppressed a groan, seeing the prospect of lunch fading rapidly.

'What can I do for you, Grace?' he asked as he ushered her into the office.

'I had to come over here anyway,' she said quickly as if feeling the need to explain her presence, 'so I thought I would let you know what we have so far on that piece of silk you sent over on Friday.'

Paget waved her to a seat. 'You mean the one they found in the garden?'

'Yes.' A small frown creased her face. 'Are you quite sure that's where it was found?' She opened her briefcase and pulled out a sheet of paper, and Paget saw it was a copy of the garden grid at Bracken Cottage.

She leaned across the desk and turned the grid for him to see. 'This is where they said it was found, but I find that hard to believe.' Paget leaned forward to see better, and became aware of her perfume. It was very delicate, and he rather liked it.

'So what's the problem with it?' he asked.

Grace tapped the grid with a slim finger. 'It's out in the open,' she said. 'No shelter anywhere close by, and yet there is no sign of this material having been out in the weather. I checked with the meteorological people and they say that at least nine millimetres of rain fell in that area between March 12th and last Friday, yet I would swear that none of it fell on this.' She pulled out a clear plastic envelope containing the fragment of silk.

Paget leaned back in his seat and looked at her across the desk. Tregalles was right; Grace Lovett was a very attractive woman, and he wondered idly why he'd never noticed that before. And dedicated to her work. This was twice she'd taken the trouble to come to him personally to explain her findings.

His stomach grumbled quietly. 'So what are you suggesting?' he asked.

She sighed. 'I don't really know,' she admitted. 'Perhaps there was a mistake in reporting where it was found. Perhaps the wind carried it out of a sheltered place. Or perhaps it was put there deliberately more recently.'

Paget thought about that for a moment. 'Is that blood on it?' he asked.

'No, it's rust. Which is odd, because I can't see what caused it.'

Paget's stomach growled insistently, and this time he was sure she heard it for she smiled. 'I'm keeping you from lunch,' she said. 'I'm sorry.' She rose to her feet. 'Perhaps we can go into this some other time when you're not quite so busy.'

Paget pushed his chair back and stood up also. 'Sorry about that, Grace,' he said. 'Didn't mean to be rude. It's been a long time since breakfast.' He felt awkward. 'Look,' he said. 'I'd like to pursue this with you because it could be important. But could we do it over lunch? I was just going across the road to the pub, but if you'd care to come, we could talk this through. On me this time,' he added as he saw her hesitate.

He smiled, and it seemed to Grace that he looked ten years younger.

She returned his smile. 'Best offer I've had all day,' she told him happily. 'And the pub sounds just fine.'

SIXTEEN

'It's IMPOSSIBLE to be certain, of course, but the silk is of the same quality as all of Lisa Remington's other things. And the colour is right for her. My guess is that it's part of a nightgown.'

Grace Lovett sat back in her seat and picked up her drink.

'But you think someone planted it in that bush for us to find?'

Grace hesitated. 'Not really,' she said slowly. 'I know this all sounds a bit tenuous, but take a look at the top edge of the material. When you look at the fibres under a microscope, you can see where the material has been pulled away from rusting metal. Now, look at the rest of the material. Not a fibre out of place. I went out there myself, yesterday, to check the bush itself. It's a pyracantha, and there is no way that this material could have been caught up in that bush without there being some evidence of it. I examined the bush carefully, but I couldn't find anything to suggest that this silk was ever on there. And, as I said before, the fibres on this piece of material are undisturbed except for where they were caught on the rusty metal. This other mark down here is where the man who found it pulled it away. Unfortunately, he had dirty hands—you can see the outline of his thumb there opposite the rust mark. But there are no other tears or pulled threads anywhere, so I'm forced to conclude that this was caught on metal, not a bush.'

'That's an old cottage,' Paget said ruminatively. 'Isn't it possible that the nightgown—if it was a nightgown—could have been caught on a rusty nail or something like that? I mean, why would someone lie about where they found it? What would be the point?'

'I'm not saying that someone lied. I'm just saying that I'm not sure we have all the facts, and if that is the case, then anything we conclude from the examination of this material could be misleading.'

Paget sighed inwardly, and wondered whether any of this mattered. Grace might be right, but did it really have a bearing? It wouldn't be the first time that a forensic technician had tried to convince him that two and two made five.

'I'll look into it,' he promised. 'I'm going out there now, so I'll have a word.'

As if by mutual consent, they both rose, and Paget helped Grace on with her raincoat. It was a cool day, and the threat of rain hung in the air. His hand brushed her hair as she flipped it over the collar, and he caught the fragrance of her perfume.

'You're welcome to come along, if you wish?' he said, and immediately regretted the invitation. It was an impulsive thing to do, and quite pointless. It wasn't as if she could be of any help out there. She had told him everything he needed to know. 'But you probably have work to do,' he added hastily, 'so...'

Grace turned to face him. 'Thank you, Chief Inspector,' she said, smiling. 'I'd like that very much. And thank you, too, for the lunch. If you'll just give me a minute, I'll phone Charlie to let him know where I am.'

TREGALLES had spent the morning with Len Ormside in the mobile unit at the back of Bracken Cottage. Together, they'd been over every scrap of information gathered by the team assigned to the local area, but the results seemed hardly worth the effort. No one, it seemed, had seen anything that had a bearing on the case, although a woman from Chedstone, who travelled the road regularly, had seen a dark blue car leaving Bracken Cottage one morning about seven o'clock.

'I remember it quite clearly,' she said, 'because he came out right in front of me. I had to put the brakes on or I would have hit him. I almost rang the firm and reported him, but then it slipped my mind, and when I thought about it again there didn't seem much point. I mean, they stick together, those people, don't they?'

'Which people are you talking about?' the constable who had interviewed her had asked.

'Why, those young computer people. I saw the name on the car. Protronics, it was. I remember it quite clearly. Well, I should, shouldn't I? He couldn't have been more than ten feet away from me when he shot out into the road.'

'Did you get a good look at the driver?'

The woman nodded emphatically. 'Like I said, young—fair hair. And cocky. Waved at me. That's what he did. Gave me a big smile and waved at me. Young devil. Late for work, I expect.'

'Do you remember what day that was?'

But the woman couldn't remember. The best she could do was either the very end of February or the beginning of March, and that it wasn't a weekend. When they checked those dates with Foster's appointment book, they found that he had been away from home from February 26th to March 1st.

'It's not conclusive,' Ormside said, 'but it's as near as dammit. Gray was having it off with Lisa Remington whenever Foster was away for a few days.' He rubbed his jaw thoughtfully. 'I can't say as I altogether blame Foster if he came home and found the two of them in bed together. But the thing I can't work out is what he did with Lisa's body.

She has to be dead. If she's alive we'd have found her by now.'

The two men assigned to checking the hotels and pubs at which Merrick might have stayed—always assuming that he was telling the truth, and that they were on the right road—had so far found no record of the man. 'We'll give it one more day,' Ormside told Tregalles. 'If they haven't come up with anything by then, chances are that Merrick's lying, and they're probably wasting their time.'

PC YATES arrived in a state of apprehension. He had only just returned to regular duty when the call came through for him to report to DCI Paget at Bracken Cottage, and he couldn't help wondering why. Not that he'd done anything, he told himself. At least, he couldn't think of anything he'd done to warrant such a summons, but one never knew what funny ideas a DCI might get. Perhaps it was to do with that piece of cloth he'd turned in. Perhaps it was the very clue they needed, and he was the one who'd found it. He perked up at the thought. There might even be a commendation in it; DCIs didn't call you for nothing.

Paget and Grace Lovett arrived shortly after Yates. Tregalles and Ormside, who were standing by the window, exchanged knowing glances.

'She's definitely after him,' Tregalles said. 'I thought she had her eye on him the other day. Not that she'll get anywhere with Paget. Got a shell around him like case-hardened steel. Take more than our Gracie to crack that. She's wasting her time.' He drew back from the window before Paget saw him. 'I doubt if he's even noticed that she's a woman,' he concluded.

Sergeant Ormside, a contentedly married man of many years, sighed. 'I noticed it right away,' he said wistfully. He squeezed in behind his desk and made himself busy as

Paget opened the door for Grace and ushered her inside. Yates jumped to his feet as Paget entered.

The chief inspector wasted no time. 'I want you to come with me and show me exactly where you found that piece of cloth you turned in on Friday,' he told Yates. He made no attempt to introduce Grace Lovett.

Yates led the way to the spot where he'd been digging. 'It was here, tucked in under that bush,' said Yates, bending to indicate the spot. The bush was, as Grace had said, a pyracantha.

'You're quite sure?' Paget said.

'Quite sure, sir,' said Yates. He felt proud of himself.

'Tell me,' said Grace, 'did you have to pull very hard to get it out of there, Constable?'

Yates shrugged modestly. 'It was in a bit,' he confessed. 'Scratched my hand getting it out. Good thing I spotted it, though.' He became bolder. 'We'd been working around it most of the day, but nobody else saw it.'

'Could I see your hand?' Grace held out her hand.

'Oh, there's nothing to be seen, miss,' said Yates. 'The scratches have gone now.'

'I'd still like to see your hand.'

Yates glanced at Paget, but the chief inspector's face was impassive. Grudgingly, he lifted his hand. 'See, there's nothing there.'

'Yes, you're quite right,' Grace agreed. 'Where *did* you find that piece of silk, Constable? It certainly wasn't underneath that bush, was it?'

Yates swallowed nervously. She couldn't know. How could she? Unless… That had to be it. His mates had turned him in. Bastards! Some mates! Well, bugger them. 'It was right there where I showed you,' he blustered. 'Just because I was the one to find it when it wasn't more than a foot from their faces, they probably…'

'That's quite enough, Yates.' Paget's voice cut across his

protestations like a knife. 'I don't know what your reasons were for lying about where you found it, and I'm not sure I want to know, but I do want the truth. It's important, and I want it now.'

Yates shifted uncomfortably. 'But I'm not...' he began, but something in Paget's eye told him it was better to stop now before he dug himself in any deeper. 'I didn't mean any harm by it, sir,' he whined. 'I mean, we hadn't had a break for hours—well, it seemed like hours—and I just nipped round the corner for a smoke while the sergeant was away. Then, when he came back and nearly caught me, I told him that I'd found that piece of stuff there.'

'Where did you find it?'

Yates breathed slightly easier. Perhaps he'd escape without a rollicking after all if he showed them. 'It was round here, sir.' He led the way around the side of the house to the water butt. 'I sort of tucked myself in here, you see, and it was stuck on the side of the barrel.' He moved aside as Grace moved forward and peered into the narrow space.

'Ah, yes, I see,' she said. 'That's more like it. There's the metal band, rust and all, and it's sheltered.' She bent to examine the ground. 'I'll need to take samples,' she told Paget, 'but I think we might find evidence that someone took shelter here.' She straightened up and dusted off her hands. She smiled at Yates. 'Thank you, Constable.'

Yates almost returned the smile, but the look on Paget's face stopped him, and his heart sank when Paget said, 'I'll be having a word with your sergeant, Yates. That's all. You can go.'

'I KNOW there's not very much to go on,' Grace Lovett said, 'but I think it's possible that Lisa Remington escaped from the house and tried to hide behind the rain barrel.' She looked at the three grave faces in front of her and spread her hands.

'It seems I'm always saying that, doesn't it?' she said wryly. 'But there isn't much else to go on, is there?'

Paget had to admit she was right. The whereabouts of Lisa Remington was the key to this whole maddening business. If Grace was right, then where could Lisa have gone? Everything pointed to the killing of Gray having taken place at night, but where would a woman go clad only in a nightgown? Was she hurt? If so, how badly? They had searched the area thoroughly, but there had been no sign of her. On the other hand, whoever was supposed to have searched behind the water butt hadn't done a very good job, so perhaps other evidence had been missed as well.

A wild thought occurred to Paget. 'Did anyone look inside the water barrel?' he asked. 'The damned thing is big enough to hold a body.' Three pairs of eyes stared at him blankly.

Tregalles was the first to recover. 'I'll check it right away,' he said.

They waited. No one spoke. None of them knew quite what to hope for. Alcott would have his balls for breakfast if they'd overlooked such an obvious hiding place, Paget thought. He tried to remember how full the barrel was, and couldn't. It was set up on bricks, and it was difficult to see inside without standing on tiptoe.

The minutes ticked by with agonizing slowness. They saw from the window Tregalles coming back. He came up the steps of the unit and stepped inside, brushing off his hands.

'Not there,' he said. 'And I remember now. The water was siphoned off that first day to make sure nothing had been dropped inside. It's only a little over a quarter full now from the rains we've had since.'

The release of tension was palpable, and Paget said, 'Thank God' beneath his breath. But if Lisa Remington wasn't there, where the hell was she?

TOM TYSON stared unblinking at the road ahead, his mind preoccupied with what he had to do. He hadn't slept for weeks, or so it seemed. There had to be another way. There simply *had* to. But he knew there wasn't. The more he tried to reject the idea, the more it became embedded in his mind.

This would be the third time he'd made this journey. He had been unsuccessful twice, but now…

He didn't know whether to feel elated because he'd got what he was after or sickened by the fact that now he had but one choice to make. He slid his hand inside his jacket and felt the small package nestled there. Unconsciously, his broad fingers counted the tablets sealed in their sterile cells. Six. The number registered, and yet there was no need; it was burned inside his skull.

He felt the sweat across his brow; felt his features crumble as tears spilled down his weathered face.

He let himself in quietly, but she was waiting for him, demanding to know where he'd been.

'I told you, Emily,' he said wearily. 'Don't you remember? I went in to pick up the gear-box I took in last week. Stripped gear, it was. You remember?'

The woman grunted, hoisting herself painfully from the daybed to cross the floor, sticks thumping hard against the tiles. Thud!…Thud!…Thud!… The sound echoed in his brain. It seemed his heart had slowed to match the rhythm. Thud!…Thud!…

He held his hands to his ears and closed his eyes, thankful that her back was turned. 'I'll do it,' he said belatedly, knowing it was no use.

'It's woman's work, getting the tea,' she snapped. 'I know my duty. There's devil's work for idle hands. Get washed up.'

'I was just going to…' he began, but Emily Tyson's bitter laugh stopped him dead.

'To see the boy?' she finished for him. 'Aye, I know he's up there. Skulking around when he thinks I can't see him. He was up the top of the field again today, watching. Can't leave the place alone, can he? She was another one. I told you then and I tell you now. She was one of them.'

Emily Tyson leaned so far forward on her sticks that she looked as if she would fall. 'You thought you'd hide him up there, didn't you? Up there in the old barn. Thought I wouldn't know. But I can *feel* him. Feel his evil. He's a curse, Tom. I've told you before and I'll tell you again. He's a curse upon this house, and will be while he lives.' She spat contemptuously. 'An evil child inside a grown man's body. I tell you, Tom, it's the devil's work. He has to go!'

'GOOD-NIGHT, then, Frank,' said Peggy Owen. She stood there in the doorway of his office, hesitating. 'Are you sure there's nothing you want me to do? I can stay behind if...'

'No. No, thank you, Peggy.' Frank Porter wished she'd go. Everyone else had gone and he wanted to be alone to think. 'I shan't be long. Just want to finish up one or two things. See you in the morning.'

'Well,' Peggy said doubtfully. 'If you're sure.'

'Quite sure, Peggy,' he said.

It wasn't like Frank to work late, the secretary thought as she made her way to the door. She hoped there was nothing wrong. He'd been acting strangely, lately. Well, perhaps not *strangely,* exactly, but different. He seemed edgy, distracted. Had done ever since that Chief Inspector Paget had talked to him. He'd gone home early that day. Said he was a bit off colour.

Peggy let herself out, making sure to lock the door behind her. Frank would leave by the back door, and he always checked the lock there. Couldn't afford to make mistakes these days.

But it was a bit odd. Frank was never ill. It wasn't as if he'd liked David Gray. But he'd looked ill that afternoon. It couldn't be because... No. Peggy dismissed the idea out of hand. Not Frank. On the other hand, he and Mike *had* rushed off that day. She brushed the thought away. That was the way Mike was. Mercurial. Up one minute, down the next.

That heart attack had scared him. He tried to pretend it hadn't, but it had. He'd gone inside himself. Wouldn't talk the way he used to. Moody. He'd even snapped at her a couple of times and he'd never done that before. She wished he'd take more care.

Peggy Owen sighed heavily. It was all changing. It wasn't like it had been in the old days. Hadn't been ever since David Gray had joined the company. All charm and determination. Making a name for himself and the firm. He had impressed Mike. And Janet. But it hadn't taken Peggy long to see his game.

Her face was grim as she continued on. David Gray would have destroyed Mike Freeman had he lived, she thought. She was glad that he was dead.

INSIDE THE OFFICE all was quiet. Frank Porter swung his chair around to face the window, and he saw the car. It was one of the company cars, in its place as usual, but his mind flew instantly to that day. That fateful day when David Gray had left the office, whistling.

He'd thought the worst when he saw Paget there this morning. He'd gone cold all over. He was sure the man was coming back to see him, but he'd gone in to see Mike instead.

'Stop worrying,' Mike had told him when Frank went in to see him later. 'The man's just doing his job. It's not as if you've done anything wrong. It's this chap Foster they're after, but they have to check everything out. You'll see. Relax, Frank. It will be all right.'

AT HOME, Janet Freeman and her father ate their meal in almost total silence. It had been that way for days, now, and it wasn't like him to be so quiet. On the other hand, she'd been withdrawn herself. Withdrawn! She almost laughed aloud. That was hardly the word for it, she told herself miserably. How could she have been so utterly stupid? How could she have been so blind? Everyone knew but her, she thought bitterly, yet no one said a word.

It had taken every scrap of courage she could muster to go back into the office yesterday. Everybody looking at her. Whispering behind her back, no doubt. Silly woman. Acting like some lovesick youngster; planning to get married while all the time David was...

The tears came without warning. Blindly, she left the table and ran to the stairs. Behind her, Mike half rose from his seat, then slowly subsided. There was nothing he could do. Let her get it out of her system. Grim-faced, he pushed his plate away. Like Peggy Owen, he was glad that David Gray was dead.

THE GREY-HAIRED MAN shivered. He turned on the electric fire. Just one bar; had to watch the pennies. It had begun to rain again and he could feel the chill inside the room.

It was a cheerless room, but better than that other place. He shivered again, but this time it wasn't cold he felt within his bones. He sat before the fire and stared at the shimmering glow of the copper-clad reflector behind the bar, and saw figures there. Figures from another time and place.

He sucked in his breath. She was there! He watched, excited now. He closed his eyes. He didn't need to see, for she was there inside his head. He raised his hands and caressed his face as if he held her there.

JOHN TREGALLES would have been surprised if he could have read Paget's thoughts as he drove home that evening. Contrary to the sergeant's opinion, Paget *had* noticed that Grace Lovett was a woman. A very attractive woman, and he'd rather taken to her. She had a good mind. Analytical. Got a bit carried away with it at times; stretched her theories pretty far, but that was the way detection worked. Facts were important; logic was important; hard evidence was important; but so, too, was intuitive imagination, and Grace had that in spades.

It had been pleasant there for an hour this afternoon, relaxing over lunch with Grace. He'd enjoyed her company, but he'd found himself comparing her with Andrea. He hadn't even realized it was happening at first. It was when he was helping her on with her coat. The hair. That's what it was, it was the way she flipped her hair over the collar.

Andrea used to do that. The same sort of action, and it immediately took him back. Paget grimaced to himself inside the darkened car as he thought what might have been.

He thought, too, of Jill. No one, not even Andrea, could ever take her place. Jill belonged to another part of his life, a very special part, but that part of his life was over. He sighed. It had taken him a long time to accept that.

Andrea McMillan belonged to a more recent part of his life. A very short part, he thought bitterly. He'd been an idiot to let her go.

But it hadn't been his decision to make, had it? It was Andrea's decision to leave, and he couldn't blame her. Life could be cruel, he thought bitterly. No, not just cruel. Life could be vicious! First Jill, then Andrea. No one's fault; no one to blame except fate. Or God. But where was the satisfaction in that?

And where, he wondered, was Andrea now?

SEVENTEEN

Wednesday 10th April

MOONLIGHT FILTERED through the ragged clouds and made patterns on the window. Emily Tyson flung the blanket aside and pushed herself upright on the bed. She was fully dressed right down to her thick-soled shoes. She slid off the bed and gasped at the pain as her feet hit the floor. She breathed deeply, girding herself for the task ahead. Slowly, she made her way across the room to the door, her two stout sticks silent on the tiles for once as she placed each tip carefully ahead of her.

Tom's coat was there as it always was on the peg behind the door. She propped herself against the wall and struggled with the coat, almost crying out with pain as she forced her arms into the sleeves and pulled the coat around her.

She managed the buttons without too much trouble, but the door was hard. Reaching up to undo the top bolt was almost too much, but it gave way at the very last second, and she fell back against the wall to rest until the pain subsided.

Emily Tyson closed the door behind her. The night air was cold, but she raised her face to it and breathed it in. It felt good to be outside. So long. So very long.

But there was work to do. She placed one stick ahead of the other and began the long, slow journey, eyes fixed firmly ahead.

In the darkened bedroom above, Tom Tyson stirred uneasily in the big bed where he had slept alone for so many years. Perhaps it was a dream, perhaps it was a sound carried on the breeze from the partly open window, but it was there, deep inside his troubled mind.

Thud!…Thud!…Thud!…Thud!…

PETER FOSTER couldn't sleep. He wandered from room to room, unable to settle to anything. Constance had telephoned again. Shrieking epithets as usual.

'I gave up my life for her, you odious little bastard,' she screamed at him. 'I worked—I slaved for her, pushed her, made her what she is. She'd have been nothing without me behind her. And she had ten more years ahead of her. Ten more years! And she threw it all away on you!'

Her voice dropped. 'And you killed her, didn't you? You couldn't stand the thought of her being with another man, could you?' Unexpectedly, she laughed. 'If only you'd known how many men she'd had, you stupid little man. Do you think you climb that ladder on good looks alone?'

He could hear her gathering breath for another onslaught, and he felt the blood draining from his face. Furious, he slammed the phone down. 'I hope it breaks your bloody eardrum!' he yelled at the silent instrument.

Her words echoed in his head as he stood there now in the darkened room. From the stand of trees across the road came the eerie hooting of an owl, and he pictured it swooping on silent wings to scoop up some small animal foolish enough to venture out at night. That's what he was waiting for, he thought. They would come along and scoop him up soon. It was only a matter of time.

He wandered back upstairs and opened the large wardrobe. Lisa's clothes were still there. He felt the softness of them; buried his face in them. They smelt of her.

As if in slow motion, Foster took out the dresses one by one and tore them into shreds.

THE LAND SLOPED gently upward from the river, but to Emily Tyson it felt more like a mountain. She rested for a moment, sucking in the cold night air and praying for the strength to carry on. Her frail legs trembled and she longed to rest, but she must go on. She must! She fixed her eyes firmly on the outline of the barn. Not far now. Not far.

She thrust her body forward; stick first, then the leg; stick first, then the other leg; stick first...

The barn loomed over her, blocking out the moon. Exhausted, Emily Tyson leaned against the wall, panting hard. She had no conscious memory of the last hundred yards. Only pain. Every muscle screamed in agony; every drop of blood coursing through her veins shrieked in protest; but with it came the knowledge that soon it would be over.

The door was on the latch. She eased it open carefully, stopping short as she saw the light. It puzzled her. There shouldn't be a light inside the barn. Very carefully, she opened the door wider.

The heater. Wouldn't you just know it. There was that great hulking boy asleep and he'd left the heater on. A waste, that's what it was; a waste. Tom always was too soft, especially with the boy. He'd always favoured him; always stood up for him.

Rage welled up inside her as she thrust her deformed body forward, the heavy sticks thudding into the hard-packed earth. The boy stirred in his sleep; moved uneasily as if sensing what was about to happen. His mother reached him; stood over him, stick raised high...

The stick came slashing down, aimed at Eric's unprotected head. It came down hard, but Emily all but lost her balance at the last moment and it landed on his shoulder. A sound burst from him as he came awake, eyes wild as consciousness struggled to return. A second blow slashed across his ear and he howled with pain.

'Devil's spawn!' his mother shrieked as she slashed at him again. 'Down on your knees! Down!' Spittle flew from her mouth as she swung the heavy stick again and again while Eric struggled to free himself from the blankets and stagger to his feet. The blankets fell free and he flung his hands over his head to ward off the rain of blows.

His childlike mind couldn't comprehend what was happening. It didn't occur to him to fight back. He must have done something terribly wrong, but he didn't know what it was. But he must obey his mother. His father had made him promise long ago that he would always obey his mother.

He sank to his knees, but the blows continued to fall. He didn't know what to do. The end of one of the sticks sliced across his hand and the blood streamed down his face. He sank lower, whimpering like a dog. Where was his father? Why didn't he come?

The *thing* before her refused to die. She had to kill it; had to destroy the thing that had cursed their house; cursed their life; subjected her to a life of pain. In fury, she raised both sticks and swung them hard...

She didn't realize she'd fallen until it was too late. Hardly felt the searing flash of pain as she fell backwards across the heater.

She screamed as fire engulfed her. Paraffin spread across the floor, the straw exploded into flame, and she felt the air sucked out of her as the fire swept toward the walls. She struggled to get up, but she couldn't move. There was no air, and her lungs were burning...

PETER FOSTER thought it must be the moon at first. Standing there in the midst of a pile of shredded clothing, he felt drained. Tears ran down his cheeks, and he was barely conscious of the flickering light. It was only when he turned toward the window that he saw the blaze atop the hill.

He stood there, stunned, uncomprehending for a moment. The old barn was going up in flames. He watched for perhaps a minute, fascinated by the spectacular sight, before it occurred to him that someone must have started the fire. Probably the same lot that had thrown the stone through his window. He should let somebody know.

TOM TYSON ran out of the house and up the hill toward the fire. The barn was blazing like a torch, sparks flying high into the air as pockets of trapped moisture exploded from the ancient timbers.

Emily was gone, and he knew with a terrible certainty that she was up there. Eric was up there, too. The heater. He should never have let Eric have the heater. He'd thought it would be all right. The boy was always careful; it was only around his mother that he had trouble, dropping things, breaking things. Just the same, he shouldn't have left the heater.

He pounded up the slope, boot laces slapping at his ankles. He put up his hands to shield his face from the heat as he came close to the barn. Only a burning skeleton remained. The barn was almost gone.

'E-e-e-r-r-i-i-c,' he called despairingly. He felt the tears streaming down his face as he cupped his hands around his mouth and called again.

He heard the sound of pounding feet, and turned to see Foster coming up the hill. 'The fire brigade is on its way,' Foster panted as he came up to Tyson. Belatedly, he realized what Tyson was doing as the man screamed Eric's name again.

'Oh, Christ!' he said, staring at the flames in horror. If Eric was in there, there was no way he could have survived. Tyson began to run around the barn, still calling at the top of his voice, and Foster, not knowing what else to do, followed him.

They circled the barn, but there was no sign of the boy. Tyson was becoming frantic, and Foster took hold of him, afraid the man might try to run into the flames. Tyson tried to shake him off, but Foster hung on.

Lights were appearing on the hillside, and moments later the first unit of the fire brigade came bumping over the coarse grass. With it came a police car. A policeman jumped out of the car and ran toward the struggling men outlined against the fire.

'Hold him back,' Foster gasped. 'He thinks his son might be in there.'

'Bloody hell!' The policeman grabbed Tyson, and, together, he and Foster dragged him to the police car. 'I'm sorry,' the constable apologized as he forced Tyson into the back of the car. 'But there's nothing you can do. Are you *sure* your son's in there?'

Tyson put his head in his hands. 'I think my wife might be in there as well,' he choked.

Foster and the policeman looked at each other, then looked at the fire. 'Bloody hell!' the policeman breathed again, and Foster, staring at the flames, could only silently agree.

THERE WASN'T MUCH the firemen could do. By the time they had run their hoses down to the river, the barn had been reduced to a charred skeleton; still burning, but dying quickly. There was little wind, so it was merely a matter of hosing it down and keeping an eye on it for the next few hours. As for searching for anyone who might be inside, that would have to wait until the heat subsided. More lights began to appear at the bottom of the hill as people arrived in cars, awakened, no doubt, by the passing of the fire engine, and one of the policemen radioed in to ask for another car.

It was one of the firemen who found him. A fireman by the name of Stubbs. Having been called out in such a hurry, he'd not stopped for anything, and the pressure of last night's drinking at the pub was making itself felt.

The dying fire still gave off a surprising amount of light, and Stubbs scrambled down a small gully to where clumps of bushes bordered a small stream. He stood with his back to the fire, staring out into the night.

'Aahhh,' he said softly as the pressure eased, and for a moment he thought he heard an echo. Not likely, he thought as he zipped up his trousers. The sound came again. A snuffling sound.

Stubbs scrambled away from the bushes and fumbled for his torch. The beam swept across the ground and stopped.

Eric Tyson lay naked, half in, half out of the stream. Even in the light of the torch, Stubbs could see the welts across his shoulders, and the blood. The boy lay hunched over, whimpering like some small animal in pain, and he shied away as Stubbs approached.

The fireman scrambled up the slope and began to run for help.

EIGHTEEN

'ANOTHER SUSPICIOUS DEATH. Bit of a coincidence, don't you think?' Alcott growled. 'Especially with Foster within a stone's throw of the place.'

'He was the one who turned in the alarm,' Tregalles pointed out. 'And he rang Tyson.'

Alcott turned his back on the still smouldering barn and eyed the distance to Bracken Cottage. 'What would it take?' he asked rhetorically. 'Five minutes? Foster could have set the fire and been on the phone five minutes later.'

'He could,' Paget agreed, 'but to what purpose?'

'The woman's dead,' Alcott said flatly. 'If it is Mrs Tyson,' he added. 'Foster's had us on that merry-go-round before. But if it is Mrs Tyson, it could be because she saw something; knew something.' He turned to Tregalles. 'According to your report, the woman was very observant. Seemed to know a lot about what went on up there. She could have been holding back. Perhaps using it as a lever to get that access to the road Tyson's been after. Or worse.'

Tregalles frowned. 'Blackmail?' he said. 'I'd say that's a nonstarter, sir.'

'I wouldn't,' said Alcott bluntly.

Paget shot the sergeant a warning glance. Superintendent Alcott was dead set on blaming this on Foster. He might be right, but it didn't add up to Paget. But there was no point in arguing with the man, especially at seven o'clock in the morning.

'Sergeant Ormside is with Foster now,' he told Alcott, 'and I'll be going down there myself when we're finished here. But I think Tyson's explanation sounds more likely.

The lad has been severely beaten, and the woman appears to have been mad. We'll know more when they've had a chance to examine everything in there.'

'Mrs Tyson was violent,' Tregalles put in. 'She went after young Eric while I was there and Tyson had to restrain her.'

Alcott grunted. He looked unconvinced. 'Where is Tyson now?'

'He's at the hospital with Eric. The boy was terrified, and the only one he'd let near him was his father. We'll be taking a full statement from Mr Tyson later in the day.'

Charlie Dobbs, who had been pacing around the perimeter of the barn like a bird dog quartering, came over to them. He looked cold, his narrow features pinched and grey, and his hands were thrust deep inside his coat pockets.

'There's something back here I think you ought to see,' he said as he drew near. 'Don't know what it means, yet, but I have an idea it might be connected to what happened down there.' He nodded toward Bracken Cottage.

Alcott perked up. 'Ah-ha!' he said softly. 'What did I tell you, Paget?' He tapped the side of his nose with a forefinger. 'Trust your instincts, man. Trust your instincts. What have you got, Charlie?'

'Come and have a look for yourself.' They followed Charlie around the barn to a ragged clump of bushes. Those closest to the barn were scorched and charred, and the leaves had either burned or fallen to the ground. A thicket of blackened twigs remained, but now that the leaves were gone, they could see a small patch of grass, now grey with ash, that lay beyond.

But that was not what drew their attention. In the middle of the grass was a mound of what had once been colourful blooms, but they too were now covered in ash. Blooms

Paget recognized instantly, for there were many just like them surrounding Bracken Cottage.

It took no more than twenty minutes to lift the body from its shallow grave. That it was the body of Lisa Remington there could be little doubt. It had been wrapped carefully in a sheet and a blanket before burial, but beneath the wrapping, still well preserved, the body was clothed in a nightdress, torn at the shoulder. One glance convinced Paget that it would match the fragment of silk Grace Lovett had shown him the day before.

Alcott took one look, stuck a cigarette in his mouth, lit it, and jabbed a finger at Paget. 'Foster,' he said grimly. He turned on his heel and set off down the hill. 'I'll be in my office,' he called over his shoulder. 'Let me know when you bring him in.'

DR STARKIE arrived within the hour, red in the face and gasping from having to walk up the hill carrying his heavy bag. But after examining the body, he flatly refused to discuss time of death or its possible cause. 'Tomorrow at the earliest,' he told Paget. 'But more likely it will be later. The body is decomposed; I have no idea how she died, and I'll need time. Sorry, but that's the best I can do.'

The investigating fire officer refused to allow anything in the barn to be disturbed until later in the day, and that included the body of Emily Tyson. When Starkie learned this, he threw up his hands.

'I'm not lugging this lot up the hill again today,' he said flatly, indicating his bag. 'If you want me back again, then you'll have to have someone meet me to help me carry it up.'

'You'd be a lot better off if you'd get rid of that gut,' Charlie twitted him. 'Good God, man, you're supposed to be a doctor and look at you.' He leaned over and patted Starkie's ample stomach, an action he knew infuriated the portly little man. 'You should be more like me. Look at that.' He patted his own almost non-existent stomach. 'Now that's the way a stomach should look.'

'You don't have a stomach,' Starkie snapped. 'Six feet of bloody sewer pipe; in one end, out the other, that's you.' He slung his bag on his shoulder and, with a curt nod to Paget and Tregalles, he set off down the hill.

'Have a nice day, Reg,' Charlie called after him. 'See you up here later.' Starkie's reply was unintelligible. Which was, perhaps, just as well.

'FOSTER'S STATEMENT seems straightforward enough,' said Ormside. 'I was just going over to the cottage now to have him sign it. Would you like to take a look?'

Paget and Tregalles each took a copy and read it swiftly. 'As you say,' said Paget. 'It seems straightforward enough, but we'll take it over to him, Len. There are a couple of other things we have to talk to him about.' He told Ormside of the shallow grave they'd found up on the hill. 'Superintendent Alcott is convinced that it was Foster who buried her up there,' he ended.

Len Ormside settled his long frame into his tilter chair and leaned back against the wall. 'I don't see it,' he said at last. 'Not Foster. What would the girl weigh? Seven, maybe eight stone? Something like that?'

'Pretty close,' Tregalles said. 'Not all that heavy to carry.'

Ormside shook his head. 'Dead weight,' he said. 'No pun intended. You might do it,' he told Tregalles. 'You're in good shape, but I reckon you'd be huffing and puffing by the time you got up that hill with eight stone on your back. I can't see Foster managing it. He damn near falls over himself when he lifts one of those stones out there. And why would he go all the way up the hill when it would be easier to go down to the river? Softer ground down there, and it's screened from view. Or he could have just put weights on her and dropped her in. It runs deep in that bend.'

Paget and Tregalles looked at each other. 'Eric?' said the sergeant.

'Eric,' said Paget. 'My first thought when I saw the flowers. The first time I saw him he was collecting them from the rhododendrons along Foster's drive. The question is: did Eric find her out there and carry her up the hill on his own? Or did he do it under instruction from Foster?'

'Or,' said Ormside softly, 'did young Eric do the shooting?'

Paget nodded gravely. 'It's certainly a possibility,' he agreed. 'By all accounts, he was very fond of Lisa, and he had a habit of walking into the house unannounced. He carries that shotgun around with him, and the cartridges he uses are identical to those used by Foster. Who knows what his reaction might have been if he'd found Lisa in bed with Gray? He's a child in many ways. Would he be jealous? Would he think she was being attacked? More to the point is how do we find out what really happened? The only way we can talk to Eric is through his father, and his father can tell us anything he likes, and we'd never be any the wiser.'

FOSTER LOOKED EXHAUSTED when he finally answered the door. His clothes were rumpled, his eyes were bloodshot, and he hadn't shaved. He shaded his eyes and squinted at them as if unsure about who they were, silhouetted as they were against the sun.

'Oh, it's you,' he said listlessly. 'Sorry. I must have fallen asleep. I was up all night.' He turned and wandered into the living-room, and the two men followed him inside. Foster stood there as if in a daze, then abruptly sat down and put his head in his hands.

'I told Sergeant Ormside everything I know about the fire,' he said. 'I can't tell you any more.'

'We brought the statement for you to sign,' Paget told him. He held out the papers to Foster. 'Please read it over, then sign on every page where it's marked.'

Foster took the papers and glanced at them, then looked around vaguely. 'Do you have a pen?' he asked Paget.

'You should read it carefully,' Paget cautioned him. 'If you don't feel up to it now, I'll leave the statement with you and have someone come over later and witness your signature.'

Foster sighed as if a great weight had been taken from him. 'Thanks,' he said, and tossed the statement aside. It fell on the floor and he left it there. Tregalles picked it up and put it on the table.

'We have found Lisa,' Paget said quietly.

Foster didn't seem to hear him for a moment, then suddenly his head jerked up. 'What was that you said?' he whispered. 'You found Lisa?'

'Yes. I'm afraid she's dead.'

Foster continued to stare at him, then slowly nodded. 'I knew she must be,' he sighed, 'but I kept hoping...' Tears began to trickle down his face. 'Where...? How...?' He looked from one to the other. 'You mean... Up on the hill?'

'Now why do you say that, sir?' Tregalles asked.

Foster looked confused. 'I—I don't know. I just thought... That's where you've been, isn't it? Up there at the barn?'

'But why would you think that Miss Remington might be up there?' Tregalles asked. 'I mean, we've had a nation-wide search going on for days, now.'

Foster buried his face in his hands once more. 'I don't know,' he mumbled. 'I just thought...' His shoulders heaved and he stifled a sob.

'We believe she was probably dead when someone carried her up the hill from here,' Paget said. 'What can you tell us about that?'

Foster raised his head and stared at Paget. 'Go to hell!' he said. 'I've told you over and over again everything I know. I'm not saying another word.'

'Have you had anything to eat, recently?' Paget asked him.

Foster blinked as if he didn't understand the question, then shook his head.

'See if you can find Mr Foster something to eat,' he told Tregalles. 'And a cup of tea or coffee. Which do you prefer, Mr Foster?'

Foster jumped to his feet. 'Get out of my house,' he screamed. 'Bugger off. Just leave me alone.' He pushed them toward the door.

Tregalles flashed a questioning glance at Paget, but the chief inspector shook his head. 'I'll have someone come over later for your statement,' he said quietly as they reached the door and stepped outside, but Foster made no answer. Instead, he slammed the door in Paget's face, and they could hear him sobbing on the other side.

'WHY DON'T YOU COME IN and have a cup of tea, love? You look like you could do with one and it's just made.'

Molly Forsythe glanced at the list in her hand and thought about the number of houses in the avenue still left to check. The backs of her legs ached—she should never have worn these shoes with the higher heels today, but she'd just felt like a change. She'd already decided to nip home at lunch-time and change them, but there was almost another hour to go before she could do that.

'Thank you, Mrs Arkwright, I'd like that,' she told the owner of Number 38 Sidbourne Avenue.

The woman smiled and stood to one side. 'Elsie,' she

said. 'Call me Elsie. Come along in, then. What's your name, love?'

'Molly. Molly Forsythe.'

'Molly. I had a friend called Molly, once,' the woman said. 'That was years ago when we were at school.' She laughed. 'That was a long time ago.'

Elsie Arkwright led the way down the narrow hallway to a bright and cheerful kitchen. 'Sit yourself down, then,' she said as she busied herself with the tea. 'Would you like a scone? They're fresh baked this morning.'

'I'd love one,' Molly said. The smell of fresh baking was partly why she had accepted the woman's offer of a cup of tea.

'They haven't caught him yet, then?' said Elsie as she poured the tea. 'No, of course not or you wouldn't be here, would you?' she went on, answering her own question. 'Scary, isn't it, knowing someone like that's out there. People like that ought to be castrated. That's what my Albert used to say. That'd give 'em something else to think about, wouldn't it?'

'You live alone, now, do you, Elsie?'

'Yes. Help yourself, love. You like butter or marg? Here, have a bit of butter; it won't hurt you. It's not as if you're fat, is it? Yes, Albert's been gone, oh, it must be going on six years, now.'

'I'm sorry.'

'Oh, don't be, love.' Elsie Arkwright laughed. 'He isn't dead. Oh, no. He went off with a woman from across the road. They live just two streets over. I see him every now and again down at the supermarket. He works there, you know.'

'Oh.' Molly could think of nothing else to say.

'Oh, it was all quite friendly,' Elsie went on. 'Except I don't know what he sees in her. But I'd sooner be on my own. I mean, marriage is all right when you're young and foolish, but it wears a bit thin after a while, doesn't it? He liked the sex, but I wasn't all that keen. I mean, it wears you out, doesn't it? Especially with Albert. Every night, regular as clockwork. Tell you the truth, love, I was glad to see the back of him.'

Elsie broke off into peals of laughter. 'Glad to see the back of him,' she chortled. 'I was and all. I'd seen more than I wanted of the front of him. You married, love?'

Molly laughed. 'No, and I'm not sure I want to be after hearing your experience.' She took out her notebook. 'Do you know if anyone such as I described has moved into the street recently?' she asked.

The woman shook her head. 'No. Can't think of anyone,' she said slowly. 'Well, except for my lodger, Mr Trent. He moved here from somewhere near Newcastle, I think he said. Came here to be closer to his daughter. Doesn't have anyone else, you see, not since his wife died. But you won't mean him. Ever such a quiet gentleman, he is. No trouble at all. I hardly know he's there.'

'How old a man would he be?'

'Sixty, perhaps sixty-five,' the woman hazarded. 'He's retired, now. Used to be a butcher.'

Molly felt the hairs on the back of her neck actually *move*. Coincidence? Or had the fates led her to the very house in which the man was lodging? She suppressed the excitement she felt within her. She didn't want to alarm her new-found friend.

'I saw someone like that in the street earlier,' she said casually. 'What's he look like?'

'Oh, no, love. I don't think that would be him,' said Elsie Arkwright. 'He went out in the car this morning. Went off to see his daughter again. What's he like?' The woman thought about that. 'Well, he's a bit taller than me; a nice face; kind, you know. He's got grey hair, of course, cut nice and short. Keeps himself very nice, too.' She shrugged and made a face. 'I don't know what else I can tell you, love. He hasn't got any, what is it you call them? Distinguishing marks; that's it.' Elsie giggled. 'Least not on any of the parts I've seen, but you never know, do you?'

Molly smiled. 'Do you know where his daughter lives?'

Elsie pursed her lips. 'I believe he did say when he first came,' she said, 'but I'll be dashed if I remember. But you can't think that Mr Trent... Oh, no, love, I wouldn't have anybody like that under my roof.'

'He lives upstairs, does he?'

The friendliness in Elsie's eyes was fading. 'Yes,' she said cautiously, 'but you can't think...'

'Would it be possible to see his room, do you think?'

Elsie bristled. 'I couldn't do that, love,' she said. 'It wouldn't be right.'

Molly nodded. 'I know how you must feel,' she said, 'but I'm thinking of your safety as well as that of children. Sometimes the most innocuous-looking men can be, shall we say, disturbed. If I could just take a look, perhaps I could set both our minds at rest.'

Elsie Arkwright was plainly troubled. 'I wish you hadn't said that, love,' she said plaintively. 'You've put a doubt in my mind, and I shall always be wondering.'

'Then, perhaps the quickest way to set that doubt at rest is to take a look,' said Molly. She stood up. 'Shall we go up and see?'

NINETEEN

APART FROM A TORN EAR, which now had eight stitches in it, Eric Tyson had managed to protect his head. But the rest of his upper body and his arms had taken a vicious beating.

No bones were broken, his doctor said, but it would be some time before Eric would be able to move without pain. As for the psychological damage... The doctor merely shrugged and shook his head.

They found Tom Tyson in the patients' lounge. He was sitting on a couch, elbows on his knees, head in his hands, staring at the floor. He looked up as they came in, and Tregalles was shocked by the change in the man. His broad face seemed to have shrunk, and he looked old. Old and very tired.

'I reckoned you'd come,' was his only greeting.

'I'm very sorry about your wife,' Paget said gently. Tyson nodded but remained silent. 'Have you seen Eric since they brought him down?'

'Aye. They tell me he'll be all right, but you should see him. My God! she made a mess of him. He's black and blue all over his back and arms, his head is cut, and his ear...' He stopped, unable to go on.

They waited.

Tyson straightened up and looked Paget in the eye. 'You'd best get your notebook out,' he told him. 'I should have told you before, but I didn't.' He sighed deeply. 'I got the boy almost killed because I couldn't bring myself to do what needed doing. It wasn't her fault, you know, it were mine.'

Paget and Tregalles pulled up chairs and sat down. 'What

was it you couldn't bring yourself to do, Mr Tyson?' Paget asked.

Tyson shook his head slowly. 'Have her put away,' he said so quietly that Paget barely heard him. 'Dr Bradley—he's the one Emily's had ever since, well, ever since Eric was born—he's been trying to get me to do it for a year or more. But I said no; she was my responsibility and I'd look after her.'

He looked down at his hands, examining them closely, and it seemed to the two men that he was asking himself why he'd failed. 'It got so I couldn't leave the boy alone with her,' he went on softly. 'She had it in her mind that he was the cause of all her pain; all her suffering. And she has suffered, Mr Paget. She has indeed. It's no wonder her mind went as it did; day in, day out, dragging herself around on those two sticks.

'She was a good woman,' he went on earnestly, glancing up to make sure they understood. 'Very religious. Read the bible every day, and it seemed to help her earlier on when Eric was little. He was late, you see. She were nearly forty when she had him, and something went wrong inside. And then something happened to her bones. It was a sort of arthritis, the doctor said.' He searched for the right word.

'Osteoarthritis?' Paget put in, and Tyson's face cleared.

'Aye, that was it,' he said. 'And it was painful, Mr Paget. Some days she was off her head with pain, and the tablets didn't seem to help her. She prayed, Mr Paget. She believed that God would heal her if only she could pray hard enough. But then, as time went on and she got worse, something happened to her.'

Tyson buried his head in his hands once again. 'It was as if she were twisted, somehow. She got it into her head that she was cursed. She even had the vicar over and pleaded with him to do one of them things they do to get rid of evil spirits, but he said he couldn't do that. He tried to tell her it wasn't evil spirits at all, but she wouldn't have it and told him to get out. She said he was one of *them.*

'That's when she started blaming Eric for everything, and it's been getting worse ever since. The doctor told me a long time ago that I should put her in a place where she could be treated, but I couldn't do that, Mr Paget. She was my wife. I couldn't do it.'

Tyson sighed heavily. 'But she started lashing out at Eric whenever he came near, and when she started talking about killing him to get rid of the curse, I knew I had to do something. Dr Bradley made an appointment for her to see this psychiatrist weeks ago, but she refused to go. Screamed at me; called me everything she could lay her tongue to. So I waited for her to calm down and suggested that she at least have Dr Bradley in to explain things to her, but that just set her off again.

'Yesterday, I went to see him again, and he gave me these tablets. He said to put two in her cocoa at bedtime, then put two more in her tea next morning. He said it would make her go all drowsy like the stuff they give you in hospital before an operation. Then he said I was to take her straight over to Collington mental home, and they'd do an assessment of her there. He said he expected they would be keeping her there.'

Tyson shrugged apologetically. 'But I couldn't do it,' he said simply. 'I had the tablets in my hand, but I couldn't put them in her cocoa. And now she's dead. I don't know; perhaps it's for the best. She would have hated it in there. But in a fire…' He shuddered and turned his face away.

'Tell me how Lisa Remington died,' said Paget.

For a moment, it seemed as if Tyson hadn't heard, but then he slowly nodded. 'I thought you'd be asking about that,' he said. 'But she was dead, you know. I mean, when Eric found her there by the wall.'

'You mean the wall between your field and Bracken Cottage?' Tregalles said.

'That's right. I made him show me where he'd found her. The wall is very low there, so maybe she climbed over.' Tyson looked up at them. 'I can't always get it right, you see,' he went on. 'Not with Eric. He does his best, but it's not easy to understand everything he says.'

'When did this take place?' asked Paget.

Tyson thought back. 'It would be the Wednesday. Eric found her early morning; must have been before seven, but it was close to ten when I first saw her. See, Eric thought she was hurt, so he carried her up to the barn and made a bed for her in the straw. He does that with animals and birds he finds, and I suppose he thought it was the same. When he realized she was dead, he did what he thought right. He put flowers round her like he'd seen us do when his Granny Tyson died. Then he came and took me up there to show me what he'd done. I couldn't stop him bringing flowers even after she was buried, and I was afraid someone would catch on if they saw him.' He looked from one to the other and saw doubt there on their faces.

'If anyone's at fault, it's me,' he said. 'I'm the one who buried her.'

'How do you think Lisa died?' Paget asked. 'You saw the body; what do you think killed her?'

Tyson grimaced. 'She'd taken some shot in her left eye,' he said. 'There wasn't much on her face, and not much blood, but that left eye was gone. I reckon the shot must have gone up into her brain.'

'Was the body stiff or flaccid when you first saw it?'

'Her arms and face were stiff,' Tyson told him. 'But her legs weren't when I rolled her into the sheet.'

'What time would that be?'

'Between ten and eleven that morning. Eric had been

pestering me since about eight, but I had things to do, so I didn't go up till later.'

'And when did you bury her?'

'Not till dark. Should have done it earlier because she was as stiff as a board by then.'

Paget did a quick calculation. He'd have to talk to Starkie, but his own guess was that Lisa had probably died sometime between midnight and three o'clock Wednesday morning.

Tyson was speaking again. 'I know I should have reported it,' he said tonelessly, 'but I was afraid. Afraid they'd take Eric away. The lad only did what he thought was right. I didn't want him put away like some animal in a cage. He's a good lad, is Eric.'

'Are you quite sure that Eric didn't kill Lisa Remington?' Paget asked quietly. 'I'm told he was very fond of her, and he might have become enraged if he walked into the house and found her in bed with a strange man.'

Tyson was shaking his head violently from side to side. 'Eric's never hurt anything,' he insisted. 'He was just trying to help. And he would never have killed her. No matter what else she might have been, she was always kind to Eric. He practically worshipped her.'

'It could have been an accident,' said Paget. 'Eric kills rabbits with that shotgun of his. The man who was killed died from a shotgun blast.'

'See? See?' said Tyson as he scrambled to his feet. He stood there breathing heavily. 'That's what I mean. Because he can't defend himself, you'll try to say he did it, and he didn't. I *know* he didn't.'

'How do you know, Mr Tyson?' It was Tregalles who spoke.

'Because,' said the man, 'Eric may not be able to speak, but I understand him, and he's never lied. Even when he knew I'd be cross with him, he always showed me exactly what he'd done. He was never in that house that night, believe me. He was trying to help, that's all.'

Paget wanted to believe him. There was no doubt that Tyson was convinced of his son's innocence. But no matter how much faith the man had in his son, the possibility remained that Eric *could* have killed Lisa Remington.

Another thought crossed his mind. 'When I first saw Eric at the cottage, he seemed to be afraid of Foster,' he said. 'Foster seemed surprised by that. Do you know why he would act that way, Mr Tyson?'

Tyson nodded slowly. 'Eric was never that keen on Foster,' he said. 'It was Miss Remington he liked. She was good to him. Patient, like, you know.' Tyson paused, and when he continued, he seemed to be choosing his words carefully. 'It could be that he thinks Foster killed the girl. I don't know that, mind, but it could be. I do know he's stayed clear of him since that day.'

'Perhaps there's a good reason for that,' Tregalles said. 'Perhaps he saw something. Can you find out?'

Tyson shook his head. 'It takes me all my time to understand the boy on simple things,' he said. 'Things like that...they're too complicated. Sorry.'

FRANK PORTER followed Mike Freeman into the office and closed the door behind him. 'The police are asking questions about the car,' he said worriedly.

Freeman hung up his coat and turned to face Porter. He looked tired. 'So?' he said. 'Isn't that their job?'

Porter shook his head. 'You don't understand,' he said. 'They've been round to the neighbours, asking questions. The chap next door told me last night. Said he was sorry to hear we'd had a car stolen last month. He said the police were going round asking everyone if they'd seen anything suspicious. They know, Mike. They must! Why else would they come round asking questions like that right next door? What are we going to do, Mike?'

'*Do?*' said Freeman as he sat down. 'We're not going to do anything, Frank. Stop being such a bloody old woman. The police have nothing.'

'Nothing?' Porter squeaked. 'For Christ's sake, Mike, they must have something to be sniffing round like that.'

Freeman leaned back in his chair and put his hands behind his head. 'So the police have been round the neighbours. What is there for them to find out? You haven't done anything stupid, have you, Frank?'

Porter flushed. 'Of course I haven't done anything stupid,' he shot back.

'Then why are you worrying? Even if they find out, what can they do? A slap on the wrist for obstruction, but that's about all. What else can they prove?' His face darkened. 'Unless someone talks out of turn, Frank.'

Porter's mouth opened but no sound came out. He didn't like the way Mike Freeman was looking at him. He found his voice. 'No one's going to do that, Mike,' he said hoarsely.

Freeman continued to hold his gaze. 'Good,' he said. 'So forget it.' He drew a sheaf of papers toward him and began to read.

Porter stared at him. 'Forget it?' It was almost a yelp. 'For Christ's sake, Mike, we...'

Freeman sighed heavily. 'I said forget it, Frank. Now get out of here. I've got work to do even if you haven't.'

'MERRICK STAYED two nights at the Beechwood just outside Ludlow.' DC York produced a photocopy of the entry in the hotel register. 'March 11th and 12th. The receptionist remembers him well. She said he came in limping badly, and there was blood on his coat and trousers. She offered to ring the doctor, but he swore at her and told her to mind her own business. Said he'd been in an accident, but he didn't need her help, then made straight for the bar.'

Sergeant Ormside looked at the entries. 'Sounds like Merrick, all right,' he said. 'Resting up, was he?'

York nodded. 'That's what it looks like. The receptionist said he stayed in his room all the next day, just sending down for meals and drinks. She said he must have left during that night or very early the next morning, because he was gone when they took his tea up at seven. Left the room in a right old mess, though. Bath in a mess and towels all covered in blood.'

'So he *could* have gone back the next night,' said Ormside ruminatively. 'Found Lisa in bed with Gray, and shot him with Foster's gun. Lisa must have been wounded in the process, but managed to get away. Died later, if Tyson is to be believed.'

Somebody, he thought, would have to talk to Merrick again; check out his story; look for anything that would connect him to Bracken Cottage on the 12th or later. He yawned and stretched. Time enough for that in the morning, he decided. At least Merrick was safely in custody in London. Thank God for that, at least.

BODY OF TOP MODEL FOUND? was the headline, but it was the picture of Lisa Remington that first caught Sean Merrick's eye. Out on bail, he'd stopped in for a take-away and the paper was on the counter. He snatched it up and scanned the article, tearing the paper almost in half in his haste to turn to page two.

'Hey! Watch it, mate,' said the man behind the counter, but Merrick paid no attention. He read on. The article was short on detail, but there could be little doubt that the body was that of Lisa.

Merrick crumpled the paper in his hands. Foster. He was

to blame for everything. It was all his fault. Merrick clenched his fists. He'd pay, the bastard! By God, he'd pay!

The man behind the counter reached over for the paper. 'I said watch it,' he said threateningly. 'That paper…'

Merrick grabbed his arm and pulled hard. 'You shut your face unless you want this paper rammed down your bloody throat,' he snarled. The people waiting on either side of him moved hastily away as he slammed the paper down. No one said a word as he shouldered his way to the door, fists balled and ready to smash anyone in his path.

'MOLLY THINKS she might have a suspect,' Tregalles said. 'She wants Olivia to have a look at him to see if it's the same man.'

Audrey's hand flew to her mouth as if she was afraid of saying something she shouldn't. She felt a coldness creeping through her even as her mind told her not to be so silly.

'I don't want her near him,' she blurted. Her voice was high, on the verge of panic. 'I'm sorry, John, but no. It could frighten her.'

John Tregalles set aside the tea-towel and put his arms around his wife's shoulders, but Audrey shook them away. 'Stop it, John. My hands are all soapy. Can't you see I'm doing the washing up?' She knew she was being irrational, but she couldn't seem to stop herself.

Tregalles pulled her gently away from the sink and handed her a towel. 'We can't do anything until we are sure it's the right man,' he said gently. 'And Olivia would be inside a car.'

'But…' Audrey gnawed at her lower lip, trying desperately to think of a reason for saying no. 'She's so young, John. I mean, you hear of this sort of thing coming back years later.'

'It's not as if he's done anything to frighten her,' Tregalles pointed out. 'In fact, Olivia hasn't shown any sign that it's bothered her a bit. Sitting in an unmarked car, watching for this man, would probably seem like a bit of a lark to her. Something to talk about at school.'

'You *want* her to do it, don't you?' Audrey said. 'You've already decided.'

Tregalles shook his head. 'You know better than that, love,' he said.

Audrey eyed him doubtfully. 'Could I be there with her?'

'Of course. It could be a long wait, though, for both of you.'

'And he'd be arrested there and then? If it's him.'

Tregalles wished Audrey hadn't asked that question. 'It doesn't work like that,' he said. 'You see, as far as we know, he hasn't done anything wrong. He's...'

Audrey bristled. 'He tried to take Olivia,' she said, but Tregalles was shaking his head.

'That's just it, love. He didn't do anything apart from walk with her and talk to her. Then he left. There's no crime in that. Olivia wasn't frightened. In fact it made so little impression on her that she only mentioned it casually later on.'

'But he could have. He might have been going to take her when something frightened him off.' Audrey's voice was rising again. 'John, the man could be dangerous. He ought to be arrested.'

'Perhaps he should,' Tregalles agreed, 'but until we have more evidence, we can't do anything. The thing is, if Olivia tells us that's the right man, we can watch his every move, and when he does try it on, then we have him.'

Audrey stared at him. 'You mean you'd leave him loose so that he could do...whatever it is he does?' Her eyes grew larger. 'Are you saying he could still come after Olivia?'

'He can still come after Olivia, as you put it, now,' said Tregalles reasonably. 'This way, at least we'd know who to watch.'

Audrey turned back to the washing up. 'I'll have to think about it,' she said, not looking at him. 'I—I understand what you're saying, and you're probably right. It's just...' A tear ran down her nose and splashed in the water, and she wiped her cheek with the back of her hand.

She didn't know why she was crying.

TWENTY

Thursday 11th April

PC MAYHEW loosened his tie and undid the top button of his shirt. He slipped his boots off and put his feet up on the desk. It was after midnight, and no one would be coming round to check at this hour. For that matter, he hadn't seen why he should have to be here at all, stuck out in the back of beyond in the mobile unit, but Ormside had soon set him straight.

'Every thief in the country knows this unit's here,' he'd said. 'They'd have it stripped in no time if we left it out here unguarded. That's if they didn't tow the whole damned unit away during the night.'

Still, he was on overtime, and he could use the money. Mayhew switched off the light above the desk, rested his head against the wall, and closed his eyes.

PETER FOSTER came out of a deep sleep to the sound of pounding on his door. The room was pitch dark. The noise disoriented him, and he couldn't think where he was for a moment. As memory returned, he sat up in bed and switched on the bedside lamp. His heart was pounding hard, and he felt dizzy as he swung his legs out of bed.

'All right! All right, I'm coming,' he shouted as he stumbled down the stairs. 'What's wrong now?'

'Police!' bellowed a muffled voice, and Foster quailed. 'Oh, God,' he prayed. 'What now?'

The pounding began again.

Foster unbolted the door and fumbled with the latch.

The door smashed inward, catching his knee and foot as it knocked him backward into the wall, and a dark figure hurled itself inside. Before Foster had a chance to catch his breath, blows rained down on his head and he felt himself slipping to the floor. Hands gripped his throat, choking him, and he gasped for air. Instead, he sucked in the foul smell of beer and smoke and whisky. He struck out with his hands and connected with a face. His fingers found soft flesh and dug in hard, clawing, scratching…

The dark figure cursed; the pressure eased, and Foster struck again. His fingers found an eye and he thrust with all his strength. The figure screamed, fell back against the door, and Foster scrambled crabwise across the floor. His hand came in contact with the doorstop, a heavy, cast-iron replica of a flat-iron used in summer to prop the door open. He grasped it by the handle, turned and swung it hard.

The long, piercing scream brought Mayhew wide awake. He scrambled to his feet, searching in the darkness for his boots. He listened as he found the switch and turned on the light, but the sound was not repeated. Probably a fox or something like that, he tried to tell himself as he shoved his feet into his boots, but there had been something very human about that cry. Jesus Murphy! Ormside would have his balls on a plate if something had happened over at the cottage.

His wavering torch picked out the black Volvo in the driveway, and he slowed his pace. Mayhew wasn't one to walk blindly into an unknown situation. He inched cautiously toward the front door of the cottage and saw that it was open. He shone the torch inside.

The body of a man lay on the floor, and beyond him sat Foster on the bottom step of the stairs. He was clad only in pyjamas. One sleeve had been torn away, leaving his arm bare from shoulder to elbow. His head was in his hands, and he was shaking so hard his teeth were chatter-

ing. Blood oozed from beneath his chin. It soaked the front
of his pyjamas, and even as Mayhew watched, the dark and
ugly stain grew larger.

'Jesus Murphy!'

Mayhew didn't realize he'd spoken the words aloud until
Foster looked up. 'I think I'm going to...' he began, but
choked on the words and toppled forward on to the floor.

FOSTER WILL BE in hospital for several days at least,' said
Paget. 'His windpipe is damaged; and an artery was nicked
during the struggle. It wasn't all that serious, but he did
lose quite a lot of blood. Fortunately, Mayhew knew
enough first aid to keep it from becoming worse prior to
the ambulance arriving.

'As for Merrick, he has a concussion, and he has a damaged eye. He's lucky, though. If that flat-iron had done any
more than clip the side of his head, he'd have been dead.
As it is, the doctors say he should make a full recovery.'

Christ! What a balls-up. Alcott looked grim as he
squinted at Paget through a veil of smoke. 'All right,' he
said wearily. 'Let's run through it all again. You say you
can place Foster in Chester as late as nine o'clock on the
evening of March 12th, and he paid his bill at the hotel at
seven thirty the following morning.'

'Right,' said Paget. 'He left the hotel and went directly
to a meeting with people from British Rail and the adver-
tising firm hired to do the brochures. We've spoken to the
people who were there, and they all say that Foster was
perfectly calm and focused on the job in hand. I can't see
Foster remaining that calm if he'd just killed Gray and was
worried sick about where Lisa was and whether or not she
was alive. Neither can I see him coming home that evening
and going through an elaborate charade to cover up the
killing if he'd done the killing himself. It makes no sense
at all.'

Alcott gave a grudging nod. 'What about Merrick?'

'He could have done it,' Paget agreed. 'He was close by. He could have returned to the house, found Gray there with Lisa, and gone berserk. Foster's shotgun was there to hand, and I'm sure Lisa would have reloaded after shooting at him in case he decided to come back. But we have no evidence to connect him to the killing. Foster saw to that by his meddling. We're working on it, but we've had no luck so far.'

Alcott swung round to face the window, but he was oblivious to the view across the playing fields. 'You say Foster's a nonstarter,' he said irritably, 'and we can't question Merrick. What the hell *can* we do?'

'There are several things,' said Paget more confidently than he felt. He pulled his chair closer to Alcott's desk. 'Melrose has been busy trying to find out what happened to the company car that Gray used the day he went to meet Lisa. No one admits to seeing it again until it turned up at the weekend in the car-park behind Freeman Protronics, and I've always been curious about that. I think it's possible that someone in the firm could be involved in all this, and I intend to do more digging there today.'

Alcott swung back to face him. 'What about Merrick?' he demanded.

'We haven't forgotten Merrick,' said Paget quietly.

Alcott grunted. He'd hoped that Paget would have more than this. Hoped, but he knew better than to expect it. Alcott had been in Paget's shoes, and he knew how hard it was. But Chief Superintendent Brock was breathing down his neck, and he felt so damned helpless.

'All right,' he sighed. 'Get on with it, then. And for God's sake let me know the minute you get anything positive. I could use a bit of good news.'

Paget rose to his feet, pausing as he reached the door. 'Lisa's mother is coming down this morning to verify that the body of the girl we brought in yesterday is in fact her daughter,' he said.

Alcott grimaced as he pulled a pile of reports towards him. 'I hope Starkie has been able to make her look better than when we saw her last,' he said. 'Anything else from him yet about how the girl died?'

'No. Not till later on today.'

Alcott nodded gloomily. 'It'll rain tonight,' he said.

Paget searched for the connection. 'Sir?'

Alcott flexed his arm. 'Bloody elbow. Hurts like hell. Sure sign of rain.'

'I PICKED IT UP from your own notes, sir,' said Melrose smugly. 'You say in there that Porter never uses a company car. Yet I have a statement from a Miss Emma Lake—she lives in a flat on the top floor overlooking Porter's drive-way—in which she says she saw a company car parked there several days running last month. Porter's house sits back a bit, and you can't see much of it from the road because of high hedges and shrubs. But you look right down in there from her window. The only trouble is, she can't remember the dates. She knows it was around the middle of the month, but she can't swear to the dates.'

It wasn't much, but it was a start. Porter had been nervous about something throughout the interview. Perhaps this was it.

'How old is this woman?' he asked abruptly. 'And how's her eyesight?'

'She'd be about fifty, I'd say,' said Melrose. 'She's a teacher. Lives alone, and her eyesight is good. I asked her to identify several cars and tell me what people were wearing down in the street, and she was spot on every time.'

'Glasses?'

Melrose felt pleased with himself. Paget wasn't going to catch him out. 'Wears them all the time, sir. Never without them.' He waited, but Paget appeared to be deep in thought. Now, he thought, was as good a time as any to produce the prize.

'There was one other thing,' he said casually. 'Miss Lake saw the car being driven away early one Sunday morning just as she was getting ready for church. Eight o'clock service. She said she hasn't seen it since.'

'And the driver? Was it Porter?'

'Sorry, sir. She didn't see who it was. She just saw the car going out into the street.'

'Turning in which direction?'

'Ahh!' Melrose swallowed hard. 'I—er, forgot to ask that particular question, sir,' he said. Paget glanced up sharply. 'I—um, I'll ring her straightaway.'

TWENTY-ONE

FRANK PORTER was not in. 'He's been having these bilious attacks,' Peggy Owen confided. 'Keeps saying it's just a touch of flu, but I think he's got an ulcer. I keep telling him he should see a doctor, but will he?' She rolled her eyes heavenward as if seeking strength. 'Men!' she said. 'Can't tell them anything.'

Paget smiled. 'What about Miss Freeman?' he said. 'Is she in?'

'In the lab,' said Mrs Owen. 'Down the hall. Last door on the left. You'll see her through the glass.'

He found Janet Freeman staring intently at a VDU and making notes. He tapped on the glass and opened the door. 'Can you spare me a couple of minutes?' he asked her.

Janet glanced at the time. She seemed reluctant to tear herself away from what she was doing. 'I suppose a few minutes won't hurt,' she said grudgingly. She made a quick note, then swung round to face him. 'What can I do for you?'

Paget hesitated. 'One of the possibilities we are considering,' he told her, 'is that David Gray was killed, not because of his liaison with Lisa Remington, but for something that could be work-related. Tell me, was he working on anything, shall we say, sensitive in any way?'

Janet frowned. 'Do you mean something like a government contract? Something like that?'

'Not necessarily. It could be something of commercial value; a security system; something that might give a competitor an edge. I don't really know, which is why I'm asking.'

Janet shook her head. 'No. I can't think of anything like that,' she said. 'Sorry.'

Paget looked disappointed. 'Oh, well, it was just a thought,' he said. 'Thank you for your time, anyway.' He turned to go, then turned back once more. 'What about this new office in Bristol?' he said. 'Was Mr Gray involved in that in any way?'

Janet's face registered surprise, but it was quickly masked. 'Where did you hear about that?' she asked in a fierce whisper. 'That information is strictly confidential. Besides, that idea was shelved months ago.'

'Oh?' Paget feigned surprise. 'Your father mentioned it,' he said. 'In strictest confidence, of course, but I assumed that you would be aware of it.' He allowed a frown to gather as if puzzled. 'But from what he said, I got the impression that the move might be imminent. Which was why he left the office that day to discuss it with Frank Porter.'

There was a note of caution in her voice as Janet asked, 'What day?'

'The day David Gray disappeared. Sorry, I thought you knew.'

Janet smiled ruefully. 'Dad has his fingers into so many things in the course of a day,' she said. 'It's hard to keep up with him, and despite our business, communication is not one of his stronger points. In any case, I can't see what that could have to do with David's death.'

Paget shrugged resignedly. 'As I said, it was just a thought. Thanks again for your time.'

Janet Freeman waited until she was sure Paget had gone before picking up the phone. 'Where's Dad?' she demanded when Peggy Owen answered.

'You've just missed him,' said Peggy. 'He's gone to lunch with a client, and then he said he would be going straight on to Bradbury's from there. He didn't expect to be back this afternoon. You could probably get him on his pager.'

'No. It's not urgent, thank you, Peg. I'll see him when I get home.' She put the phone down. 'Damn you, Dad,' she said fiercely. 'You might have told me.'

CONSTANCE REMINGTON shook with anger as the attendant barred her way. The room was cold. Ice cold. White tiles, cracked and dulled with age, lined the walls from floor to ceiling. The floor was concrete, painted green. Chipped and scarred. It smelled of Lysol. And to those who worked there every day, it smelled of death.

'I'm sorry, madam,' the young man said again, 'but I must insist. These men must wait outside.'

'These men are my friends,' she snapped. 'They've come all this way to support me when I—' a catch came into her voice and her lip trembled '—see the body of my poor, dear daughter. You wouldn't deny a mother...'

'What is it, Graham?' Dr Starkie had come up silently behind the trio facing the attendant, and they swung round to face him.

Starkie was not a tall man, but he was impressive. And solid. He stood there like a rock, hands thrust deep into the pockets of his surgical coat—the clean one he used for visitors—and looked at each of them in turn.

'I was just telling this young man...' Constance Remington began, but Starkie interrupted her.

'I heard what you told him,' he said curtly. 'Do your friends always go round carrying tape recorders and cameras, Mrs Remington?'

The woman flushed. 'I'll have you know that...'

But again she was interrupted. 'I'll have *you* know, Mrs Remington,' Starkie said quietly, 'that this is not some sort of peep-show, and reporters are not permitted in here under any circumstances.' He turned to the two men. 'Out,' he said.

The photographer looked to the reporter for direction. The man hesitated, then shrugged. 'We'll be outside,' he told Constance Remington. 'I said they wouldn't let us in.'

Grim-faced, Mrs Remington watched them go, then turned to Starkie. 'Well,' she said, 'I hope you're satisfied. You and your petty rules have just cost me five thousand pounds. That's what they promised to pay if they could get a shot of me identifying my poor Lisa's body.'

Starkie stared at her. He'd seen almost every possible kind of reaction from relatives and friends; some grieving; some not. But this was the most callous exhibition he had ever encountered.

Constance Remington wrinkled her nose. 'Well?' she said. 'Let's get on with it. I have better things to do than stand here shivering in this stinking room all day. Where is she?'

'Now, I hope you understand, Audrey. This isn't the sort of identification that would stand up in court, but I would like to be able to tell my boss that Olivia wasn't coached in any way. So, we'll just sit here and watch the people in the street and see if Olivia recognizes anyone. All right?'

'I understand, Molly. All right, Olivia?'

'Yes, Mum.'

They waited. For the first ten minutes, Olivia sat up straight, head pressed against the window. Going through her mind were all the things she would tell her friends at school next day. What's it like inside a police car? she could hear them asking. Is she *really* a detective? Bet you were scared.

Was not!

A man on a bicycle rode past. A woman pushing a pram went by on the other side. Two women with shopping baskets came out of the corner shop and crossed the road. Olivia watched them until they were out of sight.

Forty minutes later, Olivia wriggled in her seat. She yawned. This was boring! She closed her eyes.

'Keep watching, love,' said Audrey.

Olivia opened her eyes and sighed heavily. This wasn't any fun at all. The window beside her had begun to mist up with her breath, and she drew a circle and put dots in for the eyes and nose. The mist began to clear before she could get the mouth in and she rubbed it all out.

The front door of Number 38 opened and a man stepped out. He would be somewhere in his sixties; grey-haired, and he would probably have been considered handsome in his day. He stood for a moment on the step, then began walking down the road. Toward the school.

Molly sat up straight, her eyes on Olivia through the mirror. Audrey sensed the change and drew in her breath. Her eyes went back and forth between the man across the street and Olivia.

The girl fidgeted as she watched the man, then pressed her nose against the glass and tried to look down her nose to see how flat it was.

Audrey could contain herself no longer. 'What about that man, love?' she asked, pointing. 'Is he anything like?'

Olivia looked surprised. 'The man over there? Oh, no, Mum, he wasn't as old as *that*.' She leaned over the seat and put her chin on Molly's shoulder. 'Can we go home, now?' she asked.

TREGALLES SPIED Grace Lovett in the corner as he eased his way through the throng at the bar. 'Bit off your patch, aren't you?' he greeted her as he set his plate down on the table. He pointed to the chair beside her, over which she had draped her coat. 'You waiting for a friend? Or can I sit here?'

Grace hesitated for only a second, her eyes searching the room beyond. 'No. I'm not expecting anyone,' she said. She pulled her coat off the back of the chair and folded it behind her.

Tregalles slid his plate on the table, along with his drink, and settled himself in. 'Not having anything to eat?' he asked, pointing to her drink, barely touched.

'I was going to, but I decided I'm not all that hungry.'

Tregalles took a long pull at his beer. 'Good beer, that,' he said as he dug into his pie. 'So what *are* you doing here? More to do with what we're working on? We could use a few clues.'

Grace toyed with her glass. 'No. I just happened to be over this way,' she said, 'and I thought I'd drop in. I'd never been here before your boss gave me lunch the other day, and I quite took to it.' She glanced around as if idly curious. 'He's not with you, then?'

Tregalles smothered a smile. 'No,' he said, straight-faced. 'He's off the beer and pies for a bit. Trying to lose a few pounds. You know how it is on this job.'

'Oh.' It was hard to read Grace's expression. 'There's nothing wrong, is there?' she said. 'I mean, he isn't...' She searched for a word but failed to find one.

'No. There's nothing wrong,' Tregalles assured her. 'It's just that he's a bit touchy about his weight. Likes to keep trim. Spends his lunch-hour at the gym whenever he has the chance. He's probably over there now. Pumping iron; that sort of thing. A devil for punishment is our DCI.'

'Oh.' Grace sounded surprised. And was that disappointment Tregalles detected? 'I didn't realize...' She looked at her watch and pushed her drink aside. 'I must be going,' she said. Her voice had an edge to it as if something had displeased her.

'Off to the gym, then, are you?' Tregalles asked innocently.

Colour rushed into Grace Lovett's face as she gathered up her coat. 'Very funny, Tregalles,' she said witheringly. 'Just because... Oh, never mind!' She pushed past him and made her way out.

Grinning broadly, Tregalles tucked into his pie.

DR STARKIE telephoned just after lunch. 'If you're looking for proof positive,' he told Paget, 'then you're going to be disappointed. With what I have to work with, I can only speculate on what *might* have happened. I can tell you the probable cause of Lisa Remington's death with some degree of certainty, but that's all. It will all be there in my report, but that won't get there until tomorrow at the earliest, and I thought you might like to know now.'

'Appreciate it, Reg,' Paget said. 'What was the cause of death?'

'In non-technical terms, brain haemorrhage caused by the entry of two pellets from a shotgun cartridge. Pellets identical to those I found in Gray. They entered through the left eye and travelled upward to lodge in the brain. Now, from here on it is pure speculation. The initial entry may or may not have rendered the girl unconscious. It's possible that, apart from the external injury to the eye, she could function more or less normally. Or she could have been rendered unconscious immediately. There is no way I can tell for certain. But sooner or later, the pressure from the haemorrhage would take effect and she would become unconscious, and death would follow.'

'Could she have run from the cottage and hidden herself somewhere after being shot?' asked Paget.

'It's certainly possible,' Starkie said, 'but even the slightest bump might have been enough to kill her. But understand what I'm saying, Neil. This is all speculation. It wouldn't be worth a damn in court.'

'I understand,' Paget told him. 'And thanks again, Reg.'

So Tyson could have been telling the truth when he said young Eric found Lisa beside the wall, Paget thought as he hung up. He was rather pleased about that. He'd never seen Tyson's actions as anything but an attempt to protect his son, and he hoped nothing would turn up to change his mind.

TWENTY-TWO

DR CLARENCE NUGOLD was waiting for them when Paget and Tregalles arrived at the hospital. He was very young, or so it seemed to Paget. Tall, lanky, hair falling in his eyes, he looked more like a gangly teenager than a doctor. Yes, he agreed, he was on duty the night Mike Freeman was brought in, and he had brought along the file to jog his memory.

'You understand, of course, that I cannot discuss Mr Freeman's medical history with you unless I have his written permission,' he said. 'But if I can help in some other way...'

Paget nodded. 'We understand,' he said. 'But the information I'm looking for is more general. Could you tell us, for example, what time Mr Freeman was brought in?'

Nugold consulted the file. 'He was logged in at 2.29 a.m., March 13th,' he said. 'We knew he was on his way, so we were ready and waiting to bring him straight into Casualty the moment he arrived.'

'You knew he was coming?'

'That's right. Miss Freeman phoned to tell us her father had had a heart attack, and she was bringing him in. She gave us his cardiologist's name, and she kept up a running commentary on her father's condition by car phone as she drove in. She also said she might need help getting her father out of the car when she arrived.' Nugold sat back in his chair. 'I'd say she is a very well-organized young woman who doesn't lose her head too easily,' he ended admiringly.

'And what was Mr Freeman's condition when you first saw him?' Paget asked.

'He was conscious,' Nugold said with a smile. 'Conscious enough to swear at us as we lifted him out of the car. And he told the other chap to bugger off when he tried to help.'

'The other chap?' Paget exchanged glances with Tregalles. 'What other chap, Doctor?'

Nugold shrugged. 'I don't know his name,' he said. 'I never saw him again after that.'

'Can you describe him?'

Nugold thought for a moment. 'He was a big chap; heavy-set; dark hair; somewhere in his mid-thirties to forty, I'd guess.' He shrugged. 'Sorry, but my attention was on Freeman at the time.'

'You'd recognize him again?'

'Oh, yes.'

'He was with Miss Freeman, was he?'

Nugold frowned. 'No, he wasn't, actually. He was in the second car. Red. Low, two-seater job. Don't know the make. I remember thinking it didn't seem to match the man. Pulled in behind Miss Freeman's car. I assumed he was a relative or friend.'

'What kind of car was Miss Freeman driving?' Tregalles asked.

'Looked like one of their company cars,' said Nugold. 'It had the Freeman name on the door. Why? Is it important?'

'Can't really say at the moment,' Paget said. 'Tell me, other than being conscious enough to swear, how serious was Mr Freeman's condition when he arrived? In general terms, of course.'

Nugold flipped the file open. 'He was in considerable pain,' he said, 'but that was more from the result of his fall than anything else. If he'd had a heart attack at all, it was very mild. Frankly, I suspect it had more to do with the drink than anything...' He caught himself.

'He had been drinking, then?'

Nugold frowned, annoyed with himself for having said more than he'd intended. 'In my opinion, yes,' he said grudgingly, 'but I'd appreciate it if you'd forget I said that.'

Paget smiled. 'You say Mr Freeman was in a lot of pain when he arrived?'

Nugold nodded. 'Primarily due to the pressure from the fractured rib and the severe bruising,' he said. 'God knows what he fell on. His chest looked as if it had been hammered. There were other bruises as well, but he probably got those when he fell down the stairs. Once we had the rib seen to, we observed him for the rest of the day, then sent him home. How is he doing, by the way?'

'As far as I know, very well,' said Paget. 'He's back at work and very active.'

'Good. Best thing for him so long as he doesn't overdo things.'

'THAT CAR had to be the one David Gray took to meet Lisa the day before,' Tregalles said as the two men walked down the corridor. 'The only other car was in Cheltenham for the week, so it had to be Gray's. But what was Frank Porter doing there?'

'Janet didn't mention him when she was talking about taking her father into hospital,' Paget said. 'And she most certainly didn't mention using the company car. I suppose she could have phoned Porter for help, but why were they in two separate cars? That sports car belongs to her; I've seen it in the car-park in her slot. Frank drives a white Ford. So, how did she come by the company car? And why didn't she just phone for an ambulance?'

'Sounds like Miss Freeman just went to the top of the

charts,' Tregalles said. 'Do you think she killed Gray and Lisa?'

Paget grunted. 'I don't know,' he said, 'but I do know she has a lot of explaining to do. When we get back, I want you to check on the calls made to and from the phone in that car,' he said. 'They might give us a clue about where she was calling from.'

Before they left the hospital, they checked on the condition of Foster and Merrick. Both, it seemed, were recovering. Foster's throat and one side of his face were a mass of bruises, and he would be on liquids for some time, but there would be no permanent damage. As for Merrick, his condition was listed as serious, but no longer critical. He was conscious and all indications were that there would be a full recovery.

THE LIGHT was beginning to fade, but Audrey Tregalles was reluctant to go inside. It was a bit early to be putting out some of the plants, but the front of the house caught the afternoon sun, so they should be all right, she reasoned.

Brian and Olivia, who had come out to help her, had wandered off. Brian was busy making roads for his cars, while Olivia was talking to a friend in the street. The girl, Joy Davies, told Olivia she was going with her parents to Llandudno on the weekend to visit an aunt who was ill, and she might have to miss school on Monday. Wasn't that fab?

Still chattering away, the two girls drifted toward Joy's house four doors down, where they stood talking for a few minutes before Joy said goodbye and went inside.

Olivia didn't notice the car as she walked back. Her mind was miles away. In Llandudno. Not that she'd ever been there, but it sounded nice. She wished she could go with Joy.

She didn't pay any attention when the car door opened

behind her, and it was only when someone spoke to her that she turned round.

'Come along, Wendy,' said the grey-haired man. He spoke softly, coaxing. He held out his hand. 'Time to go home,' he said. 'It's getting late.'

Audrey stood up, stretching to ease her back. It was getting chilly. Time to go in. 'It's a bath for you, young man,' she said to Brian. 'Make sure you bring all your cars in. Come on, now, there's a good lad. Where's Olivia?'

'Talking to Joy,' said Brian. 'Can't I stay out a bit longer? It's not dark yet.'

'It's gone seven thirty,' his mother said. 'Now come on, pick up your cars.' She couldn't see Olivia. Frowning, but by no means worried, she went to the gate and looked up and down the street.

She saw Olivia. And she saw the man!

'Olivia!' Even as she screamed her daughter's name, she was through the gate and running.

THERE IT WAS. Staring him in the face. Paget gave a grunt of satisfaction as he set the file aside.

He'd spent the last two hours going through statements, looking for inconsistencies, and it looked as if he'd found one. He'd have to check it in the morning with Weller. But Weller was a careful man; he didn't usually make mistakes.

The chief inspector stood up and stretched. He looked at the clock and was surprised to see the time. Eight o'clock. He groaned. He should have phoned to tell his housekeeper, Mrs Wentworth, that he'd be late. He just hoped she hadn't left him something for his supper that would spoil.

He toyed with the idea of stopping somewhere to have a meal, but it would only make it that much later by the time he got home.

He was on his way to his car when a car screeched to a halt beside him. Molly Forsythe rolled the window down.

'The man we've been after showed up at Tregalles's house,' she said quickly. 'I'm on my way over there right now. Thought you might like to know.' She slammed the car into gear and was gone.

Paget raced to his car. There might not be anything he could do, but just in case they needed a hand...

IT WAS ELEVEN by the time he got home. Paget went straight through to the kitchen, turning on lights as he went. Once there, he stood in the middle of the room, not quite knowing what he wanted to do next. He should eat something, but he didn't feel like preparing anything. He'd like a beer, but he knew if he had one he'd be up in the middle of the night, so scrub that idea. He opened the door of the fridge and surveyed the left-overs with distaste. He sighed, and took out three eggs. To hell with the cholesterol.

He crawled into bed at midnight, but his mind would not let go of how close a thing it had been for young Olivia. If her mother hadn't been right there. If the neighbour hadn't come out just then.

It didn't bear thinking about. But at least Tregalles had managed to get the number as the car sped away. He'd been in the house when Audrey screamed, and he'd come running out just in time to see the car go past. He'd kept his head and written down the number, but he was still shaking when Paget arrived.

Olivia, thank God, seemed none the worse for the experience. In fact she showed no sign of fear of the man, and that alone was driving John and Audrey out of their minds.

'At least now Molly has something concrete to follow up,' Paget had told Tregalles. 'If you need some time off, John, then take it. God knows, you've got it coming.'

'Thanks.' Tregalles rubbed his face with both hands. He

looked tired. 'All right if I let you know in the morning?
I'm having a bit of trouble thinking straight right now.'

Lying there in the dark, Paget recalled the haunted look
in Audrey's eyes. It was still with him an hour later when,
at last, he drifted off to sleep.

TWENTY-THREE

Friday 12th April

TO PAGET'S SURPRISE, Tregalles was at his desk when he arrived next morning. He looked grey with worry, but insisted he was all right.

'Audrey spoke to her mother and dad on the phone after you left last night,' he said, 'and they came down by car at the crack of dawn this morning. We're keeping Olivia home today, and I feel better with Audrey's dad there. He was an RSM when he retired from the army a few years back, and I'd hate to tackle him even now.'

'How's Olivia this morning?'

Tregalles looked perplexed. 'That's the funny part about this whole business,' he said. 'Olivia doesn't seem to understand how serious this is. I mean, she's a clever kid even if I do say so myself, but she has me baffled. Do you know what she said last night when she went to bed? She said, "He wasn't going to hurt me, Dad. Really. He wasn't." I tell you, I just went cold when she said that. I don't know how to get through to her without making matters worse.'

He drew in a long breath and let it out again. 'He's a persistent bastard, whoever he is,' he went on. 'He must have followed Olivia and Audrey home from school. But why Olivia?' The sergeant's face grew dark. 'Just give me five minutes with the twisted sod, that's all. Just five minutes. He'd never go after kids again. I'd make sure of that!'

'Anything on the owner of the car?'

'I spoke to Jim Dean a few minutes ago, and he said that

Molly has a name and is following it up. He wouldn't give me the name, but he said it looked promising.' Tregalles reached for the phone. 'Perhaps I should give Molly a ring to see…'

Paget put out his hand and pushed the phone back on its cradle. 'You can still have time off if you want it,' he told Tregalles, 'but you're either here or you're not. If you're here, then let Jim and Molly do their job. It isn't going to help anyone if you keep ringing up to find out what's happening.'

A frown of annoyance crossed the sergeant's face, but it only lasted for a moment. 'Point taken, sir,' he said. 'I'm here. So who's first on the list today?'

'YOU WANTED TO SEE ME, Chief Inspector?'

'Please come in, Mrs Owen, and have a seat.'

Peggy Owen sat down and folded her hands in her lap. 'How can I help you?' she asked quietly.

The perfect secretary, Paget thought as he studied her. Efficient, loyal, patient. Peggy Owen had all those qualities, and perhaps that was part of the problem.

'I'll come straight to the point, Mrs Owen,' he said. 'We have reason to believe that you may not have been…shall we say, quite as forthcoming as you might have been regarding the events that took place immediately following Lisa Remington's telephone call to Mr Gray the day he disappeared.'

Mrs Owen moved her feet, but apart from that she remained perfectly still. 'I don't think I follow you, Chief Inspector,' she said. 'In what way was I not "forthcoming", as you put it?'

'I believe you forgot to mention that you went into Mr Freeman's office *before* Mr Gray came out to ask you to get the spare set of car keys from Mr Freeman. Was there a reason for not mentioning it?'

Her chin came up. 'Because it isn't true,' she said defiantly.

Paget shook his head. 'I have statements from others in this office saying that it is true, Mrs Owen.'

Peggy Owen's eyes never left Paget's, but there was no mistaking the slow tide of colour rising in her face. She must have felt it, because she caught her lip between her teeth. 'If I did, I've forgotten it,' she said, but her eyes betrayed her and she looked away.

'I don't think so,' said Paget gently. 'I think it was you who went in to tell Mr Freeman that Mr Gray was making arrangements to meet Lisa Remington, and that's why he and Mr Porter rushed out after him. Did he ask you to do that for him?'

Mrs Owen opened her mouth to protest, then closed it again. She began to get up. 'I have nothing more to say...' she began, but Paget stopped her.

'Sit down, Mrs Owen,' he said sharply. 'I'm sure I don't have to remind you that it is an offence to obstruct the police in the course of their enquiries. The question is a simple one: Did Mr Freeman ask you to monitor Mr Gray's calls or not? And I would remind you that lying to the police is a very serious offence.'

Peggy Owen subsided into her chair and tilted her head defiantly. 'I did nothing wrong,' she said.

'I didn't say you did,' Paget said. 'But you could have saved us a great deal of time if you had been honest with us a week ago. Please answer the question.'

Mrs Owen looked down at her hands. 'There were rumours,' she said. 'Around the office. Mr Freeman was worried that there might be some truth to them. He didn't want Janet to be hurt, and neither did I. I'm sorry, but I didn't want you to think that Mr Freeman would do anything like...' She broke off and fell silent.

'Like kill Mr Gray?' Tregalles asked quietly.

Her head came up. 'He didn't!' she said fiercely. 'He couldn't. He had nothing to do with David Gray's death. He may have followed him, but that's all. Mr Freeman is not a murderer. He couldn't have. Mr Porter was with him.'

Paget studied her. Perhaps she was right. But Mike Freeman was an impulsive man. How far would he go to protect his daughter? And how far would he go to keep her from marrying any man who might take her away from him?

'Thank you, Mrs Owen. That will be all for now,' he said crisply. 'I'll have someone take another statement from you later on this morning.'

JANET FREEMAN was not in the office, but her father was. 'I suppose I can spare you a few minutes,' he told Paget, 'but I hope this won't take long. I have a lot to do today.'

'It rather depends on you,' said Paget neutrally as he sat down.

'Oh?' Freeman's eyes narrowed. 'What's this all about, then?'

'It's about the fact that the statement you signed regarding your whereabouts on the afternoon of March 12th was false,' said Paget evenly. 'As was that of Mr Porter. My sergeant is talking to him now about that.'

'Don't have the faintest idea what you're talking about,' said Freeman. His voice hardened. 'And I don't take kindly to being called a liar.'

'Then I suggest you start telling the truth,' said Paget. 'We know you followed David Gray that afternoon. We know you had Mrs Owen monitoring his calls, and we know that she told you of Lisa Remington's call to Gray that afternoon. We also know where Gray's car was between the time he left here and when it turned up again on the weekend in your car-park.'

'Frank and I went out to talk business,' said Freeman.

'That's all. As for this other claptrap, I don't know what you're talking about.'

'The business being your proposed expansion in Bristol?'

'That's right. It's a confidential matter, and I wanted to make sure it stayed that way.'

'You told me that your daughter's a full partner in the business,' said Paget. 'Is that correct?'

Freeman eyed him. 'Yes,' he said cautiously.

'Then, how is it that when I mentioned it to her, she told me that no such move was contemplated? She said it had been considered some time ago, but was dropped.'

Mike Freeman eyed Paget stonily. 'All right,' he said at last, 'suppose—just suppose—that Frank and I did follow that bastard, Gray. So what? I had good reason. He was about to become my son-in-law, for Christ's sake. He may have been good for the business, but I could see what he was after, and it wasn't Janet. He wanted to be sitting in this chair. That was his game.'

He glared at Paget. 'So what do you plan to do about it? There's nothing criminal in trying to protect your daughter from a con man, is there?'

'There is if you kill him,' said Paget.

'I didn't kill anyone,' Freeman snorted. 'We followed him out there, that's all. That's all I needed. I had the proof, and Frank was there to back me up.'

'How do you account for the car?'

'What...? Oh.' Freeman shifted uncomfortably in his seat. 'That was a mistake,' he said. 'It seemed like a good idea at the time, but it was a damned silly one in retrospect.' He sighed heavily. 'I suppose I might as well tell you what happened, because Frank is probably spilling his guts all over the floor by now.

'We followed Gray out of here and saw him pick up this woman. They went straight out to the cottage, and went inside. I—that is, Frank drove past and parked the car, and

I got out and went back to take a look. I crept up to the window and took a look inside. Christ, they hadn't been there five minutes, and they were down on the floor already.

'I'd seen enough. Gray had parked his car just off the driveway in that little glade behind the hedge, and I had this brilliant idea.' Freeman grimaced. 'Like I said, it seemed like a good idea at the time. Why not pinch his car?—then let the bugger try to explain *that* when he got back. We all have keys to the company cars, so it was no problem. I went back and told Frank what I was going to do. But I didn't want to take the car back to the office. I wanted to find out what Gray would do; what kind of story he'd cook up when he found the car was gone. I was going to let him explain it away, then show him up in front of Janet.'

Mike Freeman grinned suddenly. 'Frank wasn't exactly happy when I said I was going to park the car in his driveway. I think he thought Gray would think it was his idea, and beat the living shit out of him. Frank is not a brave man, Chief Inspector. It was a good spot, though; private, and nobody would think twice about it if they did happen to see the car there, with Frank being an employee.'

'So you drove it back to town,' said Paget. 'I thought you weren't supposed to drive?'

Freeman shrugged. 'So what are they going to do to me for that?' he demanded.

'And you waited until Sunday morning to bring it back to the office,' said Paget. 'Presumably while you were supposed to be out for your regular morning walk?'

Freeman stared. 'How the hell do you know that?' he blurted. Paget remained silent. Mike waited, then shrugged. 'That's it, then. So what are you going to do about it?'

'Where else did you take the car?'

'Nowhere. I told you.'

'When did you tell Janet what you'd done?'

'I didn't,' said Freeman.

'Why not? Wasn't that the object of all this? Are you telling me that she knew nothing about this when she reported Gray missing to the police?'

'That's right. I didn't tell her.'

'Why not?'

'How could I? I mean, I didn't know what had happened to Gray. I expected him to turn up the next day with some cock-and-bull story about someone stealing the car. When he didn't, I didn't know what to think, so I kept my mouth shut.'

'Or was it because you knew David Gray would never return?' said Paget. 'Because you had driven out there later that night and killed him.'

'That's a lie!' The denial came out swiftly, but to Paget's ears, it sounded false. 'I told you what happened, and that's all that happened. Think what you damn well like!'

'Then, how do you account for the extra mileage on the clock? Mileage that just happens to match the distance of a round-trip journey to Bracken Cottage. And how do you account for the fact that you arrived at the hospital in that same car about two thirty the following morning? A time, by the way, that happens to be close to the time that David Gray was killed?'

Paget stood up. 'And how was it,' he asked quietly, 'that you managed to bruise yourself so badly, Mr Freeman? Could it have been when you emptied the shotgun into David Gray's face? Shotguns have a nasty recoil, especially if they're not held properly, and both barrels are fired at once.'

Paget moved to the door. 'I'm afraid I'm not at all satisfied with your answers, Mr Freeman,' he said. 'I think it would be best if we continued this conversation at headquarters.'

Freeman stood up slowly, his face chalk white. 'Are you arresting me?' he demanded.

Paget shook his head. 'No,' he said evenly, 'but I'm quite prepared to do so if necessary. Besides, it's not as if you'll be alone. Mr Porter will be there as well.'

TWENTY-FOUR

'GERALD RAMSAY. Age fifty-two. No previous—at least, not under that name. Last known address: 148 Middlesbrook Road, Cardiff, where he lived for seven months before leaving there six weeks ago. No forwarding address. Receives a disability pension, according to his landlady in Cardiff, so we're checking to see if he has sent in a change-of-address to them.'

Molly Forsythe reeled off the information with barely a glance at the sheet in her hand. 'He's described as a very quiet man; keeps himself to himself, and he's never been in any trouble. No known friends or acquaintances. He gave no notice when he left, but he paid his rent to the end of the month, which was unusual, since he rented by the week. According to Mrs Phillips—the landlady in Cardiff—he just packed up and left without saying anything to anyone.'

Jim Dean grunted. 'Did she happen to say where he'd come from before taking rooms with her?'

Molly shook her head 'She says he just appeared one day in answer to a notice she'd put in the window of a local newsagent's. He seemed all right, so she let the rooms to him. He was very punctual about the rent, but he never talked about himself.'

'What's the pension for?'

'I asked about that. Mrs Phillips said she didn't know. She said he's got all his arms and legs, doesn't limp or anything, and all in all seemed very fit.'

'What about the pension people?'

'Ah,' said Molly. 'Now they were very cagey. Wouldn't give me anything over the phone, so I've asked the locals to see what they can find out. But it sounds to me like it might be mental.'

Dean snorted. 'You're probably right,' he said. 'The way this country's run today. Handing out pensions to blokes like that who prey on school kids. Jesus!'

'We don't know that,' said Molly, but Dean wasn't listening.

'I shouldn't tell Tregalles that,' he said. 'He'll go spare.'

'I hadn't planned on it,' said Molly, drily. 'The description of the car was circulated last night, but so far we've had no reports. He may have gone to ground; probably has a garage somewhere. But he'll be back. I'm sure of it. Can we not put a watcher in the street?'

Dean shook his head. 'Sorry, Molly, but it's impossible. We don't have enough people to go round as it is. But with Tregalles's father there, and Olivia being kept home from school, she's safe enough.'

'I suppose so,' said Molly, but she didn't sound convinced. What if the man changed his tactics and went after some other child? So far, there had been no sign of violence, but you could never be sure that his behaviour wouldn't change.

Molly closed a mental shutter. To start thinking like that would do no good. Take it one step at a time, she told herself, and make damned sure you don't miss anything.

SUPERINTENDENT ALCOTT opened the door of the interview room and poked his head inside. 'A word, please, Chief Inspector,' he said cryptically.

Paget stood up, but Mike Freeman was up and around the table ahead of him. 'Just the man,' he said. 'I have a complaint to make about my treatment at the hands of your man, here. He came into my office making accusations, then dragged me down here under the threat of arrest. I'm appalled that this sort of thing can happen to someone in Broadminster. I've heard…'

Alcott held up his hand. 'In due course, Mr Freeman,' he said. 'Please sit down. I'll deal with this.'

Mike Freeman grunted. 'You'd better,' he said. 'I'll not be treated like this.'

Alcott motioned Paget to follow him. Once outside the office, Alcott turned to Paget. 'Just what the hell is going on, Paget?' he asked fiercely. 'I've just had a call from Mr Brock. He is not a happy man. He wants to know why Mike Freeman is being held, and he wants to know now! Says he had a call from Freeman's secretary. Apparently Freeman told her to ring him after you'd left the office.'

'Personal friends, are they, sir?' asked Paget mildly.

Alcott's eyes narrowed as he drew deeply on his cigarette. 'They sit on the same boards together,' he said thinly, 'and for all I know they probably belong to the same lodge. Now, why is Freeman here?'

'Because he's been lying to us,' said Paget flatly. 'He and Frank Porter followed Gray and Lisa out to Bracken Cottage that day. They've finally admitted that. Freeman pinched Gray's car and drove it back to Porter's house. He says he wanted to hear what Gray had to say when he finally reappeared, and perhaps that was the original intent. But someone drove that car another twelve or thirteen miles before it was returned to the office Sunday morning, and I am sure it was either Freeman or Porter. My guess is that it was Freeman.

'The man is hiding something,' Paget went on. 'I think he believes he can stonewall us, but Porter is another matter altogether. He's on the verge of breaking, and once he does, Freeman is done for.'

Alcott eyed Paget narrowly through a wall of smoke. 'You think Freeman killed Gray and Remington?' he asked.

'I'm not sure who killed them, sir,' said Paget cautiously.

'But Freeman is hiding something, and at the very least he and Porter have done their best to obstruct the investigation.'

Alcott looked grim. 'I hope to God you're right,' he said. He turned and led the way back to the interview room.

Freeman was on his feet at once, smirking. 'I take it I can go?' he said laconically as he moved toward the door.

'I'm afraid not, Mr Freeman,' Alcott said. 'It appears that you have lied to us and deliberately misled some of my officers. I suggest your only course of action is to co-operate fully with Chief Inspector Paget. I shall look forward to reading your revised statement. Good morning, sir.'

As PAGET HAD PREDICTED, Frank Porter was the weak link. Once Tregalles started putting pressure on him, he began to look for a way to save his own skin.

'Look,' he said desperately, 'I didn't want any part of this. It was Mike. He made me do it. I mean, I work for him; what else could I do?' Porter's hands moved constantly on the table in front of him. He seemed not to know what to do with them.

Tregalles nodded sympathetically. 'Let's just go over it once more,' he suggested. 'Just to make sure we have it straight for the record. You say the first you knew about all this was when Mike Freeman rushed into your office and asked to use your car. But you balked at that and said you'd drive him to wherever he wanted to go. Right?'

'That's right. He almost dragged me out to the car, and when he saw the back end of Gray's car disappearing, he became quite frantic. He grabbed the keys out of my hand, and jumped in the car. I only just managed to scramble in when he took off.'

Porter licked his lips. 'He wasn't supposed to *be* driving, not after his heart attack,' he went on, 'but you can't tell Mike anything when he's in that sort of mood.'

'So you followed Gray,' Tregalles prompted. 'What happened next?'

'Well, as I said, this woman was waiting for Gray. He stopped and picked her up, and when she got in the car, he leaned over and kissed her. Mike kept saying, "I wish I had a camera; I'd show Janet what her fancy boy is like." He was so excited I was afraid he might have another heart attack and wreck my car.'

'You followed them to the cottage,' said Tregalles. 'Did they stop anywhere on the way?'

'No. They went straight there. Gray parked the car behind the hedge so it would be hidden from the road, and they walked up to the house.'

'You saw all this?'

'Just as we drove by. Mike went on and parked around the corner about fifty yards up the road, out of sight of the cottage. Then he got out and walked back. He was gone so long I started to get worried, but then I saw him coming back.'

'Whose idea was it to take Gray's car?'

'Mike's, of course,' said Porter indignantly. 'He said he was going to take the car to my house and leave it there, and I was to follow him. I didn't like it. I didn't like it at all, and I told him so. But he just laughed, and told me not to be such an...' He broke off abruptly.

Tregalles raised his eyebrows. 'Not to be what, Mr Porter?'

Porter moved his broad hands across the table as if sweeping crumbs away. 'Does it matter?' he said. 'The point is, I had no choice but to do as he said. He left the car in my driveway, then I took him back to the office.'

'And cooked up this story about having gone out to talk business,' Tregalles supplied. 'Whose idea was that?'

'Mike's, of course,' said Porter swiftly.

'And when did you decide to go back to the cottage

yourself?' Tregalles asked quietly. 'Using the company car.'

'I didn't,' Porter protested. 'I never touched the car.'

'Someone did. And since Mike Freeman had no qualms about telling my boss that you were in on all this, I doubt if he's going to hold back about the second visit to the cottage.'

Tregalles leaned forward and lowered his voice. 'You've worked with Mike for a long time, now,' he said. 'Do you really think he'll admit his part in what happened? Think about it, Frank. If it's a case of him or you, he's going to drop you in it, and with Janet to back him up, I'd say you're going to be in deep shit.'

'Janet would never...'

'Janet will do whatever her father tells her to do if it's a matter of his neck or yours,' Tregalles said. 'Think about it, Frank. Like I said, you know Mike. You know what he's like.'

Porter's hands moved jerkily across the surface of the table. 'I had nothing to do with Gray's death,' he burst out. 'It was Mike.'

IT HAD BEEN a busy morning for Audrey Tregalles, but she enjoyed having her parents there. She felt more relaxed than she had for days, what with Olivia safely at home, and her father in the house. Solid and formidable, Roy Spooner had struck terror into the hearts and minds of raw recruits for years, but Audrey had always been able to twist her father round her little finger.

'You're too soft with her,' her mother used to say, and he'd agree, and slyly wink at Audrey. Olive Spooner was more practical when it came to raising children. She had to be, with four boys and a girl in the house.

'I wish you'd told us before,' said Roy for perhaps the tenth time. 'We'd have been glad to come.'

'I didn't want to worry you,' said Audrey. 'John's colleagues have all been very good and now they think they know who the man is.'

'But they haven't caught him yet?'

'No. But I'm sure it's just a matter of time.'

'I hope so,' said Olive Spooner. 'It must have been so worrying for you, dear.'

'I must admit I haven't had much sleep,' said Audrey. 'And I'm thankful that you're here now.' She was about to say something else, but the sound of the door bell stopped her. 'I wonder who that could be?' she said as she started toward the door. 'Just be a minute.'

Audrey closed the door of the living-room behind her and walked to the front door. She could see a shadowy silhouette through the frosted glass, but she couldn't make out who it was. She opened the door.

Shock took her breath away. She opened her mouth but no sound came out. Fear paralysed her, and she could only gape as the grey-haired man pushed his way inside. He spoke, but her mind refused to accept the words.

'I've come for Wendy,' he said coldly. 'I know she's here.'

TWENTY-FIVE

'THERE'S A MISS FREEMAN asking to see her father, sir,' said the duty officer, 'but I understand he's with DCI Paget, being interviewed.' The man cupped his hand around the phone. 'She's not too happy, either, sir,' he said quietly. 'What would you like me to tell her?'

Alcott looked across his desk at Tregalles. The sergeant had just given him a run-down on Porter's story. Alcott smiled. 'Tell her to have a seat,' he said. 'It may be some time before Mr Freeman is available.'

He turned to Tregalles. 'Pull Paget and tell him what you've just told me,' he said. 'Freeman may be more willing to talk if he knows Porter has caved in.'

'MR PORTER has told Sergeant Tregalles what happened, Mr Freeman,' said Paget. 'It seems rather pointless to continue to deny that you went back to the cottage later that night.'

'It's Frank's word against mine,' said Freeman hotly. 'You have no proof of anything.'

'Do you still insist that you had your heart attack in your house, and that you fell on your own stairs?'

Freeman scowled. 'That's right. Janet will tell you the same.'

'I'm sure she will. She took you to the hospital?'

'I've told you she did,' said Freeman waspishly.

'In her car?'

'Yes.'

'You were conscious throughout the journey?'

'Yes.'

'How long did it take you to get to the hospital?'

Mike Freeman gave a sigh of exasperation. 'Five minutes,' he said. 'Though what the hell that has to do with anything, God only knows.'

'I think it will become apparent, Mr Freeman, when you try explaining to me how it was that you arrived at the hospital in the company car you had previously hidden in Frank Porter's driveway? And if it only took five minutes, how is it that your daughter was in contact with the hospital, using the company car telephone, for a good twenty minutes before you arrived? We have the telephone records, Mr Freeman, and the hospital staff will verify those times.'

Freeman looked grim. He stared across the room, muscles working in his face. 'Tell me, Mr Freeman,' Paget went on, 'who are you trying to protect? Yourself or your daughter? Was it she who...?'

Freeman came half-way across the table, forefinger jabbing at Paget, and the young constable standing beside the door started forward.

'You leave Janet out of this,' Freeman snarled. 'She had nothing to do with it. And I'm not protecting anyone.'

Paget motioned the constable back. 'Sit down,' he told Freeman curtly. 'There's no point in trying to tell me that Janet wasn't involved,' he went on, 'because we know she was. Porter has signed a statement to that effect, and I'm sure Miss Freeman will confirm it in her statement. I understand that she is in the building now. She was there with you and Porter when you went out a second time...'

'No!' Freeman slammed the table with his fist. 'She came out afterwards,' he said. 'She...' He stopped abruptly, leaned back in his chair, and covered his face with his hands. 'Shit!' he said softly as if to himself. He shook his head from side to side as if he couldn't believe what he'd said. He lowered his hands.

'I had nothing to do with killing Gray,' he said wearily.

'Christ, Paget, what kind of man do you think I am? I'll admit that I didn't want him to marry Janet, but as God is my judge, I was not the one who splattered his brains all over the pillow like that. In fact I didn't know he was dead until you told me last week, and that's the truth. Neither did Janet.'

Paget eyed him coldly. 'Go on,' he said.

Mike Freeman rested his elbows on the table and leaned forward as if by doing so his words would be more convincing. 'You have to understand,' he said earnestly, 'that what I did was for Janet's sake. I didn't want to see her hurt. But the more I tried to get her to see what a bastard Gray was, the more she refused to believe me. I had to do something.'

It began, Freeman said, at dinner. He'd felt so pleased with himself that he had something on Gray at last, that he'd had a few celebratory drinks that afternoon, and Janet had commented on it.

'She didn't like me drinking,' he explained. 'Said it was bad for the heart. She was a bit sarcastic about it, and asked me what I was celebrating.' Freeman pursed his lips and shook his head. 'I should have kept my bloody mouth shut, but I started throwing out hints about having something on her precious David.' He shrugged. 'To be honest, we ended up in a slanging match. Finally, she ran off upstairs. I remember shouting after her that next time I'd get pictures.'

Freeman went on to say that he'd spent the remainder of the evening drinking and brooding about Gray. And then it hit him. Why not *get* pictures? From what he'd seen through the window, Gray would be spending the night at the cottage, and if he could get inside somehow, he'd take pictures, and *prove* to Janet what Gray was like once and for all. He didn't have a camera of his own, but Janet had an old 35mm Konica, and she always kept film in it.

Freeman said he realized now that it was a stupid idea,

and if it hadn't been for the drink he would never have considered it.

Paget wasn't so sure about that. It seemed to him that Freeman was prepared to go to almost any lengths to keep his daughter from marrying, whether it be to Gray or anyone else.

Freeman said he waited until he was quite sure that Janet was asleep, then phoned Porter and told him he was coming over. Porter, who had gone to bed, objected, but Freeman told him if he wanted to keep his job he'd better get dressed and meet him at the door.

'I wanted him to drive us to the cottage, then stay outside with the engine running in case I had to leg it,' Freeman explained.

'How did you plan to get inside?' Paget asked.

'I don't know,' said Freeman irritably. 'Like I said, I'd had a bit to drink, and I suppose I thought I'd find a way when I got out there.'

Once there, Freeman said he told Frank to park in the same place they had parked the previous afternoon. When Paget asked him what time that was, Freeman said his best guess was somewhere around one o'clock. He said he left Frank in the car while he walked back to the cottage and crept up the driveway. It was only when he got closer that he realized there was a light on in one of the upstairs rooms.

And, strangely, the front door was wide open.

Paget looked sceptical. 'Just like that?' he said. 'Open in the middle of the night? A bit convenient for you, wasn't it?'

'Scoff all you like, Paget,' Freeman said, 'but I'm telling you, it was open, and that's the truth.'

'All right, let's leave that for a moment,' Paget said. 'What about the light in the bedroom? Which room was it?'

'The one to the right of the front door as you face it,' said Freeman promptly.

The bedroom in which Gray and Lisa had been shot. 'Go on,' said Paget.

Freeman almost looked apologetic as he continued. 'I know it sounds daft now, but the light didn't bother me. It told me where they were, so I wouldn't have to go searching for them.' He frowned as if trying to remember something. 'That's when I heard this noise,' he said slowly. He looked at Paget, still frowning. 'I was standing there in the doorway, trying to see the camera to make sure it was set for flash, when I heard this noise. A sort of rustling sound.'

Freeman sighed resignedly. 'I'd had quite a bit to drink,' he confessed, 'and I suppose I was a bit slow, so it took me by surprise when this bloke came at me out of the dark. I'd only just realized that someone was there, when something slammed into my chest. God! I thought I'd been shot. I lost my breath, and I went down. It all happened so fast that I never did see who hit me. All I saw as I was going down were these trainers he had on. My chest felt as if it was going to burst, and I could feel myself blacking out, but I thought, I'll get you, you bastard, and I slammed the Konica down on his foot.'

Freeman chuckled at the memory. 'That old Konica is a heavy brute and I heard the bastard yell. And that's all I remember until I woke up in the car.'

'THE POINT IS,' said Alcott, 'do we have enough evidence to arrest Freeman? You say he admits going to the cottage, but claims he went there only to get a picture of Gray in bed with Lisa. Perhaps that's what he told Frank Porter, but it seems damned unlikely to me. It seems far more likely that he went there intending to kill Gray.'

'I'm not so sure,' said Paget. 'If he went there intending to kill the man, how did he intend to do it? He's not a big man; he's not all that strong. I'm sure Gray could have overpowered him in a fight.'

'He used what came to hand,' said Alcott. 'He saw the gun there and used it. And, as you yourself suggested, the recoil of the gun broke his ribs.'

'Frank Porter swears he didn't hear a gun go off,' Tregalles put in, 'and I can't shift him on that. He says Mike went in with the camera, and he didn't come out again. He said he waited for what seemed like hours, then went to find out what happened to Freeman. He said he couldn't find him, so he went back to the car and rang Janet from the car phone.'

'Yet Freeman says he was hit more or less on the doorstep of the cottage. So why couldn't Porter find him?' asked Paget. 'Did he go inside?'

'He says he didn't,' Tregalles said, 'and I believe him. I think he was too scared to do anything but look up the drive. I think he funked it. Probably panicked and rang Janet. She arrived about half an hour later and found her father unconscious just inside the door at the bottom of the stairs. Porter claims no one went upstairs. They got Freeman out of there as fast as they could and took him to the hospital.'

'I think we should have a word with Janet Freeman,' Paget said. 'Perhaps she can help us put this thing together.'

'Right,' said Alcott. 'Get on with it, then.' He glanced at his watch. 'Mr Brock wants another progress report within the hour, so for God's sake give me something to keep him happy.'

TO SAY THAT Janet Freeman was upset would be an understatement. She was furious at being kept waiting, and she made her feelings known in no uncertain terms.

'I insist on seeing my father,' she said. 'He's a sick man. I cannot allow him to be treated this way. Where is he?'

She looked around as if she expected them to produce Mike Freeman out of the air.

'I'm afraid that's not possible at the moment,' said Paget quietly. 'Would you come this way, Miss Freeman?'

'I'm not going anywhere until I've seen my father,' she fumed.

'Both he and Mr Porter have told us what happened the night David Gray was killed, Miss Freeman,' Tregalles said. 'But we do need confirmation before we can release them. As it stands, I must tell you it looks very much as if he went to the cottage with every intention of killing David Gray.'

'That's utterly ridiculous! My father could never kill anyone.'

'Not even to prevent you from marrying Gray?' Paget said quietly. 'He admitted having a violent argument with you about Gray that same evening. And he admitted he'd been drinking heavily. But there are one or two points that need clarification. Particularly concerning Mr Porter's role in all this. I understand he called you from the car that night?'

Janet Freeman's mouth formed a thin line at the mention of Porter. 'He panicked,' she said flatly. 'He went to pieces. He was almost crying when he rang me. I couldn't understand what he was talking about. Woke me out of a deep sleep and started babbling.'

Paget moved aside as a uniformed constable brushed past. 'Perhaps we should move out of the way,' he suggested as he eased Janet Freeman toward an open door. 'The sooner we can clear this up, the better it will be for everyone.'

Grudgingly, she allowed him to usher her into a small room. Tregalles closed the door and they sat down.

'Now, then, Miss Freeman, you were saying that Mr Porter was babbling, I believe?'

Janet shook her head as if in despair. 'I've always known that Frank was not exactly the heroic type,' she said, 'but to leave my father lying there without even attempting to help him is something for which I shall never forgive him. It took what seemed like ages before I could get him to calm down enough to explain what had happened. The long and short of it was that he was too scared to go up to the house by himself. If he had, he'd have seen Dad there. If it had been up to him, Dad could have died there,' she ended bitterly.

'You drove out there?' Paget prompted her.

'Yes. Once I'd managed to get some coherent directions from Frank. I was worried sick. I had no idea what I'd find. I couldn't understand what they were doing out there in the first place. Fortunately, Dad was all right, and we got him back to the car and to hospital in time.'

'You went into the cottage?' Tregalles asked.

'Just inside the front door. Dad was lying there at the bottom of the stairs.'

'Weren't you afraid that someone would come out to see what was going on? I mean, you *were* in someone else's house.'

Janet shook her head impatiently. 'According to Frank, only David and the girl were there, and if what Frank said was true, I didn't give a damn about either. My father was hurt, perhaps dying. I had to get him to hospital. Besides, Frank was there.' She grimaced. 'Not that he'd have been much good if it came right down to it.'

'Did you see anyone while you were there? Hear any movement?'

'No. The place seemed deserted, and once I found my father, the only thing I wanted to do was get out of there.'

'You didn't go upstairs?'

'Of course not. Why should I?'

'And you saw no sign of the person your father says attacked him?'

'I didn't know he had been attacked then. It was only later when he regained consciousness in the car that he told me what had happened. I assumed the person who had attacked him was David.'

'And you neither saw nor heard anyone else?' Paget persisted.

'I told you, no,' said Janet wearily. 'There wasn't the slightest sign of life; not even a car went by. Except, of course, for the one that clipped Frank earlier.'

'He was hit by a car?'

Janet Freeman shook her head impatiently. 'Clipped the car,' she said. 'It happened while he was talking to me on the phone. Scraped the side of the car. Scared Frank out of his wits. He was even more incoherent after that happened.' She looked from one to the other. 'He didn't tell you about it?' She sighed heavily. 'I don't know why I should be surprised,' she said. 'God! The man is hopeless.'

FRANK PORTER seemed not to have moved since Tregalles had left him more than half an hour before. He looked up as the sergeant and chief inspector entered the room, then looked away again.

Paget wasted no time. 'Why didn't you tell us that another car hit yours while you were on the phone to Janet Freeman?' he said.

Porter looked up guiltily. 'I'm afraid I'd forgotten about that,' he said. They waited. 'Why? Is it important?'

Paget sighed. 'Just tell us what happened,' he said.

Porter's hands began to move across the table once more. 'I was on the phone to Janet when it happened,' he said. 'You see, I was parked just up the road from the cottage. There's this blind corner, and I was half on the grass verge, but the road is quite narrow there, and they drive like mad idiots on that road at night.'

He looked from one to the other, but when no one spoke, he hurried on. 'I don't even know what it was,' he said. 'I suppose it was a car, but the first thing I knew was when the lights came round the corner. I ducked down. I didn't want anyone to see me. He was coming too fast, and he only just managed to get past. But he scraped the side of the car. Rocked it as he went past. Made me drop the phone. But he didn't stop, thank God.'

'Which way was it going?'

'Toward Chedstone.'

'And you saw nothing of the vehicle?'

'No. I told you...'

'I want you to think carefully,' Paget said. 'Could it have come from the cottage?'

Porter looked surprised, then shrugged helplessly. 'I don't know,' he said. 'I suppose it could have done. I just thought it was someone on the road.'

'You didn't hear it start up? Think, man!'

Porter shrugged again. 'Sorry.'

The door opened and Alcott stuck his head inside. 'Can you spare Sergeant Tregalles for an hour or two?' he asked Paget. He looked serious.

Paget hesitated. He didn't want to lose Tregalles at this crucial point, but Alcott must have a good reason for asking. He nodded and Alcott drew Tregalles out of the room.

Outside the room, Alcott said, 'I had a call from Jim Dean. He thinks they have the man who's been bothering your girl.' He held up his hand as Tregalles opened his mouth. 'Everything's all right,' he assured the sergeant. 'No one's been hurt or anything like that, but your wife probably needs you more than we do at the moment.'

'But...'

'On your bike, Tregalles,' said Alcott gruffly. 'I'll let Paget know when he's free. Now, move it. That's an order.'

'WE WON'T HAVE any results back from the lab until at least midday Monday,' Paget said. 'But if they find what I think they'll find, then we may be able to wrap this up by Monday night.'

Alcott sighed heavily. 'God, I hope so,' he said with feeling.

The office was quiet. It was after six o'clock and it had been a long and gruelling day. Once their statements had been taken, there was nothing to be gained by holding Mike and Janet Freeman, or Frank Porter. 'It's not as if they're liable to run,' Paget had argued, and Alcott had agreed.

'Sorry I had to pull Tregalles when I did,' the superintendent said, 'but I thought it best, considering the circumstances.'

Tregalles. Good God! thought Paget, and felt guilty for not asking about his sergeant. 'What happened?' he asked now. 'Not another attempt to take Olivia, I hope?'

Alcott's face twisted into an odd smile. 'Yes and no,' he said. 'The man turned up on the doorstep. Scared the hell out of Tregalles's wife. What's her name?'

'Audrey,' said Paget. 'What happened?'

'Jim Dean phoned me a short time ago,' said Alcott. 'Apparently, this—' he consulted a notepad on his desk '—Gerald Ramsay used to live here in Broadminster some twenty years ago. His daughter, Wendy, went to the same school Olivia attends, and Ramsay used to meet her after school and take her home. But he and his wife split up, and Wendy went to live with her mother. Ramsay was devastated. He tried every way he could through the courts to gain custody of the child, but got nowhere.'

Alcott butted a cigarette and lit another. 'Wendy continued at the same school, and it seems Ramsay went there one day with the idea of abducting her. But her mother turned up just as he was taking Wendy across the road. She called to her and Wendy turned and ran back to her.

'Trouble was, she didn't make it. She was knocked down by a car and died within minutes. Ramsay went round the twist. Spent the next few years in and out of psychiatric care. He was supposed to be cured, but something must have triggered him off again. Olivia, it seems, looks quite a bit like Wendy. He never meant to harm her. He just wanted to take his daughter home. He turned up on Tregalles's doorstep and told Audrey he'd come to take Wendy home. Her father came out and grabbed the man and held him while Audrey phoned us.

'Funny thing was, he offered no resistance at all. Just sat there quietly and cried. He's been taken into care, now.'

Paget was still thinking about Tregalles and his family as he drove home that night. Thank God everything had turned out all right. They must be feeling so relieved. He'd ring the sergeant when he got home.

It was funny, though, how Olivia herself had shown no sign of fear of the man. Could it be because the child sensed that she was in no danger? Perhaps children, with their relatively unstructured minds, had insights that adults had long since lost. Whatever it was, thought Paget, he was glad for Tregalles's sake that it was over.

TWENTY-SIX

Monday 15th April

THE SMELL OF THE PLACE brought back memories, and Paget wondered whether he would ever be able to enter this hospital without thinking of Andrea. For it was here that they had met, and it was here that different loyalties had torn them both apart.

The wide doors of the lift clanked open, intruding on his thoughts. He and Tregalles stood to one side to allow a masked and gowned figure to manoeuvre a trolley into the broad corridor, then stepped inside the lift. They were silent as it took them to the fourth floor.

The results from the lab had come back earlier in the afternoon, and the evidence was irrefutable.

Paget stepped up to the desk and had a word with the sister there. 'The doctor is expecting you,' she told him. 'I believe he's in the room now.'

The two men walked down the hall and entered the room. The doctor was beside the bed, checking his patient's pulse. He looked up as they entered and stood to one side.

'I shall remain,' he said quietly. 'I trust you have no objection?'

'None at all,' said Paget. 'In fact I was about to ask you to stay.' He turned to the patient. 'I'm sure *you* know why we're here,' he said. 'You lied to us about where you were the night David Gray and Lisa Remington were killed, didn't you? Would you care to change your statement?'

The patient scowled. 'Prove it,' he said. 'I was miles away, and you can't prove otherwise.'

'I think we can,' said Paget. 'In fact I know we can. It's not a good idea to drink and drive.'

A frown creased Merrick's brow. 'You're bluffing,' he said.

'We've just received the lab report on paint samples taken from your car. They match those taken from a groove in another car that was parked some fifty yards away from Bracken Cottage on the night David Gray and Lisa Remington were killed. You claimed to be at the Beechwood Hotel near Ludlow that night, but we know that you were at the cottage.

'You went back there, didn't you? You went back to make Lisa pay for what she'd done to you. You found the door open when you got there. Lisa was always forgetting to lock it, wasn't she? You went in, and there was the shotgun, the very gun that Lisa had used on you. You picked it up and went upstairs.

'It must have come as quite a shock to you to discover her in bed with another man. Not Foster, but yet another lover. So you shot them both, but your aim was bad. You killed Gray, but you only managed to disfigure Lisa. Shot away an eye instead of killing her. You wanted her dead, didn't you, Merrick?'

Merrick's face was ashen. 'For Christ's sake let it alone!' he whispered hoarsely. 'I told you, I was miles away.'

'And as I told *you*, Merrick, we have proof that you were there at the cottage when Gray was killed and Lisa was wounded. We have a witness.' Paget reached down and whipped away the sheet that was covering Merrick. The toes of his right foot were bandaged.

'What happened to Mr Merrick's toes?' he asked the doctor. His eyes never left Merrick's face.

The doctor moved up beside the bed. 'He told me he dropped his portfolio on them,' he said. 'Apparently it is very heavy. Unfortunately, he didn't have them seen to, and two of his toe-nails had to come off.'

'More like a heavy camera,' Paget snorted. 'Is that what it was, Merrick? Still hunting for Lisa so you could finish her off, were you, when this happened? Make her suffer? Is that the way it…?'

A low moan came from the man on the bed, and he put his hands to his bandaged head as if trying to block out the chief inspector's words. 'It was him!' he growled. 'Foster. He was there. Skulking around inside. Coming down the stairs. I hit him as he came out of the door. I should have killed the bastard, but I was scared. I couldn't find Lisa. I didn't know who else was about, so I took off.'

'What did you hit him with?'

'The gun, for Christ's sake. What do you…?' Merrick stopped abruptly.

Paget sighed. 'Let's not play games, Merrick,' he said wearily. 'You were the one with the gun. Still looking for Lisa after you killed Gray. You wanted to finish her off once and for all, didn't you? Blow her away just as you'd blown David Gray away. Destroy the face that had destroyed you.'

Merrick threw his head from side to side and tears ran down his face. 'No. No. No!' he said through clenched teeth. 'It wasn't *like* that. The bloody gun went off. Both barrels. I couldn't kill Lisa; you have to believe me. She was my *life*, for God's sake. I just wanted to frighten her; make her come back to me. But when I saw this bastard in bed with her…naked…all over her, I went mad.'

Merrick lay there, chest heaving as he gasped for breath. 'I don't even remember pulling the trigger,' he went on. 'First thing I knew there was this explosion and I was on my arse in the middle of the floor, and Lisa was screaming. She was up and out of there like a flash. I didn't even know I'd hit her. By the time I realized what had happened, she'd gone. I tried to find her, but she'd disappeared. I went out into the yard, round the back, but I couldn't find her. I thought she must be hiding in the house, so I came back, but just as I got to the door, Foster came down the stairs. I hit him. Smashed him hard with the butt of the gun, and down he went. But the bastard got my foot with something as he went down, and it hurt like hell. I could hardly walk, so I got out of there because I didn't know who else might be about.'

'Foster wasn't there,' said Tregalles.

'Of course he was there,' said Merrick. 'I ought to know; I hit him. Bastard deserved it anyway. None of this would have happened if it hadn't been for him. You should be going after him. He started it when he stole Lisa away from me. We were all right until he came along.'

'Did you actually see his face?'

Merrick's eyes became guarded. 'It was Foster,' he repeated, but he sounded less sure now than he had before. 'It *had* to be Foster,' Merrick insisted. 'Who else could it have been?'

'Take my word for it,' Tregalles told him, 'it wasn't Foster. Tell us again where this person was when you hit him.'

'I told you. I heard him coming down the stairs as I was coming back into the house, so I stood to one side of the doorway and hit him when he came through.'

'So he was *inside* the cottage coming out?' said Paget.

'Christ! How many times do I have to tell you? I'm the one who's supposed to have the concussion.'

'Just wanted to make sure I had it straight,' said Paget.

Merrick put out his hand and caught Paget's sleeve. 'I didn't mean to hurt her,' he said. 'Honest to God, Paget, you have to believe me. I didn't mean to hurt her. I loved her. It wasn't my fault. You must believe that.' His hand dropped away, and he began to sob.

The doctor moved to the side of the bed. 'I think my patient has had quite enough for now,' he said firmly.

Paget stood looking down at the man in the bed. He could feel no pity for him. Lisa Remington had been bruised and battered by this man, and when she left him he'd pursued and finally killed her. And then he'd tried to justify his actions by saying that he loved her.

'I think we've all had quite enough,' he said as he turned away.

'...*WHAT KIND OF MAN do you think I am? I'll admit that I didn't want him to marry Janet, but as God is my judge, I was not the one who splattered his brains all over the pillow like that. In fact I didn't know he was dead until you told me last week, and that's the truth. Neither did Janet.'*

Paget switched the tape off. There was silence in the room for several seconds. He was in Alcott's office, and as usual the air was thick with smoke.

It was Paget who finally spoke. 'Those details were never released,' he said. 'Mike Freeman claimed to have been hit *before* he entered the cottage, but Merrick said that he heard the man he thought was Foster come down the stairs, and he hit him as he came out of the house. It was dark, and Merrick was in so much pain from having his toes smashed as Freeman went down that he didn't hang about to check on who it was he'd hit. He just assumed it was Foster. Merrick said his foot was so painful it was all he could do to get to his car. That's what made his driving so erratic. He took the corner too fast and scraped the side of the Protronics car in his hurry to get away.'

He fell silent for a moment. 'I think Merrick was telling the truth when he said he didn't know Lisa had been hit. If you recall, he was still talking about her as if she were alive when Tregalles talked to him in London.

'Merrick had no reason to lie about where he was when

he hit Freeman, but Freeman did, because he'd been upstairs and knew that Gray was dead. And he must have told
Janet, but she had to report Gray missing because it would
have looked more than suspicious if she hadn't. After all,
they were due to be married in a few weeks.

'But she couldn't tell the police what she knew without
implicating her father, and she would never do that. She
even made up that story about her father falling down the
stairs at home, and it almost worked.'

'Freeman couldn't have known for certain it was Gray,
not with his face shot away like that,' Alcott objected.

'He went there expecting to find Gray in Lisa Remington's bed,' Paget pointed out. 'Why should he think anything else, especially when Gray failed to appear the following day?'

Paget shook his head sadly. 'I can almost feel sorry for
Janet,' he went on. 'Having to cope with her fiancé's death
would be bad enough, but finding out what sort of man
Gray was must have been devastating for her. God knows
what she thought of her father's part in it all, yet she stood
by him; even lied for him. As for Porter…' Paget dismissed
the man with a contemptuous wave of the hand.

'But I would like to see Mike Freeman nailed for his part
in all this. I suppose there hasn't been a change of heart
over at New Street?' He looked at Alcott hopefully, but the
superintendent shook his head.

'Mr Brock feels there is nothing to be gained by prosecuting Freeman,' he said, obviously quoting. 'Mike Freeman seems to have quite a high standing in the business
community, and he's already putting it about that he and
his daughter are being harassed by the police. Mr Brock
feels that such a prosecution might prove counter-
productive to good public relations at a time when we need
the support of the community.'

Paget cocked a quizzical eye at Alcott, but the superintendent's face revealed nothing as he butted a cigarette and lit another. The chief inspector sighed inwardly. What it all came down to was local politics. Chief Superintendent Brock was a political animal—and an ambitious one. Don't rock the boat. Let's not do anything to spoil his chances of becoming the next chief constable. And in a region such as this, image was important.

Paget got slowly to his feet and moved toward the door. 'If there's nothing else, then…?' he said as he shrugged into his coat.

'There's still the trial, of course.' Alcott blew a stream of smoke toward the ceiling. 'And the defence is bound to call Mike Freeman and the others. In fact I'd be surprised if they don't try to prove that it was Freeman who killed Gray.'

The same thought had crossed Paget's mind, and he'd taken comfort in it. Perhaps he'd underestimated Brock, he thought grudgingly. Prosecuting Freeman and the others would be costly, and they might get off with nothing more than a slap on the wrist. Far better for Brock's 'bottom line' for the chief superintendent to sit back and let Merrick's defence counsel do the job for nothing.

'I'm not so sure that wouldn't have been true if Freeman had arrived first and seen the gun,' he said. 'It could have gone either way. If Merrick retracts his statement—and he probably will—Freeman's actions might muddy the waters sufficiently to cast doubt in a jury's mind as to who *did* actually pull the trigger.'

Alcott stood up, stretched. 'Which is why I want you and Tregalles here in my office first thing in the morning. I want to make sure that we have everything covered.' He looked at his watch. 'Good God! Is that the time?' He grabbed his coat and came round the desk. 'On your way home, are you, Paget?'

'I had thought…' Paget began, but stopped abruptly as Alcott gripped his arm and propelled him through the door.

'You're on your way home,' he said firmly. 'Marion's car is in for servicing, and she's got mine. You can drop me off.'

'I take it that's an order, sir?' said Paget wryly.

'Damned right it is,' said Alcott grimly. 'We're supposed to be going out to dinner with friends tonight, and if I'm not home by six, Marion will kill me.'

HOOK, LINE AND MURDER

A RIGEL LYNX MYSTERY

THOM ELKJER

Reporter Rigel Lynx knows zip about fly-fishing, but he needs the paying magazine piece on trout. So he hits the Northern California hamlet of Pomo Bluff for his bold foray into the unexplored vistas of steelhead... and unexpected murder.

The victim is found at a local inn where Rigel is staying. The death is ruled accidental, but soon Rigel's trying to catch a killer. And he's hooked—to a mystery that seems to involve the entire town. Casting his lures, he discovers fishing's greatest truism: the ones you catch can't compare to the ones that get away....

Available October 1999 at your favorite retail outlet.

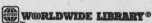 **WORLDWIDE LIBRARY®**

Visit us at www.worldwidemystery.com   WTE323

Ronald Weber

The Aluminum Hatch

A MICHIGAN MYSTERY

Link Pickett's tourist season ended before it had even begun. The fishing guide met his grisly end as he canoed down the Borchard River and was nearly decapitated by a wire strung across the river.

Most have decided that Verlyn Kelso—Link's fierce business rival—is the killer. Department of Natural Resources agent Mercy Virdon, who happens to be Kelso's ex-wife, thinks otherwise.

Soon Mercy is up to her neoprene chest waders in a mystery as turbulent as the churning river waters—and twice as deadly.

Available October 1999 at your favorite retail outlet.

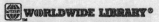 **WORLDWIDE LIBRARY®**

Visit us at www.worldwidemystery.com   WRW324

HARVEST OF BONES
A VERMONT MYSTERY

NANCY MEANS WRIGHT

Ruth Willmarth, busy working to keep her rural Vermont
dairy farm in a manageable state, is plunged into a mystery. It
starts with a finger bone, and leads to a skeleton.

New neighbor Fay Hubbard has just opened a farmhouse
B&B and finds her home invaded by its original owner, a
gutsy septuagenarian who announces the dead body is that of
her husband—whom she murdered twenty years ago.

The bizarre discovery puts Ruth and Fay in the middle of a
twisted history of hatred, blackmail and murder, as deep and
dark as the rich Vermont soil.

Available October 1999 at your favorite retail outlet.

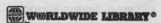
WORLDWIDE LIBRARY®

Visit us at www.worldwidemystery.com   WNMW325